# SECRET GARDEN

––––––––

Find descriptions of all Cathryn's books at CathrynParry.com

# SECRET GARDEN

## A SAGE FAMILY OF SCOTLAND ROMANCE

### CATHRYN PARRY

SECRET GARDEN

Copyright © 2015 by Cathryn Parry



This edition published by Brave Cat Press
January, 2021

ISBN-13: 978-1-951076-15-3

CHAPTER ONE

*Twenty-two Years Ago*
*MacDowall Castle in the Scottish Highlands*

THE LAST PERSON Rhiannon MacDowall expected to see when she looked out the window on New Year's Eve was her friend Colin Walker, standing on her family's castle drawbridge.

Rhiannon felt a surge of excitement. Colin was her best friend, and usually she only saw him in August. Colin was American, and he came to visit his grandparents during his summer vacation. He and his parents stayed at the guard's cottage on the edge of her family's estate for the whole month.

She skipped over to him. Colin was eight, like her, and the two of them were inseparable when he visited.

"You're here!" she said, opening the heavy door and letting the cold winter air surround them both.

"I'm not supposed to be," Colin answered, not moving from the threshold.

"Why not?" She peered closer at him.

"I don't know," he mumbled, pushing his hair out of his face.

Colin had straight blond hair and his mum cut it so it was perfect all around. Rhiannon thought it was beautiful; far more beautiful than her brown, limp hair. Colin had light blue eyes, too. Her mum said it was a shame that all that beauty was wasted on a boy.

She waited patiently for him to tell her why he'd come. Finally, she decided to help him along.

"*When* did you arrive in Scotland?" she asked.

"This morning." He stared at his shoes, frowning. He seemed so sad, and Rhiannon had never seen him like this before. She'd never seen Colin in a bad mood, not in all the time they'd spent together, and Colin had been visiting since they were both babies.

But now his hands were in his pockets. He wasn't speaking. And Colin usually talked even more than she did. "Silver-tongued," his mother called him. "A chattering magpie," her dad called her. So straightaway, she knew something was wrong. Sometimes Rhiannon felt as though she could read people's minds—or at least, guess at what bothered them more than most people could—and she'd said so to her brother, Malcolm, once. He said she should keep that to herself. So she did.

"May I stay with you for a while?" he asked, finally looking up at her.

"Of course!" She opened the door wider. They never stood on ceremony between them. Colin had let himself in nearly every day in the summer. They'd been in charge of watering and haying the ponies, so he came over very early in the morning. Sometimes he went upstairs to her room and woke her up, which didn't bother her because she was used to having an older brother around. Boys didn't always *think*, as her mum would say.

"Will you come to our party tonight?" she asked Colin, leading him inside. She twirled around in her red dress, which was special, because it was New Year's Eve. Hogmanay, they called it in Scotland.

Colin just shrugged, still looking sad.

"We're all going first-footing afterward," Rhiannon said. "And they're letting me stay up late and sing 'Auld Lang Syne.' We've been practicing the verses all day."

Colin gazed at the Christmas decorations still on the walls, his expression relaxing a bit. She remembered how much he loved her family's castle. Colin lived in Texas, which she thought was fascinating. She followed his gaze to the empty spot over the fireplace.

"Do you want to see our swords?" she asked him. "We took them down so Dad could clean them."

"You took *all* the swords down? In the whole castle?"

"No, we're just cleaning those two fancy ones with the jewels in the blade."

Still, Colin was impressed. "Those are my favorites."

"Mine, too." She bounced up and down on the balls of her feet. "Come upstairs in the library and see them. I think the bigger sword might be like the one Robert the Bruce used."

Colin's head tilted in interest. The two of them had spent so much time this summer running across the moors and through the woods, Rhiannon pretending to be Robert the Bruce and Colin playing Davy Crockett.

She ran up the wide staircase, knowing that Colin would follow her close behind.

But just as they reached the first landing, the castle door below them swung open. The winter cold came rushing into the great hall again. "Yoo-hoo! Is my son here?" called a high-pitched, female voice.

Colin's mum, Daisie Lee Walker. She was tall, with wavy blond hair. Daisie Lee always wore cowboy boots—some red, some beige, some with sparkly decorations—and once

Rhiannon had curiously asked her why she did that. Daisie Lee had replied that she'd been born in Texas on a working ranch and that gave her the right. Rhiannon liked her. "A force of nature," Rhiannon's mum called her. "Outspoken," Colin's grandmother said. Colin didn't say much about her either way. But when he visited, he seemed to spend most of his time with Rhiannon and her family. Once, he'd told Rhiannon that he liked that her parents were so calm.

But tonight, Colin grabbed Rhiannon's hand and quickly pulled her down into a crouching position, hiding from Daisie Lee. With the way the big staircase curved, there was a small box on the landing where they were hidden from view, but they could watch everything the adults did in the great hall below.

Kneeling beside him, Rhiannon tucked her dress under her knees. Colin pressed his forehead against the staircase barrier, focusing on his mother.

Something was wrong.

Rhiannon's mum hurried from the kitchen to greet Daisie Lee. Rhiannon could see them both clearly, too, from the tiny carved-out slits in the lattice wood. Her mum was dressed for New Year's Eve, and she looked beautiful. She wore a long white dress that was decorated with bits of gold lace. She was so pretty and it made Rhiannon hope she could be like her, too, one day.

"Why don't you come in?" Rhiannon's mum said to Daisie Lee. "You're welcome to join the party tonight."

Rhiannon whispered in Colin's ear, "I hope your mother says yes." In the living room, her older brother, Malcolm, was sitting on the bench with their dad, and they were playing "Auld Lang Syne" on the piano, practicing the words. Malcolm always got to stay up late and sing, but this was her first time. "Then you can stay up late with me, Colin."

But Colin only shook his mop-top head. She peered closer at him. Beneath his shaggy bangs, his eyes seemed wet. His mouth was scrunched. She felt sad because she only really knew Colin as somebody who laughed and played jokes and had fun. Colin didn't like to feel sad.

Rhiannon's mum ushered Daisie Lee farther into the castle, directly below them. Colin stayed down when his mum glanced in their direction, not knowing that they were in their clever hiding spot. Both Rhiannon and Colin squinted through the scrollwork in the old, dark wood.

"I'm not here for the party, I'm here to fetch Colin." Daisie Lee sounded angry. "Have you seen him? I've looked everywhere and I can't find him."

"No, we haven't seen him." Rhiannon's mum took Daisie Lee's hands in hers and peered closer. "How are you? Are you visiting for the holiday?"

Rhiannon glanced at Colin. He seemed awful eager to hear what his mum would say.

"No, we're not *visiting*. We just got here, and we're flying back tomorrow," Daisie Lee said.

"That's a short trip," Rhiannon's mum remarked kindly.

"We came because I *caught* him," Daisie Lee said. "Did you know my husband is seeing someone?" she demanded. "He's been calling her for months now. I think he met her in August. At that pub he always goes to." She spit out the word *pub*.

"Oh, dear," Mum said quietly.

"He had the *nerve* to fly back here over Christmas. He had the excuse that Jessie was ill. Ill, my foot. His mother is healthier than I am. She should be—she has no stress. Her son is *my* problem, not hers."

"I'm sorry," Rhiannon's mum said mildly. "I haven't seen Dougie here at all, Daisie Lee, if that helps you."

"Well, he came here to see *her,* and I knew it. I knew it in my bones. So I packed up Colin and flew *his son* over to see him. We caught him with her today, just now. That son of a..."

Rhiannon glanced at Colin. He'd gone pale. His hands were trembling against the barrier.

"He doesn't care about his *own son,*" Daisie Lee said, her voice rising. "He never has, really."

Colin went rigid beside her. Rhiannon could barely breathe.

"Oh, Daisie Lee, I'm sure that's not true," Rhiannon's mum murmured.

"He said it to his *face,*" Daisie Lee hissed. "I was *there.*"

Colin's neck and shoulders seemed to droop.

"Colin's not *enough* for him," Daisie Lee was saying, "and I told him so, and he agreed as much. He agreed, and now he's leaving us. How am I going to raise a son alone?"

Whatever Rhiannon's mum said in return, it was muffled as she led Daisie Lee off, crying now, into the family kitchen.

Rhiannon glanced at Colin, but he just sat there, his forehead against the wooden railing, and not saying anything.

Rhiannon couldn't imagine how she would feel if her mum had said those things about her and her dad. It made her stomach hurt to think about it. It was too scary.

Hesitantly, she placed her forehead on the latticework beside Colin's.

"I think my dad is leaving us for good," Colin mumbled.

Her stomach churned with the thought. She didn't know what she would do in his place. "What will happen to you, Colin?"

He lifted one shoulder in a shrug. "My mom said we're moving to my grandmother's ranch. My *other* grandmother," he clarified. "The one in Texas."

"You really will be a cowboy," she remarked. Everybody called him a cowboy anyway, because of living in Texas and his mum's cowboy boots. Now it would be true.

Colin hung his head lower. Rhiannon was sure that he

would rather everything went back to the way it used to be. It was what Rhiannon would have wanted.

She peered through the latticework, but her mum and Daisie Lee hadn't come back.

She finally dared to ask, "Where will your dad live?"

"I don't know." Colin's voice was a whisper.

Rhiannon thought about that. Colin's dad had been part of their summer world at the castle for as long as she could remember. He was a funny man. Round-faced and quiet, he'd always been with Daisie Lee and Colin—a unit, even if they did shout and make rows. Daisie Lee, Dougie and Colin. That was their family. They stayed at the cottage on the edge of Rhiannon's family's property. Jamie and Jessie were Colin's grandparents—Dougie Walker's parents—and they worked for Rhiannon's family. They always had.

It fit together like a puzzle with the pieces all there, and with Colin's dad gone, it just wouldn't feel right anymore. Nothing would be the same again.

"Maybe he'll move over here and live with Jamie and Jessie in the cottage," she mused.

Colin didn't answer.

And then a terrible thought occurred to Rhiannon. *"You'll come back, won't you?"* she asked, horrified at the thought of *that* changing.

Colin didn't answer again. He covered his eyes with the heels of his hands.

A cry tore out of her. She didn't know where it came from. Rhiannon just remembered their happy times, coming at her in snippets of memory, all at once.

Running over the grounds with Colin. Helping his dad repair a car engine. An outing at Loch Ness, she and Colin searching for Nessie with her dad's binoculars. Takeaway suppers from the local pizza shop. Swimming at the beaches near Aberdeen. Golfing with Jessie at the public course at Kildrammond.

What if it never happened again? What if they couldn't be friends anymore?

She put her arms around Colin and laid her cheek on the back of his shoulder. His skin was warm and he smelled the way he always did. She squeezed him tighter, wanting him to stay with her. "I don't want you to go," she whispered.

He stiffened at first. She remembered that he was a boy and she was a girl, and even though they were best of mates, they should never touch like this.

She pulled back. "Sorry," she said. "But I wish it didn't have to change. I wish nothing ever changed. It's perfect as it is. I can't bear it to be any different."

"Me, too." He gave her a meaningful look. She and Colin thought so much alike, sometimes she felt they were almost the same person.

"You're my best friend, Colin."

He smiled at her. The first smile she'd seen from him today. At that moment, her brother and her dad chose to sing aloud with the music they'd only been playing on the piano until now:

*Should auld acquaintance be forgot,*
*And never brought to mind?*
*Should auld acquaintance be forgot,*
*And auld lang syne!*

The words were sad, especially in her dad's deep singing voice. Rhiannon couldn't help sighing. She glanced at Colin and saw that he was listening, too.

"That's what we'll sing together at midnight," she whispered.

"We sing it at home, too," Colin answered.

They both grew quiet, listening to her dad and Malcolm

sing. So far away from them that the words were somewhat muffled.

Rhiannon joined in with them, singing the words clearly. Some people didn't know all the words to the song; they just mumbled on the harder parts. But Rhiannon's dad had taught her all of it. She knew what that song meant, every phrase.

Colin took her hand. He held it in his, and smiling gently at her, he whispered the words to the song, too. But his voice didn't sound like hers. His accent was American.

*For auld lang syne, my dear,*
*For auld lang syne,*
*We'll take a cup of kindness yet,*
*For auld lang syne.*

This was the ending chorus, the part when they would hold hands and all rush into a big circle. It was brilliant fun. But instead of smiling or acting silly about it, Colin got quiet.

She gazed at him. Now was also the time when everybody was supposed to kiss. She'd never stayed up so late before to get any kisses at midnight.

Colin seemed to read her mind, too. He turned to her and kissed her then, straight on the lips. Fast and firm. With *conviction,* as her dad would say.

Her heart jumped a little, and she looked into his light blue eyes.

"I'll never forget you, Rhiannon," he said fiercely.

Her heart seemed ready to burst. August was much too far away.

"If I write to you, will you write back?" she asked him softly. Suddenly, she felt shy with him.

His face flushing again, he nodded. "I will."

"If you see Colin, tell him I need him, now." Below them,

Daisie Lee had reappeared and was saying her goodbyes to Rhiannon's mum. Daisie Lee was sniffling and she looked terribly upset. Rhiannon's mum was doing her best to comfort her, but...

Colin stood. "I have to go now." But his gaze was still on Rhiannon.

"Do you *promise* to write me back?" she whispered.

"Right away, as soon as I get your letter."

Then he took her hand and squeezed it. He ran down the staircase toward his mother without looking back.

"Colin! Where have you *been?*" Daisie Lee wailed.

"Looking at swords up in Rhiannon's room," he lied neatly. "Her dad has a massive collection." He gave Daisie Lee a huge grin as if nothing at all was wrong, as if he wasn't upset about his father, as if he hadn't just kissed Rhiannon.

Rhiannon touched her lips.

But Daisie Lee smiled at him, happier now, because who wouldn't smile when they were with Colin? He was special. There would never be anybody else like him.

Rhiannon stood so that she wouldn't be hidden anymore and watched Colin leave, ushered through the door by her mum.

Colin turned back to Rhiannon as he crossed the threshold, and he gave her a secret smile.

A lump formed in her throat but she forced herself to smile, doing for him what he had just done for his mother. She would not show pain or fear. She lifted her hand in a wave. *I will write to you,* she mouthed to him.

———

BUT RHIANNON NEVER did write. Because shortly after that New Year's Eve, her life changed, too.

Rhiannon lay in a hospital bed, her whole world turned upside down. She hated seeing people, because all they did was ask her questions and make her feel even more frightened. And even though she thought about Colin all the time, she wouldn't want him to see her like this.

It wasn't until weeks later that she was finally allowed to return to her castle. And once she was there, she never wanted to leave again. She never left the grounds of the estate, and she rarely saw visitors.

Staying in her own special world made her feel safe and in control. Everybody in Scotland knew that. She supposed Colin knew, too, and she took comfort from the fact that he would understand.

For years afterward, Rhiannon believed that Colin left her alone precisely because he understood her so well.

And she was grateful.

# CHAPTER TWO



*Present Day, Central Texas*

COLIN WALKER HAD A MOTTO in life: take nothing seriously and keep everything light.

On a lazy summer's Monday afternoon, he was doing just that—strolling the fairways at Sunny Times Golf Academy in Winwood Springs, Texas, sizing up the lay on a chip shot and aiming to enjoy the day with his caddie and best friend, Mack. That was when he became aware of Mack's cell phone buzzing.

He turned toward Mack, who stood beside Colin's golf bag. Mack stared at his phone, a concerned look on his face.

Colin was a tour pro. In his and Mack's world, there was protocol. A caddie who wasn't paying attention to the game was not to be tolerated. But Colin just shrugged. He figured that Mack was a grown-up, and if something needed his attention, then Colin wasn't going to get upset.

Instead, he ambled over and pulled a nine iron from his bag. Normally, this was Mack's job, but Mack was busy with his text message. A party of four was on the course behind them, so Colin needed to keep playing and stay with the flow of the game.

He approached the ball, knelt and squinted at it where it lay in the rough beside a green that sloped downward in a steep, thirty-degree pitch to the cup, marked with a red flag.

The flag hung limply, no movement, no breeze. Colin wiped the sweat from the back of his neck. It was hot, a humid June afternoon, and it might have been Colin's imagination, but waves of steam seemed to be coming off the fairway.

Straightening, he strolled back to Mack. "What do you think of the lie?" Colin asked, nodding toward the gopher hole his ball was nestled against. "Nine iron, or should I use a wedge?"

"Seven," Mack said absently, and Colin had to laugh, because a seven iron was absurd. But his caddie didn't even smile, busily tapping out a text message, and not paying attention to the game at all.

"And people wonder why I've slipped to one hundred in the rankings," Colin said with a laugh.

"One hundred twenty-four," Mack muttered.

Colin turned. "Seriously?"

"It was on the Golf Channel this morning."

Colin took off his glove and stretched his hand, then put the glove back on. He was trying not to think about that. To *keep it light.*

Mack gave him a look. Mack had risen from the college world to the minors tour to the big show—the pro tour—with Colin, and Mack knew exactly what was at stake. If Colin slipped below number 125 on the "money list," then he would lose his tour card. If he lost his tour card, he lost his ability to play in the tournaments with the big purses and the big attention.

The tour card was the golden ticket. People dreamed of it, prayed for it, gave up everything for it. Every golfer remembered how he felt the day he'd earned it.

A sick feeling settled in Colin's gut, as if things were spinning out of control. He knew that if he wasn't careful, then he was somehow going to be abandoned again. Dropped, as if he was nothing. And then everything would change for the worse.

Colin looked away from Mack, toward the red flag flying over the eighteenth hole, trying to clear his head.

"We still have the New York Cup ahead of us," Mack said quietly. "Everything will come together. That tournament is good luck for you. Remember last year?"

"Yep," Colin said tightly. He'd *kept it light* and they'd come in second place. It had been his best showing and had confirmed that he was right not to take anything too seriously. Being laid-back about life was how he'd ended up on the pro tour in the first place.

He glanced at Mack, who had turned back to his cell phone. "What are you texting about, anyway?" Colin asked, leaning toward the screen. "Did you meet a girl last night or something?"

"Nope." Mack shoved his phone in his pocket. He seemed cagey, giving a smile that Colin knew was fake. Colin had roomed with him his first two years at college, and of all his friends on the golf team, Mack was the only one that Colin had introduced to Daisie Lee. Daisie Lee adored Mack like a second son. "Colin-clone," she called him. Maybe he was. Mack didn't take anything too seriously, either.

"Go take your shot," Mack ribbed him.

"I will when I'm ready."

"It's an easy chip shot. You do those in your sleep."

"Now you're really making me worry. What's on your damn phone?" Playfully, Colin reached for it, but Mack swatted his hand away.

"Okay, fine." Mack sighed, taking off his cap and wiping his brow. "I was going to tell you after you finished the hole, but "if you've got to know now and ruin your game, great— It was Leonard, letting you know he's here for a noon meeting."

Leonard was Colin's accountant and business manager. "What's so bad about that?" Colin asked. Leonard's management company ran Colin's website, made his travel arrangements, took care of all the stuff that Colin didn't enjoy doing. Leonard had even snagged Colin a few endorsements—nothing big, one with a sportswear company that was little more than a struggling start-up, and another with a ball company that, admittedly, spread money around to pretty much every tour pro, just to flood the tour as much as possible with their brand of golf balls. But every dollar counted.

"It's nothing," Mack said. "It's just business."

Colin hoped their business was still okay. He'd become used to the lifestyle—a far better living than they'd had on the minors tour. That first year in the pro tour, Colin had made close to a million dollars, and he'd bought Daisie Lee a house and a new car. He'd spread the wealth to Mack, too. Stepped up their accommodations on tour.

The thought of losing that made his guts ache.

He just...needed to keep this gig going. Keep the wolf from the door. Do what made everybody happy.

Colin gripped his nine iron and headed toward the ball.

Truth was, his game *had* been slipping lately. There had been magic in Colin's game once. Time was he'd pulled off amazing feats, with seemingly little effort. Every so often he still had glimmers of that, and if he just focused hard enough, maybe he could find it again in time for the next tournament. Make the final cut, and thus earn a slice of the purse money, which would automatically boost his ranking again.

Mack crossed his arms and watched silently.

*Don't think.* Colin gave the ball his usual address, whistled under his breath, swung...

And completely undershot it.

He stood there, staring at the dead ball for a while. He honestly didn't know how to begin to fix this.

He turned to Mack. All the greats had caddies who helped them with this sort of thing. Made coaching comments, or had swing coaches on call. "Any tips?"

"Seriously?" Mack laughed. "You hate tips."

Yeah, well, that was true, too. Colin typically avoided overanalyzing things. He'd always thought that was the secret to his success, and his college golf coach had been fine with it. Mostly, Colin was allergic to critical people who weren't helpful. "Anything *constructive?*"

Mack ran a hand through his hair. "How about I videotape you, and then you take a look at it yourself?"

Colin paused. He hadn't done much of that lately. When he was young, he'd been videotaped a lot. "Sure. Let's do it."

"Tomorrow," Mack said.

"Right."

Colin took his putter from Mack and prepared to finish up the hole. Two putts later, he sank the ball in the cup, for a bogie on the eighteenth and final hole. Overall, he was three shots under par, which was great for an amateur golfer, but not so impressive for a tour pro.

Pensive, Mack took out his pencil and filled out Colin's scorecard.

"I've got two more weeks to prepare for the New York Cup," Colin said. "I'll be fine."

"Yep," Mack agreed. But he didn't meet Colin's eye. He was lying, and Colin knew it.

Not feeling like himself, Colin headed toward the Nineteenth Hole, Winwood's combination pro shop and bar-and-grill. Mack followed with the golf bag slung over his shoulder. But a few yards from the gravel path that led from the golf cart rental stand, a foursome of ladies Colin knew from the club—Doris was the blonde ringleader—stopped their cart and hurried over to hug Colin.

He didn't show the ladies a hint of his worried mood. Instead, he gave them each a smile, a kiss on the cheek, a few "shooting-the-breeze" good words. Because at the end of the day, Doris and her friends were Colin's people, and he appreciated their support. He was *supposed* to be here on the golf course at Winwood. He never had a doubt about that in his mind.

Sometimes, though, his motto failed him, and he had a fear that he had some kind of defect. That he would waste whatever gift or talent he'd been given.

"Yo, Walker!"

On the steps to the clubhouse stood Doc Masters, one of the stars of the pro tour, ranked number five. The muscular bald guy had skin on his neck so burned by the sun that it was textured like an alligator's. As always, he was surrounded by his entourage.

Cocking a hand on his hip, he said to Colin, "I saw you on the roster for the New York Cup."

Colin turned slowly, the grin still on his face. Sensing trouble because they knew Doc, Doris led her friends to their tee time.

"Yes," Colin said to Doc. It seemed as if everybody was waiting to see if Colin could pull it off again. Including him. "I'll be there."

"Good," Doc said. "My wife's sister is coming in to town, and she's a fan of yours. She wants to hang with Colin's Crew."

*Colin's Crew.* The merry band of fun-loving, young-at-heart supporters who followed Colin along the fairways in his tournaments as he played each successive hole. Golf being mostly a staid sport, spectators tended to stay put at a hole, watching all the golfers as they played through. But not Colin's Crew. Colin had never encouraged it; it had just sort of happened back in the early days.

Colin made it a point to sign everybody's autographs. Shake everybody's hands. High-five the little kids, especially. He wanted to make everybody feel good about the game of golf. Maybe it tripped up his focus a bit, but that wasn't so bad. All told, he was pretty damn lucky in his life, and he knew it.

Colin shrugged. Spending time with Doc and his sister-in-law wouldn't be a hardship. "Sure. We'll meet up for drinks afterward."

"You can hang out with her on Sunday."

Colin stared at Doc. Outwardly, there was no malice in his statement. It hadn't even occurred to Doc that in assuming Colin wouldn't make the final cut—that he would be eliminated before the final day of the tournament—he was insulting Colin.

Doc walked off. Usually, Colin would have laughed it off. But some old spark of commitment, of competitive spirit seemed to rebel. "Sure," he called after Doc. "When the network guys interview me with the trophy, I'll be sure to bring her up to the press box with me."

Doc paused. Then he turned and let out a guffaw. "That's a good one." He rubbed his chin. "Hey, do you need a ride on my private jet? Anytime, just give me a call."

"We will," Mack interjected. Colin didn't blame him. Traveling by private jet was better than flying commercial.

"Call me," Doc said to Colin. "We'll keep in touch."

Colin leaned back and gave him the good ol' boy smile he'd learned after they first moved to this part of Texas when he was a kid. Acting as if nothing riled him. As if he was just an easygoing guy. No drama, no pain.

"That guy is an ass," Mack said, once Doc was well out of earshot. "But he's an ass with a private plane."

"Yep," Colin agreed. He headed into the clubhouse and then directly toward the conference room where he habitually met with Leonard. "But I'm not going to waste my time worrying about him."

Mack grabbed Colin's arm, stopping him. "Actually, Colin, now that we're finished with the round, I, uh, need to tell you something."

"Is this what the texting was all about?"

"Well...yeah."

"See?" Colin said, pointing his finger at Mack. "I know you."

"Can we just step over here?" Mack asked, nodding to a table in the far corner of the snack bar.

"Why? Is *Golf Digest* here to grill me? Am I being waylaid?"

"No, it's not *Golf Digest*." Mack laughed nervously. "Your mom's here. Daisie Lee is upstairs in the conference room with Leonard."

*"What?"*

"She needs to tell you something important, and she wants to do it in person," Mack said quickly. "She texted me from Leonard's phone—they were already in the conference room. I had nothing to do with that."

"Oh, great. She saw the money list." In his opinion, Daisie Lee spent entirely too much time following his life. Yeah, she was his mother. He loved her, and he'd always worry about her, too, but barging in on his business meetings was too much. "Thanks for warning me."

"There's more." Mack blew out a breath.

"She's upset, isn't she?"

Mack gave him a look. Great. Now he would have to calm her down. Get her to smile. Make her laugh.

That was his job.

Colin glanced around them. They were in the middle of the crowded snack bar at lunchtime. People in golf shoes and polo shirts walked past carrying trays. Golf school was in session over on the far driving range, evidently.

He glanced toward the stairs. "You said she's up in the conference room?"

"She is. But, Colin—"

"I'm on it," Colin interrupted, and headed up the stairs to the private second-floor room that management let him use for his meetings. He was just about to open the door and reassure his mom when Mack blocked him with a hand.

"Look, I didn't want to have to tell you this," Mack said, "but...you probably have to go to a funeral this weekend."

"*What?* Whose?"

While Mack just mouthed, *I'm sorry,* the door opened and his mother said in her loud twang, "Honey, I came as soon as I heard."

Colin groaned inwardly. "What happened?" he asked in as calm a voice as he could manage.

His mom crossed her arms and looked at him. But instead of being upset, she seemed strangely pleased. "Your grandmother called me."

"Mimi?" Colin asked, his heart pumping harder. "What's wrong?"

"With our people? Nothing!" Her eyes widened at the thought of that. Then her mouth turned down. "Your *other* grandmother called," she said coolly. "The one in Scotland."

Colin's pulse slowed.

He hadn't heard from his father's family since he was a kid. Then, suddenly, when he turned pro a few years back, his grandmother—Jessie—had sent him a note through his website. Leonard had told Colin, but Colin had informed him that he wasn't interested. He'd pushed that part of his life out of his head as if it had never existed. He'd figured it would freak Daisie

Lee out if he started up any kind of relationship there, and that was the last thing he wanted.

Colin steadied his nerves and entered the conference room, where Leonard sat in a rumpled suit, a bunch of papers likely showing Colin's reduced financial circumstances spread before him.

Leonard stood clumsily, his face perspiring from the lack of air-conditioning.

"Colin," Daisie Lee said, following him inside, "there's good news, too. You're getting an inheritance—a sizable inheritance—and all you have to do is show up for it."

Colin stared. He felt as if life was moving in slow motion. Nobody in his father's family had money, as far as he knew. Then again, he'd been just a kid when he last saw them. Eight years old. "Whose funeral is it?" he asked. "Is it Jamie's?"

His grandparents would be elderly now. Colin hadn't heard from his grandfather since the divorce. He still remembered that Jamie had stood by Colin's father when he left them. Colin would never forget that day.

Daisie Lee waved her hand. "No. And I don't blame you for not wanting to see *those people* but you'll just have to endure it. They offered to let you stay at their house. That ugly little crofter's cottage."

"That ugly little crofter's cottage" had been heaven to Colin once—if only because he got to see Rhiannon when he went there. He closed his eyes at the memory.

So if Jessie and Jamie were both still alive, that meant...

Colin took off his cap. Stared into Daisie Lee's eyes, which were bright with animation. "Are you telling me that my father died?"

"Yes." She nodded. "He had a heart attack. That's why Jessie called me."

He couldn't focus. His vision seemed to be swimming and he blinked hard to clear it. Somehow he remained stubbornly on his feet.

"No," he said. Mack and Leonard were staring at him, so he sat. "I'm not going to his funeral."

"Colin, there's a *million-dollar inheritance.*"

Colin closed his eyes. He felt sick. He hadn't wanted to think about any of this stuff from his childhood. It was easier to pretend that it didn't exist. He sure as hell didn't want his father's money.

"I'm a tour pro," he said. "Last year I grossed almost that much myself."

There was silence in the room. Leonard cleared his throat, but Colin caught Mack giving him a look. *Don't fight it,* the look said. *Just go, and take the money.*

"I know my tour card's at risk," Colin bit out. "But I still don't want anything from him."

"Oh, Colin," Daisie Lee whispered. She seemed sad, and that tore him up inside, the way it always had.

Gritting his teeth, he walked to the end of the room and grabbed a paper cup, pouring a drink from the watercooler. Somebody in the hall outside came over to wave and smile at him through the conference room window, but he just couldn't muster up that old, carefree Colin attitude to wave back at them.

He was all tapped out. Didn't care about keeping up his cool. When it came to the subject of his father, nothing was light, and never would be.

His hand shook as he raised the cup to his lips. For so long he'd thought that someday he'd bump into his father at a tournament, maybe. Show him that he'd been wrong. Rub it in, even.

It had been a secret, stupid desire, something he'd never shared with anybody, or even really dared to admit to himself, because it was petty. And it was sad, too, because a part of him really had wanted his dad to say he'd made a mistake. That he did love Colin.

Now it was too late.

*My father is dead.*

Colin heard a choking sound, and he was shocked to realize that came from him. He pressed his palm to his forehead. He didn't want to *feel* this.

His mother came over to him and put her hand on his shoulder. "Colin, honey, I know it's hard. What he did to us when he left...well." She shook her head, collecting herself, and pushed her phone toward him. "The most important thing now is that we need to be practical. If you lose your tour card—"

He turned to her, suddenly furious. "I *will not* lose my tour card."

"Of course you won't, Colin. I know. The inheritance is... Think of it as a contingency plan."

He turned and stared out the window. "Then tell Jessie to mail me the check."

"I did, but she said you need to be there, for lawyers and signatures and whatever else. Then she mentioned Mr. Sage, Jamie's employer. Colin, I looked him up on the internet. Do you remember the family?"

Colin shook his head, ignoring her outstretched hand, cradling the phone. He didn't like that she was getting so excited about this. For too long, Daisie Lee had cried over the divorce, and Colin, even as young as he was, had been the one who'd had to lift her spirits.

"Don't frown, Colin. Surely you remember the MacDowall family that lived in the castle? Rhiannon, the little girl? She was so sweet to you. The two of you were so close back then."

Of course he hadn't forgotten her. Rhiannon had been the one great thing about that place. The best thing, actually.

But then, Rhiannon had never written to him the way she'd

promised. Colin couldn't help thinking that he'd done something wrong, because he'd believed her when she said that she would write him.

She'd seen everything that had happened, though—had heard what his father had said to him, and Colin had always figured that in the end, it had affected her decision to keep in touch.

"Rhiannon's mother," Daisie Lee continued, "was a Sage. The Sages of Scotland—you've heard of them? They own that big shampoo and cosmetics empire?"

Daisie Lee didn't wait for his reaction. She just kept talking, an excited look on her face. "Colin, they're now about the wealthiest people in Scotland. Can you believe it?"

"I really don't care about that," he said coldly. Because he didn't.

"Their company is called Sage Family Products. Here, I looked it up. They sponsor professional athletes."

He saw where this was going, all too clearly. She was trying to ensure his financial stability in the event that he crashed and burned on the pro tour. She was just being a mother.

He sat down at the table and put his head in his hands. He just wanted to keep his tour card and his dignity. No amount of money could save that.

Daisie Lee's voice was softer now, but she was still revved up. Apparently, she really was convinced that Colin should return to the place that she'd scorned for so many years.

Not that he'd blamed her. Daisie Lee's life had been tough after the divorce. The laughter had died in their little home. For a while, they'd been living in a trailer in her mother's front yard, next to a chicken coop. Daisie Lee had cried herself to sleep every night, and he'd heard it because the trailer had been so small.

But the worst thing of all was that his father hadn't once asked how they were doing. Colin hadn't heard a word. Not a card on his birthday, not a call at Christmas.

He could never, ever forgive that.

Colin stood. Everyone was staring at him. Mack, Leonard, his mom. In a sense, they all depended on him. Colin had never thought of himself as someone big on commitment—he'd expressly avoided it, in fact—but when it came right down to it, he was fast realizing that he *was* a committed man.

He had a team to support. A caddie, a business manager, his fans, his sponsors... They were all good to him—friends—and Colin didn't desert his friends.

Maybe it was just important to him that he end up being the good guy that his father hadn't been.

Mack was watching him, waiting for his decision.

Leonard rolled his pen in his fingers. He looked sorry about the whole thing. Daisie Lee was filled with crazy hope. Mack too, probably.

Colin didn't like his options. Either go to Scotland and renew the relationships he had no interest in cultivating, or stay here and watch an opportunity to help his team slip away from him.

If he lost the tour card, if he ended up back on the minors tour, or worse, working in obscurity as a club pro, knowing that he'd failed his talent and he wasn't worth it, then he would need money for his support system. He loved them.

"I'll go," he said quietly.

"You will?" Daisie Lee asked.

"Sure." He would be responsible and bring home the income stream that would keep them all going. He would do it, but he wouldn't like it.

While Leonard nodded, Colin took another drink of water. Crushed the cup with all the fury he had inside him.

Mack rose. With a quiet voice he said, "I'll talk to Doc about hitching a ride on his plane. I know he's going to a charity tournament in the Highlands this week."

"Thanks," Colin said. "I appreciate it."

## CHAPTER THREE

TWO DAYS LATER, Colin sat beside Mack on the large, comfortable seats of Doc Masters's private plane, and prepared for takeoff.

Back in the conference room at Sunny Times Golf Academy, the plan had seemed simple. Fly in. Meet Jessie and Jamie. Go to the funeral and collect his check, then fly home.

But now... Wednesday morning was when Doc needed to leave for his charity tournament, so Colin would be arriving four full days before Sunday's funeral. That meant spending more time in his grandparents' company than Colin wanted. To make matters worse, he'd finally sucked it up and emailed his grandmother. She'd responded immediately with the address of a restaurant where she wanted to meet at six o'clock local time, after he landed.

He had no idea what he was going to say. Whatever happened, he was determined not to let it get to him. He wouldn't care too much about it. *Keep everything light.*

The flight attendant stopped by, bringing Colin a drink from the bar service. Colin drank it gratefully and, without asking, she promptly brought another one. He finished that one, too.

Colin wasn't a big drinker—he was an athlete first—but the comfortable, mellow glow that the alcohol gave him helped dull the edge of his anger. He was even able to tolerate Doc and his small, sarcastic digs.

He didn't even mind too much when Doc sprang on them that they were making a detour to Iceland to pick up somebody's wife or girlfriend—this wasn't exactly clear to Colin. All he knew was that it added more than an hour to their flight time.

Then, once they did finally land in Scotland at the small Highland airport, there was a short delay before they could disembark. Something about their plane's manifest needed to be straightened out before they could clear customs, and that made the delay that much longer.

By the time the pilots finished the formalities, it was a few minutes past the time Colin was supposed to meet his grandparents.

"Are you *sure* you don't want to come with us to St. Andrews?" Doc Masters asked Colin as he reached for his bag.

Colin would have given anything to head off to the famous golf course. But it wasn't possible with his schedule, and frankly, he was glad to get a break from Doc. "Thanks, but if you don't mind, I'll just hook a ride back with you on Sunday night."

"I'm sorry about your father," Doc's wife said.

Colin thought about being truthful, telling her that he hadn't really known his father well, but what was the point? So he just nodded silently and went through the motions of grabbing his stuff and disembarking from the plane.

Once out on the tarmac, standing beside their pile of luggage, Colin realized this was the first time he'd been on Scottish soil since he was eight. All he kept thinking about was the way he'd felt that day. He'd been just a little kid, and he'd been scared and upset and ashamed. His whole world had blown apart, and his grandparents had sided with his father against them.

At least, that was what his mom had always said. To contact them and maybe find out otherwise had always seemed disloyal. So Colin had avoided it.

Given the choice, he would still rather avoid it. No doubt about it, he didn't see how this reunion could possibly be pleasant, for any of them. They had a lot of old, bad feelings to deal with.

"Where to?" Mack asked.

"I booked a hotel for us," Colin said. "But first, I need to meet my grandparents at a restaurant in town."

"Okay. You mind if I tag along?"

"Mind? Hell no." Colin was just grateful that Mack was willing to be a buffer for him.

Colin dug the address out of his wallet, and they flagged a cab. The driver was an old-timer and Mack shot the breeze with him, especially once the old-timer saw Colin's golf clubs. Colin signed his autograph, but didn't say much otherwise. It wasn't like him, but he was starting to feel kind of distracted and crappy.

Honestly, would he even recognize his grandparents? All those years with no contact had dulled his memory. Yes, his grandmother had tried to get in touch with him and maybe he shouldn't have ignored her. But when he was young and vulnerable, he'd always thought that his grandparents could have picked up a phone or hopped on a plane to see him, and they hadn't. So he was determined not to feel guilty if he couldn't identify them right away.

He and Mack finally found the restaurant—they were late because of the diversion and the holdup at the airport—and the server at the counter told them they'd missed Jamie and Jessie by a half hour.

"They *left* me?" Colin asked, incredulous. "They couldn't just eat dinner and wait an extra few minutes to see their grandson?"

The server looked apologetic. She gave them a slip of paper that Jessie had left, with their home address and telephone number written in neat script.

Colin's forehead was throbbing. He knew he might be over-reacting, but given their history, it was understandable. He stared at her address in disbelief. His grandmother expected him to stay with them, it appeared.

Or maybe Daisie Lee had given her that impression. Colin hadn't really talked with his grandmother about the sleeping arrangements—he'd just exchanged that one email about his estimated time of arrival, because frankly, it was all the contact he'd been able to take for the moment. He was filled with resentment, it seemed, and this wasn't like him. He hated feeling this way.

He was also sobering up.

"Are you going to phone them?" Mack asked.

"Not yet." Colin needed to calm down first. He was a mellow guy, laid-back. That was his reputation. That was what kept him sane.

"Let's sit here, get a drink first," Colin said. There was a pub attached to the restaurant, so they headed over to check it out. A three-person group was performing. Guitar, vocals, drums. Celtic music—they were pretty good.

Colin and Mack found chairs at a table. Before Colin knew it, two local women gravitated toward them. Mack talked with them—Colin was too busy getting his mind comfortably numb again to interact much. One song flowed into another. One beer flowed into another.

Somewhere along the line Colin noticed that one of the women was sitting on Mack's lap. By now, there was lots of laughter. He kept forgetting the names of the people they were talking to—the faces started to blend. Mack was getting friendlier with the two women... Bonnie and Clyde...that was what Mack was calling them. Colin was clear that Bonnie was the tall redhead currently sitting in Mack's lap, and the other woman wasn't really named Clyde, but Clara or Cassandra...something along those lines. Still, Mack coined them Bonnie and Clyde, which the two ladies thought was hilarious.

Mack was wearing his cowboy boots, and the more he drank, the more pronounced his Texas drawl became. Bonnie especially seemed to like that.

After the pub closed, the party moved to a local house. Even though it was well after midnight, Colin didn't feel tired at all. His body clock was seven hours behind the local time. Mack took the front seat of Bonnie's car, and Colin crowded in the back. Colin wasn't going to end up with either of the women—that would be stupid for someone with his profile, and he wasn't stupid, he was just prolonging the inevitable pain of meeting his grandparents.

In the back of his mind, he knew he had to deal with a potential confrontation that he just wasn't ready to face.

He also felt sick, and sad, and he didn't want to be. His father was dead and he was too late to do anything about it. This wasn't a jam Colin could talk his way out of. A problem he could smooth over with a laugh and a joke. He was here, in Scotland, and he needed to somehow get beyond the anger.

Because he wasn't a kid being manipulated or dragged around any longer. Those days were over. It was years ago that he'd overheard his parents arguing on that last trip to Scotland. Overheard his father telling his mother that it just wasn't worth it. His mother screaming back, "What about your son, isn't that reason enough?" His father answering, "No, that's not enough. It's not enough!"

All those years, deep down, Colin had spent feeling guilty

and ashamed, as if it were his fault. Anger, because rationally, he knew it *wasn't* his fault. He'd felt sad, for his mom and for him, too, because their lives had changed so drastically.

Or maybe he was slowly making up his mind to decide to get over it. To forgive his grandparents for not reaching out earlier —and himself for reaching out only now, when it was too late. Maybe he should just start the weekend with a fresh slate. Colin still wasn't sure, though. Mack obviously sensed his inner turmoil, and seemed to be steering clear of Colin's mood, or of any discussion regarding it.

"Do you want us to drop you off at the hotel?" Mack asked him finally. "Because I'm gonna stay over with Bonnie. She said she's got a couch you can stay on, too, if you want. When we wake up, I'll help you call your grandparents. How about if we just arrange a time to meet them before the funeral on Sunday? Will that work?"

It was the coward's way out, and it was tempting. Colin could avoid the whole three-day wait this way and then meet them at the funeral.

But now that he was sobering again, something bothered him. Avoiding his grandparents sounded too much like running away from the problem. Colin wasn't irresponsible. He didn't want to be like his father.

Especially not like his father.

"No," Colin said, "I need to talk with Jamie and Jessie. I'll head over there now. They always were early risers." Hopefully, they still were.

In the end, Bonnie drove him to his grandparents' cottage. She went slowly and carefully, weaving her way down a single-lane Scottish country road and playing Fleetwood Mac on the stereo—old stuff Colin hadn't heard since he was a kid. "You Make Loving Fun." None of it fit with the fact that he was the estranged grandson returning to Scotland for the funeral of a father he hadn't heard from in twenty-some years.

Colin pressed the heels of his hands to his eyes. The sun was streaking over the horizon. The digital clock on Bonnie's dash told him it was six o'clock in the morning.

"Jamie always liked to get up while it was still dark," Colin said, to no one in particular. Snatches of memory were coming back to him. From what little he remembered of his grandfather, he was set in his ways and brooked no nonsense.

"Would you mind turning down the music?" Colin asked as Bonnie pulled up beside the whitewashed cottage. Now that he was here, he felt completely sober. They were out in the middle of nowhere, in the Highlands. Somehow he had to get along with his grandparents for four more days. Then he could leave.

With the music subdued, Bonnie and Mack climbed out and hauled Colin's two bags to the dewy grass in front of his grandparents' cottage. The zippered bag holding his golf clubs made muffled clanking noises. Colin glanced at the cottage, studying it. It looked so much smaller than it had in his memories.

He'd never felt more alone than when he stood on the roadside in the silent, cool morning, his belongings dumped on the pavement.

"You gonna be okay?" Mack asked.

"I doubt it," he said drolly.

Mack laughed. Colin smiled. They hadn't said a damn serious thing all night anyway—even though his father had died and he was here for his funeral. Why should they start now?

His grandfather stood on the porch with his hands on his hips, watching everything. Fittingly, it had started to rain. There was no more delaying the confrontation, and Colin felt as if he'd reached rock bottom. In his heart, he was ready to consider that maybe it was both their faults that nobody had kept in touch.

Not just his fault. Not just his grandparents' fault. Just one big, snowballed mess that they might begin to melt together with a face-to-face conversation.

He took off his wet cap and turned to the grandfather he hadn't seen or heard from since he was an eight-year-old boy. He didn't know how to begin, except to say, "Granddad?"

"Where the devil have you been?" his grandfather thundered in return.

Colin wiped his hand on his pants. So much for the triumphant celebration of the prodigal grandson returning to the fold. He shrugged in a *what can we do?* pose and gave his grandfather a wayward smile that usually worked for him. "You know how plane travel is."

"No, I don't." His grandfather's answering scowl sent chills through Colin. "And don't you have a mobile phone?" he demanded.

"Ah...somewhere. I hope." Colin patted the side pocket of his cargo pants. Yeah, the hard plastic lump was there. "Sorry. I should've called to warn you I was running late last night."

His grandfather glared harder. Maybe Colin should give him the benefit of the doubt. Colin's father had been this man's—Jamie's—son. Jamie was no doubt grieving his son's death.

"I should leave you out here in the rain," Jamie said. "Let it soak some sense into you."

The illusion of being greeted with open arms was pretty much shattered. The rain spit harder. Colin rubbed his arms, but his grandfather wasn't inviting him inside. On the contrary, he seemed to be guarding the door.

"Wait here," Jamie said. He disappeared inside the cottage, shutting the door behind him.

While Colin waited for his grandfather to reappear, he searched his mind to remember something good from his childhood...a common, shared happy memory. But the only night that was coming back with any clarity was the last one. New Year's

Eve. The day his mother had confronted his father with his infidelity and he'd finally snapped, washing his hands of them. There had never even been a formal goodbye, just a general loading up of a small suitcase and then a car roaring away from the side of the dirt driveway.

Colin remembered crying. He remembered feeling powerless. And then he remembered running to the castle across the field, and later, crouching on the staircase beside the only person who had seen through him—who had cared to see through him—who had made him feel that somebody saw his pain and understood it.

Jamie reappeared on the doorstep, quietly closing the front door behind him.

"How's Rhiannon?" Colin asked, before Jamie could say anything.

"Rhiannon?" His grandfather's face turned red. "What do you care about her for?" he snapped, stalking toward Colin's position on the grass like a gnarled, stooped-over boxer.

"She was a good friend when I was a kid," Colin said. "I'd really like to see her again."

Maybe it was crazy, but he wanted to know why she hadn't written him when she'd promised. He'd waited to hear from her, and nothing had come. Maybe if she had, things would have been different.

No, he couldn't blame any of this on her. "I'll look her up tomorrow," he mused. He gave Jamie a smile. "Do you know if she still lives around here?"

His grandfather's eyes narrowed. "You leave her alone. She's not interested in seeing the likes of you."

"How do you know that?"

Jamie seemed to be fighting to keep himself from blowing up. He hadn't been all that warm and cuddly when Colin knew him, and the years had only seemed to make him crankier. He wagged his finger at Colin. "Because she's married and has five wee bairns. Her...husband would right kill you. Or at least break your arms. Then how would you play your golf?"

Colin pushed his irritation away because he didn't want to be angry anymore. He'd liked Rhiannon a lot. He remembered her as a skinny girl with pigtails and a soft, shy voice. What had made her special to him had been her spirit. Her fierce, sweet, independent spirit.

Maybe it was disappointing to hear that she was married, but he could still check in with her. Maybe she would go with him to the funeral. She'd known his father, too.

And then the sadness of it all hit him in a crushing wave. His whole body feeling shaky, he drew a ragged breath. "I'm here because my father is dead." His voice sounded small and pained, like a boy's.

Where had *that* come from?

His grandfather got even more furious. "Aye, you should feel bad about it!" he shouted.

Colin felt his mouth dropping open.

"Did you even think once about your grandmother?" Jamie said in a more hushed tone, making a guilty, backward glance at the closed cottage door. "About the pain this brings her? Despite everything, she sat up all night waiting to see you. Waiting, and crying. Now she's asleep, tired of waiting for you lot."

His grandfather waved a gnarled hand, and Colin felt ashamed. "Now you can wait for her to wake up and take you in. She asked me to drive her to the store yesterday, because she wants to cook your favorites for breakfast. And she will! But until she's awake and in her kitchen, you'll just find a hotel. I'll not let you in to see her, smelling like a brewery. Sleep it off and get yourself clean. Maybe then you can think to yourself about what you've done tonight."

*Think* to himself? That was all Colin had been doing. That was his problem.

But the ancient door to the cottage closed again, and Colin was left alone, in the elements, with a canvas bag containing funeral clothes, fast getting soggy, and his ever-present set of golf clubs.

Colin hadn't really thought about why he'd brought his clubs. It was more a reflex or a habit. Something he always lugged around with him because he wanted to. He liked golf. He liked the feeling of competence it gave him, especially since he'd gained his tour card. Made him feel valued and accepted.

He tucked the golf clubs into a dry spot under the overhang to the roof. Behind the cottage was a long, rolling field. The Highlands. Paradise of his childhood summers.

The landscape looked the same, held all the promise that he'd remembered. He'd used to range over this land, racing with sticks aloft—pretend swords—in the company of Rhiannon MacDowall.

Shaking his head, smiling again—at last—he grabbed a fairway wood and a handful of practice balls from his golf bag. Traipsing through the squishy grass, he headed for the rolling field beyond. It smelled like rain and heather and fresh, wide-open air.

He remembered this place in his bones. This feeling of peace. The mist rose off the grass even as the rain came down. It was so quiet it seemed holy. Not another soul was awake with him.

He dropped the practice balls and lined up his stance so he was facing a copse in the distance. That way had been Rhiannon's castle.

Winding up, he hit a ball with a solid whack. It reverberated through him, centering him.

Calming him.

———

THE FIRST THING Rhiannon MacDowall did every morning when she awoke was to visit her garden in an effort to center herself and reconnect with a feeling of peace.

Afterward, she climbed the stairs to her art studio with the view over her family's property. This was the same terrain Rhiannon had been taking comfort from for most of her life. On an easel beside her was her latest landscape painting, done in oils and nearly completed. Her uncle was coming to collect it in a week; one of his wealthy friends had commissioned it.

Art was what she did with her life. She loved it. It calmed her.

She tilted her head and observed the large canvas.

*I want to add a cottage to it.*

The thought stunned her because it was so different from her usual style. But it felt right.

Her yellow tabby cat hopped off the window ledge. He landed gingerly, shaking his front paws. *Poor Colin.* She picked him up and hugged him. He was twenty-one, old for a cat.

Her whole world seemed to be changing of late.

Mum and Dad had been gone a week now—rare for them —with eight more weeks to go on their vacation. For the first time Rhiannon could remember, she was living alone in the castle. Just Paul, their longtime butler, Colin the aging cat and her.

Even her brother, Malcolm, was newly married, and her cousin Isabel—now her closest female friend her age—had just sent her a "save the date" notice for an autumn wedding invitation. A wedding that Rhiannon would attend by video monitor, of course. Rhiannon wished Isabel well, but if she were honest, the invitation had set off a tinge of dissatisfaction within her. Maybe a wee bit of envy?

Perfectly natural. But, as always, she would control it until she was content again.

Rhiannon found her camera and grabbed a warm raincoat for her walk outside. The weather was misting a bit and alternating with rain, not atypical for Scotland in early June, so she laced up her waterproof boots and tucked the camera inside her front pocket.

She had the perfect picturesque cottage in mind, and it was on the edge of their two-hundred-acre estate. Usually, Rhiannon worked from memory, but the last time she'd seen the cottage was, well, before she'd become agoraphobic. Just the thought of approaching the boundary lines and the public road to see it was making her pulse race. Making this trip was daring for her. But she was ready for a change, however slight and controlled.

She went downstairs, then across the courtyard to the main castle and the breakfast room. Paul stood at the buffet table, arranging breakfast items as he had done every morning for years going back. He smiled to see her, and she relaxed somewhat.

"Good morning, miss. Would you like some coffee?"

"When I return, please, Paul. I'm going for my walk now." By habit, she reached for the dog leash, but remembered that her mum's golden retriever, Molly, was gone, too, boarded at the vet's, recuperating from minor surgery on her leg.

Rhiannon sighed. She would be walking alone today.

"I'll pick Molly up later in the day," Paul remarked kindly.

"Thank you." They'd been together so long that sometimes she thought Paul could read her mind.

He gestured to the window. "The starlings have left the nest."

"Have they? They're late this year."

"Indeed." Paul smiled mildly and wiped down their coffee machine. He was getting a bit stooped. She hadn't noticed until now. He must have been about forty when he came to them after she'd returned home from the hospital. Now he would be in his sixties.

*We're all getting older.*

And then what? What would Rhiannon do when Paul finally retired? Rhiannon was thirty. A spinster. An agoraphobic spinster, living alone in a modernized castle. Any supplies she needed, she ordered by phone or internet. But for actual contact with people, she relied on Paul. Or her parents. Even Molly.

Paul glanced at her standing there, holding the leash, and stopped tidying up. "Miss, would you like me to accompany you on your walk today?"

"No. That's quite all right." She smiled at Paul. She really did appreciate his presence in her life. "Sooner or later we all have to walk alone."

Paul blinked. "That's not necessarily true, miss."

"You don't think so?"

Paul politely gazed down at his hands. He was the help, after all, their perfect, English-trained butler. He was paid to be agreeable to her. "I wouldn't presume to know," he murmured.

"Well, for today at least, I walk alone." She patted the camera in her pocket. "I'll be back in a half hour. If I'm not, send out the hounds."

The corner of Paul's mouth twitched. They didn't have any hounds. Just a playful golden retriever, currently injured.

Rhiannon headed outside, walking her customary path past the walled garden and circling the gravel drive. Up the hill was the guard shack, and from there, all along the boundaries, a stone wall, strengthened with concrete. Surveillance cameras were installed at regular intervals, monitored by the guard on duty.

*I am safe,* she told herself, breathing deeply. She headed for the path across the open moor. Nature, cruelly, was waking. In bloom everywhere.

The cottage—the guard's cottage—was at the southern border of their large property—farther away from the castle than she'd dared to walk in years. She wasn't sure how it would affect her. She concentrated on feeling in control: maintaining her regular breathing, visualizing the peace of her garden, humming to herself.

Still, the closer she came to the cottage, the shakier she felt. She paused, tightening her grip on the camera in her pocket. She wished Molly was with her. At the very least, she wished she'd thought of carrying a large stick.

She exhaled slowly. This was the natural fallout from the brutal kidnapping she'd survived as a young girl. Ever since then she had her safe place she felt protected by—her beautiful castle grounds—and she stayed within those boundaries. Walking to the cottage would test her limits.

But she could do it. She visualized the cottage in her mind. Jamie and Jessie lived there, and had since before she'd been born. Jamie was the longtime guardsman for their family. Five days a week, he kept watch from the shack at the top of the drive. He kept a phone with a direct line to Paul in the house. There were cameras all around the property, spaced every few dozen yards. Each year, her father commissioned a security expert to review and renew their protocols and procedures.

It didn't bother Rhiannon. She was happy in her world, truly. She moved closer to the boundary, more curious than anything. How would her body react to this change in her daily walk?

She heard a roaring noise. The *whoosh* of a van passing close by on the roadway. Rhiannon froze. A white van had been the vehicle the kidnappers had used to snatch her and her brother. Her breath came in jagged spurts.

She heard a voice; someone was singing. Her pulse racing, she retreated to the edge of a copse. Then there was whistling. A man's tone. Something else was going on, too, because she heard a whacking noise. She backed away slowly, her breathing heavy. Despite the coolness of the morning, she felt heated. Her heart rate elevated. Her palms perspiring...

This was how a panic attack began. And there was nothing worse to Rhiannon than a panic attack. It was the one thing she had set her life up to avoid. She couldn't lose control of herself. She couldn't go back to those days in the hospital.

A cry sputtered out of her, and she turned to flee. But the toe of her rubber boot caught on a root, and she tripped. Her hands splayed on the wet, boggy earth beneath an oak tree.

*Get up. Run.*

But it was just like when she'd been a girl. Walking along happy, full of plans for the day, so mundane she couldn't even remember them at this point—much like painting a cottage on a landscape. She'd been caught up in herself, not paying attention to the world and skipping ahead of her older brother.

She'd seen the men—the kidnappers—before Malcolm had. There had been a split second when she could have screamed. Could have warned Malcolm. Could have grabbed his hand and made both of them run away.

But she'd done none of those things. She'd frozen instead.

Because of that, Malcolm had been taken with her, shoved into a white van parked on a busy Edinburgh street, and while she sat still, mute, Malcolm had screamed and fought.

They had beaten him, so badly that he'd lost consciousness. And even then, seeing her brother's limp, battered body, blood all about his mouth and his nose, made her feel guilty.

She could have prevented it, and she hadn't. And now it was happening again. No sound would come out of her mouth. Her body was locked in terror. The shaking started. Next came the sweating. At some point, she would pass out.

*Wham!* Something hard smashed into the ground in front of her, then ricocheted and hit her right hip bone. A muffled squeak came out of her mouth, an "umph!" rather than anything intelligible or powerful.

*Is this an attack? Scream. Why can't you scream? Run!*

But instead of yelling or fleeing, Rhiannon groaned and pitched forward. Her elbows slammed into the boggy earth; the camera at her hip hit the ground and she heard something break—the lens perhaps. The camera dug into her freshly bruised hip, sending a dull shooting pain through her. "Oh!" she moaned.

She rolled over and pulled the camera from the flap pocket. It rattled when she moved it. The camera was obviously broken.

"Hello!" a male voice called. "Is anybody there?"

Trembling, Rhiannon pushed to her knees. *Run!*

"Oh, no, I'm so sorry!" A man came into the clearing, sprinting toward her, waving. He carried a golf club in the other hand. Blinking, she glanced down and saw a golf ball on the ground beside her.

She put her hand to the sore spot. There would be a bruise. But that wasn't her immediate concern. *This man was. Run!*

*Too late.* He was there already. "Are you okay? Wow, let me help you up."

He reached for her hand, but she shrank back. He wore a gray sweatshirt—her kidnappers had worn hoodie sweatshirts—and his eyes were a pale gray blue beneath his navy blue golf cap. He also wore cargo pants and trainers. She had the impression of confident masculinity.

He pushed back the cap back from his face. Wavy, light brown hair with blond streaks. The scruffy beginnings of a beard. He gave her a boyishly charming, lopsided smile. "I'm really sorry about this."

He held out a hand to her, but she, embarrassingly, scurried backward like a crab.

"I'm a professional golfer," he said. "My name's Colin Walker."

*Colin Walker!* She almost laughed hysterically. The boy—now a man—she'd named her cat after, all those years ago.

Of course it would be Colin Walker she'd bumped into. Now, when she looked her worst—wet, muddy and bedraggled. She must have summoned him, she thought—maybe she'd conjured him up. All these thoughts about weddings and wishes for what could never be.

And he was so good-looking it was criminal. Of course she'd watched Colin on the telly; they all had. He'd strolled along the fairways as if he owned them, while his grandmother Jessie sat beside her on the couch in front of the big screen in the castle, near to bursting her buttons with pride.

Shaking, Rhiannon wiped her muddy hands on her trousers. Her right palm had nicked a sharp stone when she fell, and it stung. It was her dominant hand, and now painting might be difficult for a few days.

"At least let me take you into the house and get you a bandage for that cut." Colin reached for her other hand, but she jerked away. People knew better than to touch her. It made her panic, and she couldn't let that happen.

"No. Please. I'm fine." She stood on her own. Likely, the only reason she hadn't gone into a full-blown panic attack was that she knew who he was. Her heart was pounding with the knowledge.

His head tilted. He noticed her broken camera and picked it up from the ground. "I want to replace this for you." He tucked it into his pocket. "Do you live around here? I'm only here for a few days, but I'll order one for you and have it delivered."

She hugged herself and stepped back. "No, I'd rather you didn't do that."

"I need to. I want to, I mean..." His gaze went up and down

the length of her. She looked a fright! Her worst clothes, her scraggly, rain-wet hair, muddy boots...

"What's your name?" he asked.

Jamie would tell him even if she didn't. She had no choice. "I'm Rhiannon," she said softly. "You know me."

"Rhiannon!" Again, those charming, handsome gray-blue eyes went up and down her body. Scrutinized her face. Lingered on her eyes.

She felt herself flushing.

Did he remember her as fondly as she remembered him?

Obviously not, because he threw back his head and laughed at her. She didn't know what she'd expected, but this hadn't been it. Pity, perhaps. Quiet respect. Silence.

But never ridicule.

"I can't believe this!" he said, still laughing at her.

What, that she was a recluse by choice? That the best way to manage her agoraphobia was to cut herself off from the rest of the world?

She'd never wanted him to see her like this. She'd thought that of all people, *he* would understand.

She'd been wrong.

"What did you expect of me?" she asked quietly.

"Sorry. It's a long story." Shaking his head, he leaned toward her...*touching* her, and she jumped backward as if scalded.

What was he doing? *No one* touched her. *She* controlled her space.

"I have to go," she said.

He caught hold of her arm. "Hey, Rhiannon, wait..."

"Stop," she whispered, staring at his hand on her sleeve. She could feel her heart drumming, feel the panic returning. People didn't treat her this way. They were respectful of her dignity.

Colin looked at her quizzically, and she drew herself up,

groping for her inner peace. Control was the most important thing. "Please."

He let go of her. "Oh, Rhi, I'm sorry. You're married, huh? I didn't mean anything by it. Touching you, I mean."

*Married?* What a cruel joke.

"How are your kids?" he asked, drawling at her like a true Texan. "You have a bunch of 'em. Right?"

Something stung at her eyes. Something fierce and unexpected.

How could an agoraphobic ever bring up a child?

A strangled noise came from her throat. A harsh, suppressed sob.

"Rhi?"

Horrified, she shook her head.

Normally, she would be calm about it. Philosophical and gentle and accepting, but today...after her cousin's wedding news...she was on edge.

"No kids? Figures he lied to me," he muttered. "Well, me, neither." Colin talked blithely along as if he hadn't noticed her discomfort. "No kids. No wife. Just the traveling life." He glanced down at her. His eyes were so blue. "How about you? Do you travel?"

Colin had no idea. None. It was as if she was seeing her life the way it might have been. The way it could never be.

"Rhi?"

"I'm fine!" she shouted harshly.

His face fell. Utterly fell.

She slapped her hand over her mouth. She turned and fled back to the castle before she did anything worse.

## CHAPTER FOUR

*SMOOTH MOVE, WALKER,* Colin thought as he watched Rhiannon run away. Obviously, she'd been appalled by him. How dumb had he been, hitting golf balls into the woods? He was a trained professional and he should have known better. That was what driving ranges were for.

Thankfully, she wasn't hurt. Still, the broken camera in his hand rattled—he needed to replace it for her. Maybe his grandmother would be awake now and could help him make arrangements for that.

Blowing out his breath, Colin headed back to the cottage. The rain had stopped, but there was still no hint of sun, just gray, overcast skies. This place was about as different from Central Texas as he could imagine.

Under the overhang to the porch, he tossed his club and glove into the golf bag.

"Colin?"

Colin froze. He'd know that voice anywhere—Nana. Instinctively, a lump rose in his throat, and he turned to see her.

"Oh, Colin." Tears glistened in his grandmother's eyes. She was thinner and sadder looking than he remembered. He'd come to Scotland still harboring anger, but somehow, seeing her in person, that seemed to disappear.

Jessie's arms shook as she reached for him. He pulled her close and gave her a hug. She wore an apron that smelled like black pudding. He hadn't eaten black pudding—the Scots name for blood sausage—in ages; it had always been a favorite of his when he'd visited in the summers, because the boy in him had loved that it was made with real blood.

She stood back and held him at arms' length. "I'm so proud of you." She leaned forward and whispered, "I watch you on the telly. But you look bigger and taller in person. So handsome."

Colin couldn't help smiling. "You're looking good, too, Nana." He winked at her and lifted up her chin. He didn't want her to be so sad.

A light seemed to come on inside her, and her face appeared less tired. "Come in, dear." She opened the door and led him into her cottage.

He followed her and took his canvas bag with him. The clubs would be fine under the overhang.

The front room was as he remembered it, but the contents had completely changed. The stuffed furniture was new. The TV was a silver flat screen, and though relatively small, it dominated the space. The old childhood pictures of him and his parents weren't on the wall anymore. A large landscape oil painting hung in their place.

He tilted his head, trying to figure out why the scene in the painting felt so familiar. "Is that the clearing where Rhiannon and I built a fort?" He'd climbed those oak trees and hauled old loose boards into the limbs. He and Rhiannon used to sit and swing their feet there.

"Aye, that's Rhiannon's work."

"She's a painter?" he asked, surprised.

"She's known the world over," his grandmother said with

obvious pride, and pointed to Rhiannon's small signature on the bottom right. "She paints scenes from the estate. Wealthy collectors buy them, but this was a gift to me and Jamie."

The painting was seriously professional work—to Colin, it looked museum quality. "I had no idea," he murmured, though maybe he shouldn't have been surprised.

Rhiannon had always been creative, and she'd even sketched people with her pencils. Like him, she hadn't been disciplined then—he remembered them more as running free like wild, unsupervised children. The memory made him smile again.

His grandmother gestured for him to follow her. "Come into the kitchen and tell me about everything you've been doing."

Colin nodded. Now would be a good time to tell her how he'd seen Rhiannon in the clearing—and that he'd angered Jamie by talking about her. Also that he wasn't looking forward to dealing with his father's funeral on Sunday. Not at all.

But as he watched his grandmother shakily reaching into a cabinet, it struck Colin that she didn't seem well. He'd thought her ancient years ago, but now he realized that she'd actually been so much younger and healthier than she was now. She moved slowly, setting up a French press, her way of making coffee.

"Do you see Rhiannon often?" he asked instead, leaning against the counter and crossing his arms.

"Well..." Jessie drew the word out in the manner that Scots sometimes did, so that it sounded like *wheel*. "She takes her walks early in the morning. I used to meet her with a wee cuppie, but I've been feeling tired of late."

She *did* look tired. Maybe that was why she'd left the restaurant last night instead of waiting for him.

"I'm sorry to hear that," he said.

"Nonsense." She waved her hand. "I don't mean to talk about

me." She gazed at him, and her face brightened. "Sit down. Let me feed you some breakfast."

She rolled the *r* on *breakfast* in that delightful way that he used to emulate when he got home to Texas. Jessie's brogue was so thick and enchanting that Colin had to sometimes stop and tilt his ear to catch it all.

"Sure," he said, and pulled out the same chair he remembered using as a boy. "I'm starving." The discussions about the funeral could wait.

His grandmother beamed. She'd always loved to feed him. He enjoyed her big Scottish breakfasts.

He grinned back at her as he sat at his place in her cozy kitchen. Nothing here had changed—except maybe the appliances were modernized.

"Do you still like your eggs poached?" she asked.

He nodded. "You know I do."

"And grapefruit juice, not orange?"

He nodded again. She knew all his quirks. He *was* starving, actually.

She bustled about at the stove, opened the oven and checked on his blood sausage. But he only noticed one place setting at the table—his.

"Won't you eat with me, Jessie?"

"I'll sit with you, yes." She set down his juice, along with a bowl of oatmeal. "And here's your porridge. Jamie and I already had our wee bite."

As though summoned by the sound of his name, Colin's grandfather stomped in from the front room. He must have been upstairs. By the scowl on Jamie's face, and the tuft of white hair that was standing upright from having his hands through it so often, Colin saw that his mood hadn't improved.

Jamie addressed Jessie, pointing at Colin as if Colin weren't there. "There's something you need to tell him, woman."

She waved her hand at Jamie as if dismissing him.

Jamie made an exasperated noise. Colin averted his gaze.

"Please, Jamie," Jessie pleaded. "Let me enjoy the morning with my grandson. I don't want any unpleasantness."

Jamie glowered at Colin. There was nothing Colin could say to make this easier for Jessie, so he just remained silent, waiting.

Finally, Jamie snapped a coat from a peg on the wall and then limped toward the back door. "The sooner he's back to Texas," Jamie said, pointing to Colin again, "the better off we'll be."

His grandmother cringed and Colin's heart went out to her.

But after the door had shut, Jessie just smiled sadly and looked at Colin. He could see the tears she was doing her best to blink away.

"Don't pay him any mind," she said. "He has the gout. It's painful for him."

"Is that why you left the restaurant early last night?" Colin asked.

"Yes," she said, looking relieved and turning back to the egg she was cooking. "I'm glad you understand."

He sighed and sat back in his chair. "Nana, I should've called to tell you we were running late. I'm sorry."

She waved her hand. "Don't fash yourself." It was a Scottish phrase that meant "don't worry about a thing." His grandmother said "don't fash yourself" the same way he said "keep it light."

Chuckling, he picked up his spoon.

"What's funny?"

"Nothing," he said. "We're more alike than I'd realized."

She reached over to pat his hand. "I do wish I'd tried harder to reach you when you were younger."

*Tried harder.* Maybe she *had* called. Maybe Daisie Lee hadn't wanted her to talk with him. "My mother wasn't keen on phone calls." He glanced at her.

Jessie waved a hand. "Say no more."

He nodded again. She didn't want to revisit the past any more than he did.

Still, he felt guilty. "My manager told me that you sent some emails to my website. I'm sorry I didn't read them."

"It's not important now," Jessie insisted. She took a plate from a cabinet and arranged toast, two eggs and his black pudding on it. As she put it down at his place, he had a thought.

"You're afraid to fly," he said. "That's why you never came to Texas."

"Eat your breakfast." She sat across from him and urged him to pick up his fork.

He ate most of it; he was ravenous and it was delicious. But as he contemplated the last blood sausage, he stared down at his plate, feeling ashamed.

He was able-bodied and had enough money to pay for plane tickets. He could have flown to Scotland and visited his grandmother. His mother wouldn't have needed to hear about it, or even known what he'd done. It wouldn't have been disloyal to her.

"We're together now, better late than never," Jessie said, rolling her *r* in that delightful way.

"Aye, better late than never," he mimicked.

She laughed, swatting his hand.

"I *am* sorry," he murmured to her.

She picked up the French press, but he shook his head because he didn't need any more caffeine in his system. He was wired from the flight, from the night of drinking, from staying up late.

From hitting Rhiannon with a golf ball.

He put the heel of his hand to his head. He just wanted to make up for...everything. His father was dead, and it was too late to do anything about that, but Colin was tired of regrets. There were things now, today, he could do.

"How do you apologize to a woman?" he said aloud to Jessie.

"Oh, no. You don't need to apologize to me."

"It's for someone else, actually."

She peered at him. "What have you done?"

He stabbed his blood sausage with his fork. "I hit a golf ball and broke Rhiannon's camera, and then I inadvertently insulted her." He shook his head. "Why would Jamie tell me that she's married with kids if she isn't?"

"Oh," Jessie murmured. "Your grandfather, he's..." She waved her hand. "Never mind about him. You let me handle his temper. Now, are you saying that you want to apologize to Rhiannon?"

"I do." He thought of the landscape on the wall, the one that Rhiannon had painted. Then he gazed at his grandmother. "I don't want bad blood between us," he said meaningfully. "Not anymore."

Jessie clasped her hands and put them to her mouth. Then she took off her glasses and wiped her eyes with a tissue. Smiling at him, she stood and padded to a drawer, then came back with an old-fashioned box of notepaper and a pen.

The notepaper had a sketch of a bird on it.

He laughed. "Seriously?"

She just raised her eyes and gave him a look.

"Right." He pushed aside his empty plate and took the pen and paper from her.

So much could be said in a simple letter. He should have written. Rhiannon should have written. They all should have written.

"So...if I tell her I'm sorry, do you think that'll help?" he asked.

Jessie tilted her head. "My rosebush has budded. Cut a nice stem and strip off the thorns. That can't hurt, either."

He nodded. "Women like flowers."

"Is there no one special in your life? Another young woman, perhaps?"

"No." He clicked the pen open and then shut it. He'd never given anyone flowers. He'd also never written a personal letter.

This should be interesting.

He blinked, rubbing his fist against his eye. His vision was getting scratchy with lack of sleep.

Jessie noticed. "Aye." She picked up his empty plate. "Have you slept yet?"

He shook his head.

"I've made up a bed for you. Get some sleep, and then worry about the rest of the day. After you rest, everything else will come easier."

She was right. He really wasn't functioning well. His brain was messed-up like a zombie's.

He grabbed his bag and followed her into the front room, though he didn't need to follow her because he knew this place by heart and always would, until the day he died. He walked behind his grandmother up a creaky, steep length of stairs that she didn't navigate as well as she used to.

Inside the modest guest room was an ancient, wrought-iron twin bed, a scatter rug over a painted wooden floor and a set of drawers that had seen better days. He dropped his canvas bag on a metal chair.

"You know where the bathroom is," his grandmother said. "I've put fresh towels on the table for you." *Fresh* had that same wonderful rolled *r.*

He smiled at her, feeling like a kid again, but in a good way. In a naive way of trusting that all would be better in the morning.

She closed the door and let him sleep.

———

COLIN WOKE WHEN he heard the loud whine of weed-whacking directly beneath his window. Rubbing his eyes, gazing through the windowpane, he saw his grandfather attacking a patch of thistle, revving the motor and scowling to himself.

The perverse old dude. Colin chuckled softly. But then his grandfather glared up at his window in a manner that made Colin wonder if he was trying to disturb his sleep on purpose. The laughter died in his throat.

Jamie probably didn't even have gout. If he did, shouldn't he be resting the foot, not hobbling about on it? Colin was pretty sure that Jamie's anger had more to do with him—and his presence in Scotland—than it did with any ailment Jamie might have.

Colin couldn't think of anything he could say or do to make his grandfather feel differently about him. He was trying to be laid-back about it, but the facts didn't lie. He felt lousy. He needed to get out of here.

First, he had to apologize to Rhiannon.

After rooting in his canvas bag for his shower kit and a set of clean clothes, he took a long, hot shower, ducking his head in the low stall. When he went back to his room, he had to stoop to avoid bumping his head on the sloped ceiling. Still, he took more care than he usually did with his routine. Colin was a casual guy, not big on combs or razors, but this time he was sure to make himself as clean-cut as possible for Rhiannon.

He didn't know why—and maybe it was crazy—but it suddenly seemed critical to get her on his side again.

He sat on the bed with the notepaper for ten minutes,

pondering what to say to her. How to get across to her that he was really sorry for his rudeness.

In the end, he just wrote from the heart. Downstairs, his grandmother handed him a pair of scissors. He went to the side of the house and clipped a few of her roses. If one was good, then six were better.

It was a slow twenty-minute hike to the castle. He passed through a small copse, around a spongy moor with pale green grass and alongside a creek—"burn," they called it here. Nature had changed little except for some trees that were missing since his last visit; others were taller and fuller. It was funny—Colin couldn't specifically remember most people he met, but he'd remembered this land. The outdoors was a big part of what sustained him. Probably no accident that he'd chosen to become a professional golfer.

Colin came to the front of the castle and stood for a moment, marveling over it. A huge, gray stone facade. Still the same turrets, the same circular gravel drive. The same short, wooden drawbridge that had once fascinated him so much.

He had to clear away cobwebs before he could ring the bell, but he heard the noise echo in the great hall, so he knew it worked.

A man dressed in a black suit answered the door. "Yes?" He had a bland voice and an expressionless face.

"I'm here to see Rhiannon," Colin said.

The man coughed into his hand. Colin had no idea who he was. "May I ask who is calling, sir?"

"Colin Walker." He shifted on his feet, transferred the flowers to his other hand.

The man bowed his head slightly. He opened the door and gestured for Colin to enter. "Please wait on the couch while I phone her."

The whole thing was strange. Colin followed him inside.

The first detail he noticed was that the interior had been renovated. The great hall didn't look as much like a dank and drafty laird's castle, but a modern home with all the comforts.

Colin was led to a small anteroom he didn't remember, with a couch by a window that looked out over the front drive. At the entrance was the guard station where his grandfather worked. Colin wasn't even sure if he still worked there anymore or if he'd retired.

"I'll be back in a moment," the man said.

"Who are you?" Colin asked him.

"I'm the MacDowalls' butler. You may call me Paul."

Also surreal. Had Colin wandered onto the set of *Downton Abbey?* Rhiannon's parents hadn't employed a butler the last time he'd been here.

"Ah, will you please take these to Rhiannon?" Colin handed Paul the rose bouquet. The letter, too, just in case she wasn't inclined to see him.

Paul was gone for five minutes. Colin knew, because there was a clock on the wall and it ticked, loudly. He stood and walked out of the holding area and into the great room with its tall ceilings, about thirty feet high, and the stone fireplace with the baronial swords and shields on display. That display had been Colin's favorite part of the castle. His gaze moved to the staircase where he and Rhiannon had once hidden. The staircase had been completely rerouted now, and their hiding place was gone.

Paul's throat cleared. Colin turned.

"I'm sorry, but Rhiannon isn't seeing anyone today."

"Did she take my letter?"

"Yes, sir."

"Do you know if she read it?"

"I'm sorry, sir, but I couldn't say." Paul took a step and then paused, waiting for Colin to follow him to the door, but Colin stood rooted.

"If you'll allow me to lead you out." Paul tilted his head, signaling the end of Colin's visit.

But it bothered him that Rhiannon was avoiding him. Something was wrong. "Will she be coming to my father's funeral?" he asked Paul. "Or maybe her parents or brother?" What was his name? "Malcolm," Colin said, remembering.

Paul frowned, but Colin didn't move. He needed to know. "The funeral is on Sunday," Colin said stubbornly. He didn't know what time, though. Now he wished he'd asked his grandmother.

It made him feel terrible, still.

"Excuse me while I check for you," Paul murmured.

Colin waited, for twenty-two minutes this time. He exchanged text messages with Mack—his friend had set up a tee time for them at a nearby course, at Colin's request—to pass the time. When Paul at last returned to the small anteroom where Colin sat on the couch, watching the birds flit outside, Paul carried a silver tray with a tea service. Pot, teacup, bone china, the works.

Colin stared. He'd expected none of this. Rhiannon's family had always been more formal than his, but this was just excessive. He'd spent a good portion of his childhood living in a trailer, eating off mismatched plates and drinking out of jelly glasses.

He stood while Paul set down the tray. There was only one cup.

"Mr. MacDowall will be arriving shortly to speak with you," Paul said.

"Rhiannon's father is coming?"

"No, sir. Mr. *Malcolm* MacDowall."

Rhiannon's *brother?* Colin just felt confused. "Why did you call him?"

"Because you asked about him, sir. And since he is at his company's Byrne Glennie facility today, and is therefore available locally, he has decided to stop by and speak with you."

Colin sat, his hand on his forehead. All he'd wanted was to apologize to Rhiannon. He had the feeling he was missing something important.

Paul poured tea into a cup. "Cream or sugar?"

Colin shook his head. "I don't know. I don't drink tea." When had this gotten so complicated?

"Try this, sir." Paul used a pair of silver tongs to drop a sugar cube into the cup and then added a small amount of cream from a tiny pitcher. He passed Colin the delicate cup and saucer, but Colin just stared at him. He didn't dare touch the damn thing. What if he dropped it?

Paul cleared his throat, then placed the cup and saucer back on the tray. Straightening, he said formally, "Mr. MacDowall requested that I serve you tea, as it will be another ten minutes before he arrives." He turned to leave.

"Wait," Colin said.

Paul turned, his brow raised. Honestly, Colin just hadn't wanted to be left waiting again.

"Ah... Malcolm...he's the CEO of Sage Family Products now?" The major body-care corporation that his mother had talked about. The one that gave endorsements to professional athletes.

"No, he's the president," Paul explained patiently. "Mr. John Sage, Rhiannon's uncle, is the CEO."

---

RHIANNON SAT ON the stairs, observing Colin and Paul. Ironically, she'd curled up near the spot where she and Colin had peeked through a lattice screen. The staircase had been renovated with modern railings, and now a restored tapestry concealed her from view. But there was one threadbare place in the material that she could peer through.

She'd never expected Colin to return, or to ask to see her. She'd thought she'd scared him away. Part of her had hoped that he would stay away; that would be for the best, after all.

But then she'd been informed by the guard observing the cameras that Colin was approaching the castle. And now, watching him in person...

She put her hand to her lips, filled with amusement by his sweet but bumbling reaction to Paul's stiff formality. Her family hadn't used the services of a butler all those years ago, and it seemed that Colin wasn't sure about how to react to this foreign ritual. But he was gamely trying to put himself in Paul's good graces.

And what about the funeral he mentioned? She hadn't been aware of anything happening to his father. Then again, she hadn't spoken to Jessie in a few weeks. Jamie, either. She'd been wrapped up in finishing her painting.

"Poor Colin," she murmured. *It must be terrible.*

She was answered with a peeved *meow.* The cat in her arms had followed along behind her, more dog than catlike in his behavior. She'd been petting him when Paul arrived with the tea cart.

Now the cat struggled; he knew that the tinkling of china meant fresh cream, and Colin the cat lived for fresh cream. But she normally didn't let him have much, because he tended to get gassy. Rhiannon stood, intent on sneaking off, carrying her cat back to her painting studio with her, but he jumped down with a loud *thud.*

"*Colin,*" she whispered at him.

Colin veered from her and darted off on his short legs as best he could—admittedly, not quickly these days—down the stair-case, across the tartan carpeting and toward his namesake.

Rhiannon groaned and covered her head. Below her, Colin the cat sat by Colin the human's feet. The cat posed in a regal position and begged for cream with his most entitled *meow*.

"Colin, stop that!" Paul scolded.

"Excuse me?" Colin the human said.

"Colin," Paul said to the cat, and he bent to pick him up. "You know you don't belong here," he admonished her pet in a singsong voice.

"Wait a minute," Colin said. "Did you just call that cat by my name?"

"No," Paul said stiffly, drawing himself up. "You share a name with Rhiannon's cat."

"Rhiannon's cat?"

"Yes, sir."

"Here, pretty baby." Colin patted his lap, and her cat obliged, jumping up on him. Again, as best he could, given his age. The little devil would attempt anything to poach cream.

"How old is he?" Colin asked Paul.

"He's twenty-one, I believe," Paul said.

Colin was silent for a moment. Then he drew his hand along Colin's fur, petting him. "I never knew about him." Maybe Rhiannon imagined it, but she thought Colin looked misty-eyed.

Rhiannon sat again. Colin's letter was in her pocket. Quietly, she opened the envelope and unfolded the note inside. In a careful hand, he'd written:

Rhiannon, I'm sorry I offended you this morning. You were once an important friend of mine, and I don't want to lose that. Please forgive me. Colin.

Rhiannon touched it lovingly. Oh, what she had wished for —a letter from him—and never thought would happen.

She'd been utterly shocked when he'd come back this after-noon. Part of her wanted Colin here—but not the part that was in charge. The panic attacks trumped everything, and with them, she could never be normal around him.

More than anything, she needed her control. To be in charge of herself. Colin threatened that control. It was sad, but that was the way she was. To meet with him would be cruel, for both of them. It was best for everyone that he leave as soon as possible.

But what about his father's funeral? She would have to say something about it. She couldn't just ignore it, or him.

Just then the castle door opened—Malcolm had arrived, bringing in the smell of the early-summer air. He was dressed in his workday suit, his sunglasses on. Her older brother was a handsome man—always had been—but when Colin stood, the cat still in his arms, he managed to take her breath away.

Colin had changed clothing since she'd seen him earlier, and now wore khaki trousers and a collared shirt. He was shaven, tall and full of life, and he looked so appealing to her that all she could do was stare at him.

"Hi, Malcolm. It's me. It's Colin."

But Malcolm's jaw tightened. Slowly, he hooked his car keys on a peg beside the wall. "What's going on?" he asked in his gruff, deep tone.

Colin's smile wavered. "My father died," he said in a low voice.

Rhiannon put her hand to her mouth. She felt devastated for him.

Even Malcolm was moved; she watched him exchange a look with Paul.

"I'm sorry," Malcolm said.

"You didn't know?"

"Not until Paul told me. But I don't live here anymore—I live in Edinburgh. I'm only in the area because we own a manufacturing facility in Byrne...well, not far from here."

"Do your parents plan to attend the funeral?" Colin crossed his arms. "Because my grandmother could really use the support."

Malcolm shook his head helplessly. "My parents are out of the country. They won't be back until the end of summer."

"And Rhiannon?" Colin's voice went lower. "Is she coming?"

Rhiannon's heart seemed to pause. What was she going to do?

Malcolm's hands tightened into fists. Her brother was protective of her, and he probably always would be. It upset her and made her sad, especially because Malcolm was married now and had a new life of his own. Rhiannon didn't call to check in with him every day anymore, as she used to. It wasn't fair to him.

She wished Paul hadn't called him. The last thing she wanted were bad feelings between her brother and Colin.

"Let me talk with my sister," Malcolm said in a clipped tone. "You wait here."

CHAPTER FIVE

"THANK YOU," Rhiannon breathed as Malcolm headed up the stairs.

When he appeared on the landing, she intercepted him and put her finger to her lips, motioning him to follow her. Together they climbed the rest of the way, then went around the corner and into the library.

Inside, Malcolm leaned against the doorjamb while Rhiannon paced. She had such nervous energy. Colin's presence had affected her physically, even without the dilemma she faced regarding his father's funeral.

"You didn't need to come," Rhiannon said to her brother, keeping her voice low so Colin wouldn't hear her downstairs. "I'll manage this. I'm sorry Paul phoned you."

"Well, I'm not sorry. I was going to stop by tonight, anyway." Malcolm hooked a thumb toward the staircase. "What's going on with the Walkers? I hadn't heard anything about Dougie Walker passing on."

*Dougie.* Yes, that had been Colin's dad's first name. Rhiannon sighed. "I hadn't heard, either. It's terrible. But don't worry—I'll phone Jessie and lend my support that way. She'll understand that I can't go to the funeral."

Malcolm nodded. He seemed grim-faced. "How about you? How's everything going with Mum and Dad being gone?"

*My life is changing.* But she smiled cheerfully at him. "It's lovely."

His brow creased. "Have you heard from them this week?"

"No," she said lightly, "but they're in the Galápagos Islands by now, swimming with rare Pacific sea turtles, I imagine. Can't you just see Mum's face?"

Malcolm chuckled. "Dad's taking this retirement thing seriously, isn't he?"

"You sound like an American," she teased.

"We came back from Vermont last weekend. Kristy's getting her dual citizenship. Did I tell you that?"

"No," Rhiannon said softly. "You didn't."

They were silent for a moment. Until Malcolm had met his new wife, Kristin—Kristy was his nickname for her—Rhiannon and her brother had kept up their tradition of talking together every day on the telephone. They'd started shortly after she'd come home from the hospital as a child and he'd been packed off to boarding school in New England. Her daily phone call with her big brother had been a key part of her healing process. Sometimes all they'd shared was a *knock-knock* joke. But it had been enough.

"Rhi, I don't want you to feel you can't call me when you need to, just because I'm married. It bothers me that you're here alone. I told Mum that, but—"

"Oh, you *did*, did you?" Rhiannon had refrained from calling him because she'd been feeling protective of her brother, not wanting to disturb him during his newlywed year. But now she was a wee bit peeved by his lack of faith in her.

She folded her arms. "I'm doing fine, Malcolm. I'm taking

care of the manor and its inhabitants quite well." The dog's rubber ball rested against the leg of a chair. Rhiannon rolled it toward him with her toe. "Did you know that Molly was injured? I spoke with the vet and arranged for her care. Soon she'll be home and all will be well."

Smiling slightly, Malcolm bent over and picked up the dog's toy, covered with pet hair and tooth marks, evidence of Molly's love for her castle life. "Sorry, Rhi, I'm not trying to upset you. But I was thinking of the gathering next week." He looked meaningfully at her.

Oh, the *gathering*. Malcolm was talking about the Highland Games that were held each year in the nearby village. Rhiannon had forgotten.

Their castle had long been the place where the pipe bands assembled to begin the parade that wound through the village and on to the competition grounds. As lady of the castle, Rhiannon's mum always played hostess.

"Kristy wants to attend the Highland Games this year," Malcolm said. "She's willing to be the castle hostess."

*Kristy!* So Rhiannon was to be passed over?

Rhiannon felt a burning in her eyes. Surprisingly, it bothered her—cut her to the quick that she would be overlooked for her mum's job. Still, it made sense. Malcolm's wife wasn't agoraphobic as Rhiannon was. Kristin wouldn't be challenged by standing in the castle's front drive, greeting the pipers who marched in the bands and the villagers who came to walk alongside them.

"Rhi, I have to make a call." Malcolm glanced at a text message on his phone. "Would you like me to walk Colin out?"

"No," she answered, her voice so soft it was barely audible, even to her. "I'll do it."

Malcolm snapped up his head. "But he might ask you questions."

Meaning questions she wouldn't want to answer.

Her heart drummed. "Yes. I suppose he might."

"He doesn't know how to treat you," Malcolm protested.

"I know." And that was her biggest fear. Her life was so controlled and there were rules about who she chose to speak to and who she didn't. Colin had shown himself to be someone who didn't follow protocol. He was unpredictable and that could be dangerous.

She would have no control with him, which wasn't good for her peace of mind. And yet... "I wonder what would have happened between us if I'd never been kidnapped," she mused aloud.

Malcolm made a strangled noise.

"I'm sorry." She and her brother rarely spoke of the kidnapping; it was their unspoken pact. Malcolm had never forgiven himself for what he thought he'd let happen to her when she was eight years old. "It's not your fault," she reassured him. "It never was. You were ten. You were traumatized yourself."

"I wasn't left alone with those monsters for all that time," Malcolm bit out. "You were."

She shook her head, closing her eyes to banish the memory. "Never mind," she said quietly. "It's finished. But I have to talk with Colin because I have to say *something* about his dad. He's obviously quite broken up."

She didn't have a choice about facing him. Once, he'd been her friend. And even if he hadn't been, wouldn't her mother have done so, too, if she were here?

That was what the lady of the manor *did*.

Her hands shaking, she took a deep breath and headed for the stairs, descending with as much grace as she could muster.

When he saw her, Colin rose to his feet. Her cat jumped from his lap and crouched beneath the table, staring warily at Rhiannon. But he'd had his reward—an empty, licked-clean saucer on the floor told the tale of Colin's generosity to his namesake.

Rhiannon would have laughed if not for Colin's presence. He stood with a looming charisma that she couldn't ignore; he had a tall, rangy body, with a rugged masculinity about him that destroyed her composure.

"Rhiannon," he murmured, in a deep, husky voice.

*Nobody* spoke her name that way. A long, lazy breath of longing, of desire.

She didn't know how she dared to keep her gaze on him. She wished she could have studied him from behind a one-way mirror. That way she could look at him to her heart's content, without worrying about being touched or seen.

He smiled at her, seemingly entranced. His lips moved. So...erotic...and so dangerous, and yet she couldn't turn away. She'd forgotten that she was wearing her painting smock. Well-worn denim, old and comfortable—it was essentially a halter top that she didn't need to wear a bra with. It was a weird quirk of hers—she had so many weird quirks, it seemed—but Rhiannon hated wearing a bra when she painted; she preferred to be comfortable. Usually, no one saw her, so she wasn't concerned about the fact that she showed...well, cleavage. Possibly the outlines of everything she had.

Her face felt warm, and she imagined she'd turned a conspicuous shade of crimson. But she managed to calmly fold her hands and speak gently. "Hello, Colin. Thank you for the roses and the note. They were lovely, though not necessary."

"Yeah, they were." Colin dragged his hand through his hair. "I'm really sorry about this morning. I won't let that happen again." He gazed into her eyes, directly.

He had such remarkable eyes—she'd forgotten how light they were, more blue or gray depending on the shirt he wore. He wasn't the blond towhead he'd been as a boy. Now his hair was a rich medium brown streaked slightly with gold.

"Do you forgive me?" he asked.

She gave him a smile, though her heart was hammering. "Yes. Of course I do."

"Good. I'm glad." He exhaled. "It, uh, feels good to see you again." His gaze darted to the top of the stairs, and he licked his lips as he tore his attention from her, glancing around at the castle furnishings. "I missed this place. It meant a lot to me as a boy, and I never forgot it." He looked back at her, pleading with his eyes. "I couldn't come back. It got too difficult with my father."

"You don't have to tell me," she said gently. "I know."

Behind her the floor creaked, and she realized that Malcolm was standing there, monitoring their every word. Paul stood quietly by, as well, her sentry.

Colin subtly shook his head at her. He was bothered by the other men's presence. As children, she and Colin had their private signals. It seemed they were picking up where they'd left off, just like that.

He moved closer to her, and her heartbeat quickened. In a low voice, he said, "Can we go somewhere and talk? How about if we grab a coffee in the village? I'd love to catch up on what you've been doing."

But that was impossible, of course. And she was sure now that Colin didn't know her secret. She stiffened.

"Rhiannon?" He tilted his head. "Is something wrong?"

She was aware of Malcolm, clearing his throat behind her on the stairs, but she spoke over him, focusing only on Colin. "No." She smiled as best she could. "Though thank you for your invitation. And I'm sorry for your loss. I'll be sure to phone Jessie to give my condolences. I'm sorry for you all."

That was the very best she could do.

Her knees shaking, and feeling immensely saddened, Rhiannon turned. Without looking at Colin's face, she headed back up the stairs. Though he said nothing more, she could feel his pain and confusion.

It was excruciating to her.

———

COLIN STARED AT Rhiannon's retreating back.

Something *was* wrong. She'd just turned him down flat and he wasn't sure why, though he could guess.

He'd been an idiot. First, by checking her out when she'd come down the stairs. He'd been trying not to—he'd been doing his damnedest to keep his eyes on her face, but the outline of her breasts was stamped on his mind. Earlier this morning she'd been wrapped up in a bulky raincoat and her face covered with a hood. Now he could more clearly see her. She wasn't little Rhiannon anymore—she was a woman and she was even more beautiful than he'd realized at first.

It hadn't been his original plan, but he felt overcome by the need to talk to her again, away from the castle. Away from the people who watched them—her protective older brother and their butler. It was true Colin was only here for the weekend, for his dad's funeral—and he hated the lump in his throat that thought brought him—but he'd just wanted to be alone with Rhiannon and find out what had happened to her over the years. Get to know her again, maybe renew their friendship.

God knew, he needed a friend here. Especially now, three days before his father's funeral, back with his grandparents for the first time in over twenty years, and with all the trouble he was having with Jamie.

"Wait a minute, Rhiannon," Colin called up the stairs after

her. "Can we start over, please? I'm sorry I messed this up. I really would like to hear about what you've been doing."

She stopped, but didn't turn. She seemed to be wavering.

On impulse, he climbed the stairs two at a time until he stopped on the landing beside her. *Their* landing. Though the stairway had been rerouted, this was the spot where they'd once eavesdropped through a screen together as his world fell apart, all those years ago.

Malcolm stared down at him quizzically, as if he couldn't believe what Colin was doing. Colin knew it was sort of crazy to have chased her like this. But—ah, hell—she knew him. Or at least she had once.

He stood beside her, close enough to see faint smudges of paint on the shoulder of her denim top. He wasn't sure what to say, so he just grabbed at the first thing that came to mind.

"Jessie tells me you're a painter," he said in a low voice, well aware that Malcolm was still scowling down at him from the top of the stairs. But Malcolm didn't know about the intimacy of their past friendship. Rhiannon did. "I think it's amazing. I saw your landscape in her living room, and I could tell exactly where on the estate you painted it from."

Rhiannon slowly gazed up at him. "I really can't go with you," she murmured. Her voice was extremely quiet and serious and...sad. She wrung her hands, giving away an inner turmoil. Maybe she just didn't trust him.

"Is it because I scared you this morning? Well, I promise to be on my best behavior. How about if we go someplace where there are other people around? You can choose the venue. I'll go anywhere you want."

She paled. "No."

He paused. "Okay." That was as flat a rejection as she could give him. This had obviously been a mistake. He tried to cover by giving her a carefree grin, but it fell flat. Colin couldn't remember the last time he'd made somebody else feel awkward and uncomfortable, and it sucked—this wasn't like him. "Never mind. I'm leaving Sunday night anyway."

She sighed, sadly looking at him. "I'm sorry."

"That's...no problem."

"I do wish you all the best."

"Thanks, that's...how I feel, too." He flashed her a grin. But he had the strong feeling that she didn't think he was worth the effort. That somehow, he'd missed the mark. A sickening shame that just being himself wasn't good enough.

Before he left Rhiannon, he couldn't help glancing around the landing where they stood, the spot where the screen had once been. He'd most remembered this feeling when he'd been a kid in this place, when his father had left him and it had been clearly stated what was wrong with Colin.

Without looking back, he headed down the stairs. He had to get out of here.

"It isn't *you*, Colin." Rhiannon's voice rang clearly behind him. "It's me. I'm the one with agoraphobia."

He stopped short. Turned. She looked so beautiful standing there above him, and so sad. "What's agoraphobia?"

"It means...that I have to...that I like to stay secluded."

Secluded? *Rhiannon?*

But that made no sense to him. He remembered the vibrant girl she'd been. Rhiannon had always been a fearsome adventurer, a playmate wielding a sword of her own. Nothing back then had made her retreat.

He looked at her, confused. He couldn't wrap his head around it. He had nothing light to say, for once.

With dignity, she nodded at him. "That's why I can't be at the funeral. Or go anywhere with you to catch up. All I can do is wish you a good visit with your grandparents. They're among my favorite people on earth, and they love you. No matter what happens, please be kind to them."

"*Why* are you agoraphobic, Rhiannon?" he blurted.

Her eyes widened. He got the feeling she was shocked he'd asked, as if no one ever questioned her.

Malcolm stomped down the stairs and stopped behind his sister, his arms folded. "Enough," he growled at Colin. "It's time for you to leave."

But Rhiannon wasn't cowed. With a look at her brother, she subtly shook her head, signaling Malcolm to stand down. "I'll explain to Colin what happened. He deserves to know."

"Rhi," Malcolm said, exasperated, "you don't have to explain anything to anyone. You can just tell him to leave. You don't have to put up with this."

"I *want* to tell him," she answered.

She took a deep breath, and Colin could see the effort it cost her to face him again. Malcolm was clearly unhappy, staring at Colin with hooded eyes as if he wanted to toss him out the front door on his ass.

But Rhiannon clasped her hands in front of her and looked directly at Colin. "Shortly after you left that last time, Malcolm and I were kidnapped and held hostage for eleven days."

Colin felt his mouth drop open. Kidnapped?

*Rhiannon?*

That was horrible.

*How did it happen?* he wondered, sickened. *And what did they do to her?*

But he didn't want to show too much emotion about it. It had obviously traumatized her so much already.

Why the hell hadn't anyone told him?

Because he'd been back in America with his mom. And his mom wouldn't have known, either—back then, news didn't travel across the Atlantic quite as easily as it did today. That was in the days before the internet.

He shook his head. "Rhi, I'm really sorry. I am. I wish I'd known."

"Thank you. But I didn't want you to know. I wanted you to remember me as I was."

"I do remember." He smiled at her. "You were always so brave."

"Well." She licked her lips and looked down. "Now I'm reclusive." She started to turn again.

"Wait," he said. "When you say reclusive, what exactly does that mean?"

"Colin, I swear to you," Malcolm began.

Colin ignored him, focusing on Rhiannon. "Because... I think I can work with reclusive. I don't mind, if you don't."

She dipped her head and gazed warily at him.

"For example," Colin said, "what if I set it up so that nobody else but us was at the restaurant? Would you get in a car and go there if I could guarantee that nobody else would be there? Or what if I brought you on a horse? You used to love horses."

Rhiannon's mouth seemed to be twitching.

"Of course she's not going to get in a car," Malcolm cut in, irritated. "You're missing the point, Colin."

"I'm having a conversation with Rhiannon. *That's* the point."

Rhiannon was really smiling now. "My brother is upset," she murmured to Colin, "because you don't understand how things are."

"Then explain it to me so I do."

Rhiannon rubbed her lips. "Well, let me put it this way. I need to stay on the castle grounds, in the company of a few people I trust. It's how I choose to live, and it works for me. I'm happy with it, Colin. Truly, I am."

Then why did she seem so sad? "I don't believe you. How can

you can be happy with it if you can't leave the grounds? Does that mean you're tied to this one place forever?"

There was a general expression of shock on her face. Obviously, he'd trampled on forbidden territory. But in his opinion, she didn't deserve to be locked away.

"I get panic attacks," Rhiannon said, regrouping. "Staying on the property and controlling my interactions with other people is how I manage that. It's how I prevent getting panic attacks, which is the worst thing that can happen to me. Can you understand that?"

He snapped his fingers. "Were you having a panic attack when I hit you with my golf ball and broke your camera?"

A strangled noise came from Malcolm, but Rhiannon shook her head at her brother. She smiled at Colin, her gaze a steady, a taut line that went from one to another. They still had that connection; it hadn't been broken yet.

"I admit it's been years," she said, "and I was feeling daring in pushing the limits, but yes, that's what the beginning of a panic attack looks like."

"But then I laughed at you, and shocked you by asking about your kids, and that stopped it, right?"

Her lips twitched again. "I beg your pardon, but you're not that powerful. And you really were an eejit to me. So I think it's best we stop this conversation while we're ahead, or you'll be writing me more apology notes and picking more of Jessie's flowers. Is that understood?" She smiled sweetly at him.

Colin burst into laughter. And from the spark in her eyes, he knew she was laughing inside, too.

*That* was the Rhiannon he remembered. A little bit sassy. A little bit sweet. Always holding her own.

Colin the cat had brushed up against Colin's ankles, so he stooped to pick him up. "Okay, Rhiannon. But I have one more proposition for you." He smiled back at her, scratching behind her cat's ear.

She folded her arms. "Put my cat down. The answer is no, I'm not leaving this property with you. In fact, I'm saying goodbye to you now."

"You haven't heard my idea yet."

"It's clear what you want me to do, Colin. But I have boundaries that you need to respect." Shaking her head, she turned on her heel.

"So you're telling me you don't *dare* to go to our clearing in the forest, just a hundred yards away, and have a picnic with me and Jessie, the lady who's lived on your estate for thirty-some years?" he called to her.

"*Dare?*" Rhiannon turned. "I don't *dare?*"

He grinned. He'd hoped she would be incensed by that, because that was the old Rhiannon's personality.

"Yes, come and have dinner on the grounds with Jessie and me. If you dare."

She sighed. "It's not a matter of daring, Colin."

"I don't see why not. Because according to your own rules, how is there any danger of having a panic attack while you're in the middle of the estate grounds with Jessie?" He stared at her. "Unless you're telling me you've lost your courage and you're really just afraid."

———

AFRAID?

Rhiannon paused on the steps, shock filling her.

Nobody spoke to her this way. Nobody dared to question her when she expressed what she needed, even if he was doing it in a friendly, joking tone.

For years she'd had therapists, and she supposed that

Malcolm had, too—even living away in America at a boarding school. At the time, Malcolm had been forced to leave Scotland because of the attention he'd received over what had happened to them. Rhiannon, by refusing to leave the castle, had been spared that.

With her therapists' help, she'd come a long way since then. Initially, she'd been catatonic. She hadn't spoken to anyone—she'd only painted, her first treatment. Then, in her teens, she'd asked to stop seeing the therapists. She'd wanted to be independent—and now she was. She'd organized her life as she'd needed it, as she'd pleased. As she'd been forced to accommodate her disability of sorts. So why was Colin pushing her?

Behind her, Malcolm hovered, furious but silent, respecting her wish to speak for herself, at least when it came to Colin. Still, she'd been well aware that Malcolm had been ready to spring at the slightest misstep on Colin's part. And then when he'd mentioned the "breaking your camera" bit, she thought Malcolm would explode.

But this was her fight. Not Malcolm's. If she was to live as a free, controlled, peaceful woman—the perfect agoraphobic she claimed to be—then she needed to take charge.

She *did* need to talk with Jessie, actually, about the funeral plans, at least. Jamie was a longtime employee of her parents' estate, which Rhiannon would someday inherit. She might as well get used to taking charge of some of her mother's responsibilities now, while her parents were gone.

She considered Colin. That gleam in his eye—oh, it was maddening, but she would squelch it if she needed to. Somehow the two of them had connected again, though she was getting the feeling that the man he'd become was no more complicated than the boy she'd known and adored when she'd been a girl.

"You see, Colin," she chided, "this is exactly why I never wanted you to be told about me. You prefer me as I was then and not as I am now. How am I to compete with that? You're not listening to me, are you?"

———

"YES, I'M LISTENING to you. And I like you exactly as you are," he said. *Keep it light.* "That's why I've come up with a brilliant plan. You won't be anywhere near the property lines. That clearing where the picnic tables used to be—are they still there?"

"Y-y-yes..."

"Great." He nodded. "Then I'll pull together a basket from the house and bring it up there like we used to. You don't have to bring anything. We'll keep it low-key and simple."

She still seemed skeptical. But skeptical was an improvement over angry or terrified.

He smiled at her. "My grandmother would love to see us both together, like old times. If you'd like, I'm sure Jamie will come, too." Though Colin sort of doubted that his grandfather would be thrilled about sitting down to a picnic with him, he was on a roll, making up plans on the fly. Since Malcolm was still glowering at him, he figured *why not?* and included him, as well. "Malcolm is invited, too, if he wants." He grinned at Malcolm. "*Do* you want to come?"

Malcolm glared at Colin, then looked helplessly at Rhiannon.

Rhiannon's brow wrinkled.

"We'll only talk about good stuff," Colin promised. "Nothing heavy—we'll just catch up." *No funeral talk, no agoraphobia talk.* "You won't have to worry about leaving the property or bumping into anybody you don't know."

"I don't know, Colin..."

"It'll be okay, Rhi," he said quietly. "How about if you try it, and if you decide you don't like it, then you can leave right away?"

She expelled a breath. "When?" she asked hesitantly.

*She'd almost said yes.* His heart sped up, but he tried not to show it. "Ah, we'll make it an early dinner." That would give him time to talk with Jessie about it and win her support.

And Mack's, too.

The tee time that Mack had set up for them was in a town not too far away. A local course, but not the tiny municipality club where Colin and Rhiannon had played as children. Colin would do some chipping drills, too, but then...he would beg off from hanging out with Mack at his pub for dinner tonight. It wouldn't be good for Rhiannon to be exposed to too many people.

"How about six-thirty?" Colin asked. That was early enough to give them a few hours of light before sunset.

Her mouth twisted. She was wavering again.

"Please come, Rhiannon." He sighed and made his final appeal. "I'm leaving on Sunday night, so we won't have too many chances together. After this, if you want, you can say the word, and I promise not to bother you again."

---

SHE FELT a wee bit angry, because Colin knew perfectly well she didn't want to go, and why. And yet he kept pushing her.

But she was so tempted when she heard him say the word *together.*

As always, Colin drew her in. He fascinated her. Amazed her. Sometimes made her laugh. She couldn't *not* listen to him.

Besides, she had a duty that she needed to fulfill. If she ever expected to someday be a successor to the lady of the castle, with the same grace and capability of her mum—despite her agoraphobia—then she needed to start somewhere. Truly, there were no better people to start with than Colin and his family—for the friends they'd once been, and for the friend they needed now. She should go with Colin because his dad had passed away and she was sorry for that. Sorry for Jessie and Jamie, as well.

She nodded shakily to Colin, who'd been waiting for her answer. She supposed she could be nudged to go with him just this once. But whatever happened, she wouldn't get attached to him again. He was leaving in a few days, after the funeral, and would never be part of her life again.

"I'll do it," she said. "But only if you make the dinner for tomorrow night, not tonight."

That would give her the chance to prepare. This new role of *lady* felt so shaky and scary that she needed time to sit peacefully with her thoughts and process it all better.

"Sounds great." He gave her a lopsided smile, meeting her eyes directly. "Thank you, Rhi. I promise I won't argue if you feel uncomfortable with it."

She nodded curtly. She only hoped she wasn't making a mistake.

Breathing heavily, she lifted her chin and with dignity, she left. But this time, she walked down the stairs, away from Malcolm. Scooping up her cat and brushing past Colin, she headed directly to the back entrance. She didn't want to talk with her brother, didn't yet want to have the necessary conversation with Paul about calling *her* when there was a problem, and not Malcolm, who didn't even live there anymore.

Instead, she went outside, through the courtyard and into the building that was hers alone, the place that held her art studio.

Usually, this was her sanctuary. Today, though, all she could do was go to the window and watch for Colin as he departed, striding back through the moor and toward the guard's cottage.

Colin was the most beautiful man she'd ever seen. He was athletic. He was sexy. The way he moved his body did something to her. It was why she'd hesitated saying yes for those extra seconds. From now on, when she thought of Colin, she would never see the boy that he'd been. She would see him as he was now. With broad shoulders. A set chin. A mouth that quirked. That ever-present twinkle in his eyes.

Pacing, she sought to shrug him off. Slough him out of her aura.

But it was time to work, so she sat at her easel, which was the place where she went to lose herself, and therefore to feel calm again.

It didn't happen.

Restless, she turned away. Picking at the small bandage on her palm, she reached for a sketch pad and a pencil. She found herself sketching the outlines of Colin's face. Filling in the shape of his eyes. The placement of his laugh lines.

What was she doing? Shocked, she put her pencil down. She hadn't drawn a human face since the weeks after she was rescued, at age eight, and had needed to record the features of the people who'd held her captive, and the gentle man who'd died while saving her.

That exercise had *hurt*. It was why she'd avoided making portraits since those days. She'd kept to her landscapes ever since then.

And now here she was, rendering Colin's face.

Except, it didn't hurt to draw him. Not even physically, from the cut on her palm. Sketching Colin was rather pleasurable.

Somehow that change in herself gave her courage. Maybe his visit wouldn't be so bad after all.

## CHAPTER SIX

RHIANNON WAITED UNTIL the next morning after Malcolm had left before confronting Paul.

She sat at her mother's desk with her hands folded, the way her mother did when she gave directions to him.

Rhiannon didn't know why she felt so nervous—she'd known their butler for the better part of her life. He was the one person she consistently broke bread with. This past week, they'd been the only two people living in the castle.

Perhaps it felt strange because *she'd* never been the person in charge of the castle before. It was so new. But it weighed on her that yesterday, when there'd been a real incident requiring her decision, she'd been passed over in favor of Malcolm, who no longer even lived at the estate. Colin was wrong—she was *not* afraid of taking charge of her domain. It was a point of pride that she prove it to him.

"Miss?" Paul stopped in the doorway, the early-morning sun making him blink. For a moment he hesitated, but he caught himself and proceeded to clasp his hands in front of him, the way he did with her mother. "Did you wish to speak to me?"

"I do." She motioned to the chair in front of the desk, just as her mother would, and waited until he sat. "I'd prefer that you no longer call Malcolm when there's an issue to be resolved. From now on, I'd like you to speak to me, at least until my parents return."

"Ah." Paul nodded. If he was surprised, he hid it well. "I see, miss."

"I'm the one who'll always be living here. You might be aware that a trust has been set up so this castle will remain my home—the only one I'll ever have. I've decided that it's best for all concerned, especially while my parents are away, that I take more of an interest in what happens on the grounds."

"I understand," he said gently.

She waited, but Paul didn't move or venture to say anything more. Instead, he seemed to be listening.

"For example," she continued, "I don't want you to worry about interrupting my painting. If a matter comes up that needs my attention, then please do let me know, straightaway."

Paul placed his fist in front of his mouth and made a small *harrumph* in his throat.

He looked so comical, she nearly smiled. But she didn't, because this meeting was terribly serious, and he was behaving exactly as he did when her mother gave him direction.

"Yes, Paul?" she asked calmly.

"I beg your pardon, but the laird requested before he left that I keep *Malcolm* informed as to any issues that may arise in his absence."

"Did he?" Her heart sank. She really should have suspected as much. "Well, I'm asking you to please give me the chance to resolve any such issues *before* you bother Malcolm. I don't think that's an unreasonable request. My father would agree, were he in communication with us."

Paul gazed at her blandly. It was hard to gauge reaction with their butler; he didn't show much facial expression.

"Please, Paul. I'd like to take more of an active role in my life. Malcolm doesn't live here, and he's not likely to move back. Usually, he's three hours away."

"Indeed." Paul gazed at her sympathetically. He'd been a silent witness to yesterday's visit from Colin. He'd seen how important it was to her to represent herself well to him.

"I don't mean to pry, miss, but is this realistic?" Paul asked.

She sat up straighter. It *had* to be realistic. She wasn't turning back now. It had been an embarrassment to her that Colin witnessed her brother in charge of her life. She loved Malcolm, but that behavior would never have flown when the three of them were children.

"I *am* going to dinner with Colin and Jessie and Jamie tonight," she said softly. "I promised Colin, and I will stand by my promise."

Paul's nose seemed to twitch. He obviously had something to say about it.

"Please speak freely with me," she said.

"It isn't my business."

"I suppose we made it your business when we had our conversation in front of you on the stairs yesterday, don't you think?"

Paul sighed. "Jessie called over last night, wondering if Colin was here at the castle. But while we were speaking, Colin called her mobile phone to tell her that his workout had gone late, and he was staying at a hotel for the night, but would return in the morning."

And surely Jessie had been upset about that, though likely, she hadn't shown it to Colin.

Rhiannon kept her gaze steadily on Paul. "Is this a problem for us?"

"Technically, no. It's a minor event, true, but taking the

worried phone call from the cottage on her estate is an issue that the lady would handle, if she were present."

"I see." Perhaps there was more to the role than Rhiannon had realized. "Is this something you've discussed with Malcolm?"

Paul was silent for a moment. "No, miss. I've mentioned the incident to no one but you."

Though this was a small matter, it was another place to start. Besides, to her it was important. To Jessie, too.

"Would you like me to walk over with you to the picnic today?" Paul asked.

She smiled at him. "Thank you for offering. But no, I'll take Molly with me. Her leg seems better, and she's itching for the exercise."

Paul nodded. He didn't look entirely pleased.

"I'll be fine," she assured him.

"Be careful, Rhiannon," he said, an extremely rare warning on his part.

"I walk that part of the property every day. There's no physical danger to me."

But physical danger wasn't what Paul was worried about. They both knew that.

———

"I REALLY DO need you two to leave," Colin said.

Mack and Bonnie lounged on the edge of the picnic table as if they'd known each other for a year instead of two days. Bonnie sifted through an old-style album of photos that Colin's grandmother had insisted he cart over, while Mack picked sandwiches off the tray that Colin had prepared.

"We're going," Mack said, his mouth stuffed with cheese and

chutney, one of Jessie's culinary specialties. "Just give us a minute."

That was what they'd been saying for the past hour, after Mack had dropped Colin off from their golfing expedition and Bonnie had shown up to surprise Mack. Colin had explained in his good-guy manner—without mentioning Rhiannon—that he needed to be alone with his grandparents. He'd done his best to be diplomatic, but apparently diplomacy wasn't what this situation called for.

*"Now,"* Colin said. He glanced at the time on his phone—he only had twenty minutes until Rhiannon arrived—and turned to haul a cooler off the wagon he'd dragged from the shed behind the cottage.

Since his grandparents didn't have a barbecue grill like the one he had on his back porch in Texas, prepping for this outdoor meal wasn't as simple an affair as he'd anticipated. He gave them credit for the fresh-air picnics they'd coordinated when he was a kid.

"Is she really coming?" Bonnie asked him, holding the photo book aloft and squinting at it in awe.

Colin gazed at her sharply. "Is *who* really coming?"

"Rhiannon MacDowall, the heiress in the castle. Nobody ever sees her. She just stays in her turret tower and paints."

Colin's fists balled. He hadn't mentioned Rhiannon's name to Bonnie. He didn't want anyone spreading gossip or speaking negatively about her. "That's a lousy thing to say."

"Why?" Bonnie asked. "It's true."

"How do you know?" He took the album from her. "Have you ever met her?"

Bonnie fiddled with her sweater's buttons. "No."

"Right. Then don't say anything."

Mack gave Colin a wondering look as if Colin had lost his mind.

He was just on edge about wanting things to be perfect for Rhiannon. He'd thought a lot about her since he'd seen her last, and he'd gotten angry about the fact that she'd been kidnapped and terrorized. If there was any way for her to have an everyday picnic with his grandparents and him, then he wanted it to be so.

He put the photo album gently back in the crate. His grandmother had said that going on outings like this wasn't something Rhiannon normally did. He felt a burning need to change that.

He glanced up and saw Mack studying him. Colin regretted even mentioning Rhiannon's name to his caddie.

"You see," Colin said, "this is why you aren't invited to dinner."

Mack shook his head. Then he leaned closer to Bonnie. "Honestly?" he asked her. "You've lived in this village your whole life and you've never seen Colin's friend before?"

"No. Everybody knows what happened to her, but no one has seen her since—"

"Get out," Colin said, losing all sense of diplomacy. "Both of you. Now."

Mack gave him a funny look. Colin knew he was trying to make a joke about it. "Don't even go there," Colin snapped.

Mack turned to Bonnie. "Don't take it personally, Bonnie. He was like this when we golfed today, too."

Colin felt the slow burn. His reacquaintance with Rhiannon had *not* affected his golf game, which had felt pretty damn good, actually. He *liked* golfing in Scotland. In the past, he'd avoided coming here no matter how many times his peers had mentioned how great golfing in the birthplace of their sport was. Colin's feelings about his family had colored his opinion of the country. Now, it seemed, he was making up for lost time. Yesterday, they'd played nine holes. Today, he and Mack had joined a twosome for a full eighteen holes at a classic links course on the edge of a sea firth, not far away. The wind had rushed so hard at them that it had knocked over their bags. There'd been sea rocks and stone cliffs on three of the holes, which was crazy. If Colin hadn't been so preoccupied with thinking about tonight's dinner, he would have thoroughly enjoyed it.

"You're my caddie," he said quietly to Mack. "Where's the loyalty?"

"Come on, Colin, lighten up. This isn't like you."

This *wasn't* like him. But his father had died. His grandfather still couldn't stand the sight of him. And Rhiannon MacDowall had been violently kidnapped, and he'd never even known.

Of course he was in a bad mood and on edge.

He grabbed a checked tablecloth from the box his grandmother had packed and shook it over the table. Then he found the two globes that held citronella candles. The "midgies"—the tiny black bugs that sometimes plagued the Highlands—weren't out, but the citronella would be handy to have just in case.

"Why don't you two at least lend me a hand if you're going to stand there?" Colin had a few more minutes before Rhiannon arrived. If worse came to worst, he could toss the two of them inside the wagon and physically drag them back to Bonnie's car.

"Can't we meet Rhiannon MacDowall?" Bonnie asked him. "Pleeaase?"

"No."

"I don't see why such it's a big deal," Mack said.

Mack wouldn't; he didn't know Rhiannon was agoraphobic, though Bonnie would likely fill him in soon enough.

Colin wished his best friend would give him the benefit of the doubt. "I'm just getting to know her again myself. Grant me that one small pleasure, will you?"

Mack whistled. "You like her."

"She's a childhood friend."

Mack and Bonnie exchanged smirks.

Colin turned his back on them. He wasn't saying a word to anyone about how he felt about Rhiannon. She *was* a childhood friend. Since he was back in Scotland, he wanted to set things right for her.

What she had gone through burned him. All these years he'd assumed she'd been wary of him because of who he was. He hadn't even considered she'd been traumatized.

Just an eight-year-old girl. Rhiannon. The sweet, pigtailed kid. It infuriated him. It infuriated him even more that it had been bad enough to make her afraid to go out and live her life.

That hadn't been her personality back when he knew her. Not at all.

His foul mood must have finally sunk in to his friend, because Mack nudged Bonnie. "Let's go." To Colin he said, "Join us at the pub tonight."

Colin just grunted. He wouldn't be joining them. "Have a good time."

He glanced at his watch again. He felt antsy, waiting for Rhiannon. He killed a few minutes by hanging some lanterns from tree branches, but that still left him with spare time.

Since when did he wait around for someone like an anxious kid with a crush?

Setting out to find her, Colin took the walking path toward the castle.

The afternoon sun had lengthened and stretched and was fast sinking into evening. He set a quick pace. Whistled a tune. That way, if she was heading toward him, she would have advance notice and wouldn't be frightened.

He first saw her when he came over a slight crest. She was about fifty feet away.

"Rhiannon!" He raised a hand to her. She strode briskly, a golden retriever on a leash trotting ahead of her, slightly pulling her along.

Feeling himself smiling, he craned his neck to study her. She'd changed from the halter top he'd liked so much into a loose-fitting peasant-type shirt. The sleeves were short, with elastic around the edges so they puffed out, making her look like a Gypsy. She'd pinned one of his grandmother's rose buds into her hair, and she wore a long, jersey-type skirt that swirled and clung to her legs in interesting ways as she strode.

Just...damn.

"Hey," he said, tipping an imaginary hat to her as she came alongside him.

"Hello, Colin." Breathless with walking, she had apple-shaded cheeks. Shyly, she glanced up at his face as they both stopped. She seemed anxious, too.

"I hope you don't mind dogs," she said.

"Mind 'em? I love 'em." Colin bent to the golden retriever's height and held out his hand. The dog, skittish from what looked to be a bandaged front leg, sniffed at Colin's skin. "What's your name, pretty girl?"

"This is Molly. She's recently home from the vet. I would have left her with Paul, but she's eager to get outside again."

"Molly, huh?" The dog was now curiously licking Colin's skin. Her tongue was scratchy—it made Colin smile. "Did you name her after someone?"

"She's, uh, my mother's dog. All her dogs are named Molly." Rhiannon paused, still awkward. "Molly was the name she gave her first dog as a girl, and ever since then, she's named them all Molly. Remember?"

He scratched Molly behind the ear. "I seem to remember a Tippy, too."

"Tippy? Ye gads, you're right." Rhiannon shook her head. "I forgot about wee Tippy."

"Oh, no. Is he...?"

Rhiannon smiled sadly. "Tippy lived a long, happy life. He

was my aunt's dog. We were actually caring for him that summer while she was away."

"Ah," he said. Molly had graduated from licking Colin to now jumping up on him with her front paws. Colin stood, giving the dog's head a playful tousle.

"Stop that, Molly. Get down." Rhiannon gently tugged on the leash. "I'm sorry for her bad manners," she apologized to Colin.

"Don't be." He winked at her. "As you know, I have bad manners of my own."

She laughed again, her flush deepening. He loved that she blushed. Not enough people blushed anymore, in his opinion.

She seemed to be relaxing, and more so than she had with him at her castle.

He relaxed, too. "So, I thought I'd walk you to our picnic." He pointed the way down the path. "Shall we? Jessie's pretty excited about it. But I give you fair warning, she's broken out the photo albums."

Rhiannon smiled faintly and began to walk beside him. Molly trotted sedately along, too. "The warning is appreciated." But then Rhiannon's smile faded. They were both silent for a moment. She seemed to be pondering something. "So...your granddad and Jessie are doing okay, then?"

Colin blew out a breath and put his hands in his pockets as he walked. He'd been trying not to think about the funeral too much himself.

"It's hard to tell." He shrugged. "Jessie doesn't like to talk about unpleasant things. And Jamie is protective of her." He gave a short laugh.

"And you, Colin? How are you doing?"

He shook his head. That was a massively complicated question. "I guess you could say I'm getting through it."

"You weren't in touch with your father, were you?" Rhiannon murmured.

She said it gently. Rhiannon had a gentle spirit. He didn't mind answering her. "No. And my father wasn't in touch with me." The bitterness came out of him.

"I'm sorry, Colin."

"Don't be. I'm used to it."

He glanced at her while she deftly maneuvered Molly around a mud puddle. "Will Malcolm be coming tonight?" he asked, changing the subject.

"No. He drove back to Edinburgh last night to have dinner with Kristin. She's his new wife." Rhiannon had a small smile on her lips. Something struck her as amusing.

"What is it?" he asked.

"Malcolm's wife is American."

"Ah." He nodded. "Like me."

"Yes, and she's brilliant, too. I love her like she's my sister."

"And Malcolm is very protective of you."

"He is." She sighed, stealing a look at Colin as if deciding whether to say her next words; then she shrugged and said them anyway. "We were snatched from the street together. Malcolm has always blamed himself for letting it happen, and nothing that I or anybody else says seems to take that away completely." She hesitated. "It's why he stood by me yesterday, on the stairs." Her face flushed again.

Colin kept his pace as if it were the most natural thing. "I think most people would feel the same," he remarked, wanting to help her feel at ease, "especially since he's your older brother and he would have been the one in charge."

"Interesting you say that." She cocked her head. "You would make a tolerable older brother, wouldn't you? Did Daisie Lee have any more children?"

"No," he said, grateful that he didn't have to explain anything about his family to her because she already knew his people. "She just has me."

"Ah." Rhiannon seemed to be studying him. "That could be both a blessing and a curse, I suppose."

He chuckled because Rhiannon said it so matter-of-factly.

As they neared the picnic area, Rhiannon gently pulled back on Molly's leash. "Stay," she murmured to her dog.

She glanced up at Colin, blushing again. While Colin watched, fascinated, her cheeks turned a deep, rosy shade.

His first instinct was to gently tease her, as if they were still kids. But they weren't kids, and despite the easy, familiar conversation they'd just had, he held himself back. He wanted to be more respectful where she was concerned.

She lifted her eyes, gazing directly at him. "I...have to ask you something."

"Okay?" he said cautiously.

She licked her lips. "Is everything all right between you and Jessie? Truly?"

"Yeah." Hadn't he just told her that? Was he giving her the wrong idea? "Why?"

"Well...you stayed at a hotel last night."

"Wow. For an agoraphobic, you've obviously got spies," he teased.

She lowered her head. "Your grandparents are tenants and work on our estate. Of course phone calls go back and forth. Jessie was looking for you."

"So you've been talking to them about me?"

"No!" Her eyes widened. She sighed, as if about to make a confession. "Jessie called Paul, asking if you'd been by. She was worried."

"I called her to let her know." Colin thought he'd been doing pretty well, considering he wasn't used to accounting for his actions. "I was with my caddie, Mack, at a course we'd heard about, and it was so light outside that we didn't realize how late it was. I figured by the time we drove back, they would be asleep, so I called Jessie to give her a heads-up, then checked into a hotel for the night." He shrugged. "She didn't indicate that it was a problem. I thought I'd been reasonable about it all." Responsible, actually.

"I'm not chastising you, Colin," she said hurriedly. "I'm not your mum."

"No. You are in no way Daisie Lee," he agreed.

"How is she?" Rhiannon asked politely.

"Great. Good." Daisie Lee would have been haranguing him over it if she were present, upset about the funeral, about Rhiannon. He would've had to spend time with her, calming her down. "Everything's okay. No big problems." He grinned at her, eager to change the subject.

Rhiannon stooped to fix something with her shoe. She was gazing up at him strangely.

"What?" he asked.

She shook her head. "I was just thinking about something."

"Tell me." He smiled at her and leaned against a tree trunk.

"Do you remember that New Year's Eve when we were children, and we eavesdropped on the stairs...and then Daisie Lee came in, and you acted happy and told her nothing was wrong...?"

"Yeah?"

"Well, I was just wondering if that's what you were doing now."

"With you?"

"Yes," she said, as if relieved he understood.

"Ah...maybe I'm trying to be positive. And careful." He glanced at her. "Isn't that a good thing?"

"I'd like to know the truth." She gazed at him earnestly. "I can handle the truth, Colin."

He knelt down and petted Molly again, running his hands through her silky red fur.

"Please," Rhiannon said.

He sighed. He hadn't wanted to bother Rhiannon, but... "The truth is, Jamie's angry I'm here. If I had my way, I'd rather stay elsewhere, but Jessie's heart would be broken, so for her sake I haven't cut off relations entirely. That's the truth."

———

RHIANNON STARED AT HIM, feeling bug-eyed. This *was* a problem. An issue her mother might take on, if she were here.

Colin stood and wiped his hands. "So, you okay, Rhi?"

"I'm glad you told me, Colin."

He blew out a breath. "Okay, but it's nothing for you to worry about." He glanced over the woods, where the drone of an approaching electric buggy sounded. "That's probably Jessie now. She gets winded when she walks too far."

Rhiannon nodded. Maybe she *could* help sort this awkwardness out for him. Rhiannon had a fairly decent rapport where Jessie and Jamie were concerned.

"Colin, will you promise to always be honest with me like this, no matter what?"

He glanced at her, his eyebrows raised. "You sure you really want that?"

She nodded.

"I ask because some people just want to hear the good stuff."

"I know, but I want to hear everything."

Colin looked her in the eye. "Okay. So...only honesty between us. You promise?"

She had a funny thought, remembering that old New Year's Eve and their pledge to write to each other. "I promise, as long as you do, too," she teased him. "And this time, I really will follow up on it."

He smiled. He knew exactly what she was referring to. "Yeah, I promise, too."

The sound of Jessie and Jamie chatting with each other drifted over the hill. "Honestly," Colin murmured, "I wish it were just you and me for dinner tonight, but they're part of this shindig now, so I guess we'll roll with it, won't we?"

*Roll with it.* The phrase amused her. "Roll on." She followed Colin to the clearing where the ancient picnic table was located.

Parked beside the table was the small, motorized vehicle that Jamie used to get around the estate. Colin's grandmother sat at a folding camp chair placed at the head of the table, and Jamie stood behind her, solicitously settling her in while also gazing about and scowling.

The two spoke in low tones. Rhiannon couldn't hear what they were saying, but Colin was right, she sensed Jamie's displeasure.

The muscles in Colin's neck and shoulders visibly tightened.

Rhiannon held out Molly's leather leash to him. "Would you mind letting her sit beside you? It'll calm her."

"Sure." Colin indulged her by petting Molly's fur and guiding her to the table.

Then he moved over on the bench, giving Rhiannon room to sit beside him, on the end. This made her grateful, because in that position she wouldn't feel so hemmed in or panicked.

Rhiannon's dog settled her head onto Colin's lap and gazed up at him with big brown eyes.

"Well, you already know Rhiannon," Colin said to his grandmother. "And this is Molly."

"Your grandmother knows who Molly is," Jamie snapped.

*Oh, my,* Rhiannon thought.

"You don't have to eat with us if you don't want to," Colin said quietly to Jamie. "I invited Nana because I wanted her to have dinner with Rhiannon and me again."

Jessie looked more tired than Rhiannon had recalled. There were lines in her face and her eyes had dark circles beneath them. She also seemed to have lost weight; her blouse hung loose about her shoulders.

"Jamie, please why don't you sit?" Jessie directed him.

With a grudging expression, Jamie sat directly across the scarred wooden picnic table from Colin, whom he proceeded to shoot a glare toward.

Yes, there was surely a problem between them. What would her mother do?

Bother that. This was *Rhiannon's* situation, and she would handle it how she saw fit.

She leaned across the table and lightly touched Jamie's gnarled hand, saying gently, "I'm sorry for your loss. Please let me know if there's anything I can do for you."

———

COLIN'S PULSE SEEMED to stop. The only sounds were the birds and the rustle of leaves in the soft breeze. His grandfather's eyes were moist and shining, his lips pressed together. It brought a lump to Colin's throat.

Something had happened between him and Rhiannon during that conversation about honesty. They'd started out friendly enough. It had felt easy. But she had a way of seeing beneath the surface to what was really important.

Honestly, he did want to get along with Jamie. And it touched him that Rhiannon seemed determined to help him smooth out that relationship.

Likely, her kindness and effectiveness came from the early years they'd spent together—what Rhiannon had seen of his family back then. She'd known his father. There had to be many photos of the three of them together...

No way was Colin looking at those photo albums his grandmother had brought over. He hadn't seen a picture of his father in years, and if he did now, he might lose it.

"Rhiannon, dear," his grandmother said, eyeing him and then Jamie, "bless you for coming. Tell me how your parents are doing? Are they enjoying their tour of South America?"

"I haven't heard yet." Rhiannon politely accepted a sandwich from the tray that Jamie passed her. "They promised to send photos when they get the chance."

"The laird is keen to see the penguins in Antarctica," Jessie said to Colin.

Colin nodded. He knew his grandmother was tactfully moving the topic of conversation away from anything unpleasant, and that was fine with him. He also knew that technically, Mr. MacDowall wasn't a laird—he hadn't inherited the ancient castle, he'd purchased it. But Colin remembered liking him.

Colin spread his paper napkin on his lap and picked up his soupspoon. He'd wanted to talk to Rhiannon alone, and for a few minutes during their walk, he'd done so. She wasn't as skittish with him anymore, and he was glad for that. While he ate, he listened to Rhiannon describe her parents' travels. She seemed relaxed and happy with his grandmother.

"Do you and Jessie get together a lot?" he asked during a lull in their conversation.

"Not often enough." Rhiannon showed them her dimples.

"Several times a year, the lady has us to tea at the house." His grandmother turned to Rhiannon. "Tell Colin about the times we met in your mother's sitting room and watched him on the telly."

"I didn't know the US tour was televised over here," he remarked.

"Not every tournament," Rhiannon replied. "Sometimes we have to catch it over the internet."

"Aye. The laird sets it up so we can see it on the wide screen."

"We're technologically advanced," Rhiannon said with a smile.

"And Rhiannon went to her brother's wedding by way of the computer, too," his grandmother added.

"Really?" Colin said. "How did that go?"

Rhiannon picked up her sandwich. "Malcolm was married in Vermont last autumn. He set up an internet connection so I could watch the ceremony from home."

"That's..." *Sad,* he thought. "I'm glad you were able to participate."

Rhiannon nodded. But she hadn't been participating; she'd been observing. She had to know that.

He glanced over his soupspoon to see Jamie glowering at him still. Jessie and Rhiannon might have forgiven him for staying away, but Jamie obviously wasn't ready to forget. The man had a soft spot in his heart for Rhiannon, it seemed, and so was behaving for her sake. But as for him—it seemed Jamie wouldn't be happy until Colin had climbed on the plane back to Texas. And Colin would happily oblige him.

He reached down to feed Molly a piece of ham from his sandwich. The sooner Sunday's funeral was finished and over, the better off they all would be.

———

A LARGE, PROVERBIAL elephant-in-the-room sat with them at their open-air picnic table.

Rhiannon saw it, and it bothered her. Sunday's funeral hung over all of them, and Jessie was obviously reluctant to talk about it. And yet it needed to be addressed. Rhiannon's mother would certainly agree.

Rhiannon glanced to Colin and then to Jamie. They seemed

to be in a truce of sorts, yet she had no way of knowing if this would continue beyond the meal. She did wish she could smooth the way for Colin during his visit. This went beyond her desire to be an effective manager of the estate—it felt deeply personal.

She'd been surprised by the pleasure she'd taken in Colin's company and the ease she felt. He was also good with Molly. No doubt, they were slipping back into their old friendship, and she cherished that more than she'd expected. Maybe she'd been lonelier than she realized.

Colin was possibly the one person in the world who related to her purely as a friend. To him, she wasn't Rhiannon the recluse. Or Rhiannon the artist. Or Rhiannon the agoraphobic who needed to be protected.

And she rather liked that. It gave her courage and made her want to step a bit beyond her comfort zone and into the role her mother played. Though of course her mother would have physically attended the funeral in the village.

Rhiannon couldn't do that. She had no intention of attending *anything* beyond her castle walls. She would step into a bigger role, but a bigger role on the estate. Now that Colin truly understood that, they were better off. She liked their new "honesty" policy.

Rhiannon cleared her throat. "Jessie, what will you and Colin do tomorrow?"

*Saturday. One day before the funeral.*

Jamie sat at attention. He was interested in her answer, too.

"Why, Colin has to prepare for the New York Cup, of course," Jessie said.

Colin blinked at her. "You know about my tournament?"

"Of course." Jessie seemed insulted. "You think I don't follow your career? Everyone at Kildrammond follows your career."

"What's Kildrammond?" Colin asked.

"Your home club in Scotland. The place where I taught you to grip a club."

"I forgot about that." Colin lazily scrubbed the fur on Molly's neck while the dog stretched and preened. "Rhiannon and I went to the junior clinic one summer, didn't we?" He turned and grinned at her.

*Oh, no. Don't get me involved with that. I'm not golfing.*

"I arranged a tee time for us tomorrow," Jessie said to Colin.

"Uh...actually, Nana, that's something my caddie takes care of."

Jessie made a *pffft* noise. "He took you to Raith today. A beautiful, scenic firth-side links course, but you're an American tour professional," she chided. "You need to train on a parkland course with long fairways. Flat putting greens."

Colin crossed his arms, humor playing across his handsome face. "You know your golf. You should join my crew."

"Scotland is the birthplace of golf." Jessie drew herself up, insulted. "Of course I know my game!"

Colin laughed. "The guy I flew over here with is playing at St. Andrews this weekend."

"You want to play St. Andrews? I can see you registered at St. Andrews. Our club professional can make a phone call."

"Someday, Nana, I will," Colin promised. "The people we met in the clubhouse today told us about some small courses I'd love to try, as well."

"Aye. We have more than five hundred courses in Scotland. Most are wee, some on the honor system, all beautiful. You won't find courses like ours in Texas."

"No, I suppose not." Colin glanced at Rhiannon, and she got a bad feeling. "Give me your phone number," he said to her.

"What? Why me?" Rhiannon asked.

"I'm going to dial you up on video tomorrow. You'll go to the golf course along with me. Just for a small visit, nothing out of the ordinary."

"That's a lovely idea," Jessie said.

Colin gave Rhiannon a sweet smile, and she felt herself relaxing. *He understands.* "I suppose I could do that," she said, feeling very brave.

"Well, that's it for me," Jessie announced, rising. "I'm knackered. Jamie, will you help me pack up?"

"And then I'll walk the lassie back to the castle," Jamie said.

"But..." *You all haven't discussed the funeral arrangements,* Rhiannon was going to say.

"Ah, I made this for you, dear." Jessie passed Rhiannon a small, old-fashioned photo album. "These are pictures of you and Colin." Behind the back of her hand, she said, *"Just* you and Colin. I weeded out the ones with Dougie and Daisie Lee in them."

Flabbergasted, Rhiannon took the album from her.

With a wry grin, Colin leaned close to her. "I don't know about you, but I prefer to live in the present." He motioned with his chin. "Come with me for a minute." He unwound Molly's leash and led her dog up the path toward the castle.

Rhiannon followed Colin, not sure what else to do. When they were out of view, hidden by the leaves in a copse, she told him, "I think what's really going on is that Jamie is upset with your grandmother because she won't discuss the funeral."

Colin laughed. "Nice try. He's mad at me because I exist."

"Surely that's not true! I'll have a talk with him tomorrow and find out more."

"Sweet Rhiannon," Colin teased. "It's okay. I can't make him happy. I'm not going to try anymore, or care about it."

"You're not concerned that nobody is addressing the fact that there's a funeral on Sunday?" she demanded.

He leaned against a tree trunk, still holding the dog's leash.

Molly was scratching her neck with her hind foot. A sad smile played on Colin's lips. "I think it's enough just to be back here to catch up with you." He dug his phone from his pocket and handed it to her. "Program your number in it for me."

Hesitantly, she took his phone, still warm with his body heat. By instinct she inhaled, as if the rubber casing might carry the scent of him. Sadly, it did not.

She opened the directory to type in her name, and saw so many others. With her thumb she scrolled through dozens of *r*'s...perhaps hundreds of *r*'s. She felt herself frowning.

"Put it under *Rhi*," he said. "*R, h, i*."

She shoved the small photo album toward him. "I will, but only if you open this album and look at *one* photo."

A line appeared in his forehead.

"Are *you* afraid?" she said. "I dare you."

Scowling at her, yet taking the bait, he whipped it open. Stared at the book. And then burst out laughing.

He shared it with her. The photo was of wee Colin at a junior golf clinic, his cocky pose apparent even then. But the kicker was her. Young Rhiannon hugged him unabashedly around his waist. They were both outdoors at Kildrammond Golf Club.

"Oh, dear." Rhiannon handed the photo album back to him. "You should keep this."

"Maybe I will," he murmured. He pushed away from the tree bark, closer to her now. Too close. Closer than she let anyone get. She saw the blue of his shirt—cerulean blue, the oils artist in her automatically thought. She was at his chest height, exactly. The heat from his body was close enough to feel.

She didn't dare look up at him.

"Thank you for being here with me today," he said quietly.

"I wish I could have helped you more," she murmured. "I feel like I didn't do enough."

"Your presence is always enough." And then he leaned

forward and kissed her quickly on the forehead.

Oh, why did he do that? She gazed up at him.

His Adam's apple moved as he swallowed. He had the faintest, scattered bit of sexy razor stubble on his neck.

He chuckled at her, deep in his throat. "You were my first kiss, Rhiannon."

"And you mine, as well," she said lightly. She refused to be affected by him.

"That night during 'Auld Lang Syne.'"

All she could do was nod.

That crease on his forehead appeared again. "I should've asked. Do you...have a boyfriend?" He had a look on his face that said *probably not.*

She couldn't stand for anyone to feel sorry or make presumptions about her, especially him. "Stop it, Colin." She put her hand on her hip. "A year ago, we had a man working as a security guard for a few months on the property. I kissed *him.* No big deal."

He stared at her, his mouth open. "We said to be honest and...well, I'm jealous."

She smiled at him. "You should be."

He shook his head at her, laughing. "Rhiannon, you never cease to amaze me."

She tilted her head. "Why?"

"What was his name?" he asked instead, scowling again.

She couldn't help laughing, because his reaction was so ironically absurd to her. "Are you sure you want to open Pandora's box, Colin?" she teased. "Because I'm giving you fair warning— I'm not interested in hearing the names of all your sweethearts."

"My only sweetheart is my long-lost nana." Colin looked at her. "Honestly, who was he?" He glanced around as if the trees would give him an answer. "A neighbor?"

"His name was Colin."

"No, really."

"Yes, his name was honestly Colin." She smiled sheepishly at his disbelieving laughter. "I figured the name was my destiny. Besides, my brother was here that week when he'd first met Kristin, and well, romance was in the air. I suppose it was inevitable."

"I'm crushed."

"Don't be," she said lightly. "You're still my first kiss. Nothing can take that away."

He laughed. "Yeah, you're still mine, too."

There was an awkward moment. "You should go with your grandmother," Rhiannon said.

He nodded. "Um, tomorrow..."

"You'll be out golfing with your grandmother, and I'll be here as always."

"Right." But the awkward moment dragged on. Wanting to end it, Rhiannon leaned forward. If she were to kiss him, quickly and firmly on the lips, the same way that he'd kissed her during "Auld Lang Syne," then she would be showing him that she was fine. *No big deal.* That she could handle his presence without being silly. That she could handle a mere kiss.

She kissed him quickly. His lips were warm... And firm...

And she was lingering too long.

Her blood roaring in her ears, she drew back.

"You see," she said softly, as lightly as she could—as he would, "it's no big deal."

"Yeah, Rhiannon, it is." And then he leaned forward and kissed her. It was gentle and sweet and completely unexpected. It gave her the message that...

...that he was interested in her as a *woman.*

Stunned, she touched her lips.

"I'll see you tomorrow," he said.

He left, whistling.

She groaned, putting her head in her hands. What was she *doing,* spinning fairy tales in the air over something that couldn't be?

She was still in that position when Jamie found her a few minutes later. "Lass? I didn't want you to be involved in this."

She snapped up her head. Colin's grandfather stood alone beneath a Scotch pine. His hands in his front pockets, he was hunched over, looking grim and upset.

"Involved in what?" she asked with foreboding, wondering what he'd just seen and what he thought about it.

"It's Jessie," he said with his gravelly voice.

"Jessie? What about Jessie?" Rhiannon just felt so relieved that he wasn't talking about her kissing Colin—indeed, he hadn't seemed to have seen it—that her mind was disoriented.

"She invented the story about the funeral and the inheritance."

Rhiannon's mouth dropped open. "She did *what?*"

Jamie seemed to be bracing himself. "Our son Dougie isn't dead. He's alive. She only came up with the story to bring Colin back to Scotland."

Rhiannon felt her mouth hanging open. "Why would she *do* that?" she wailed.

It was a horrendous lie! Such a horrible, terrible *wrong* thing to do. She couldn't believe that Jessie would do such a thing.

Rhiannon clasped her head and moaned. "This cannot be true, Jamie. The Jessie I know wouldn't do this to someone."

"I know," Jamie ground out. He shook his head. "I haven't been myself since I found out what she did. I'm afraid I've been taking it out on my grandson—unfairly perhaps—but I cannot blame my wife for it, lass. I cannot."

"But...for what *reason* would Jessie possibly do this?"

"I can't say," he said grimly, "because it's her story to tell. She meant to confess to him when he first arrived, but then she said there never seemed to be the right time. She's promised to tell Colin tomorrow, when they're golfing at her club. She's pledged it to me."

"But...but..." Rhiannon struggled to find words. Colin would be devastated and furious, and rightly so. "He'll feel so betrayed, Jamie. Don't you see that? It could ruin their relationship beyond all repairs."

"Aye," Jamie gritted out. "But there's nothing we can do until she tells him."

He gazed at her, and his eyes softened. "Miss Rhiannon, you weren't supposed to be part of this. But Paul said that you must be told. That it was for you to hear, and not your brother."

She groaned, slumping against the tree. "You talked to Paul today?" she asked weakly.

"I did. Just before dinner." Jamie peered closely at her. "Is this too much for you, lass?" he asked hesitantly. "Stepping in as the lady of the manor?"

"No. I'm fine. *I'm* not the one to worry about in this situation."

Jamie clenched his jaw. "I was right—I shouldn't have listened to Paul. You shouldn't be part of this. If your father were home I would go to him."

But her parents weren't home. *She* was in charge.

She had no choice but to step up and help gather the pieces of the fallout from both Jessie and Colin, even though it could damage her relationship with Colin. "Will you *please* call me tomorrow—after Jessie has confessed to Colin?"

"Aye," Jamie said. "But don't judge my wife too harshly. She has her reasons."

Rhiannon couldn't imagine what they could be.

"All will come out soon enough, lass. In the meantime, don't tell Colin. Please let Jessie do it. Will you promise me?"

Rhiannon could only nod.

## CHAPTER SEVEN

THE MORNING DAWNED sunny and bright, a day to be taken advantage of. Colin assisted his grandmother into the front seat of his steering-wheel-on-the-wrong-side rental car, tossed their golf bags in the trunk and then prepared to head out for their grandson/grandmother tee time at the local golf club.

"Did you bring a rain suit?" his grandmother asked, carefully folding her waterproof jacket.

There wasn't a cloud in the sky, but Colin wasn't about to doubt her. Three days in Scotland, and he was already getting used to the quickly changing weather. "No, but I'll pick one up at the pro shop just in case."

"That's wise. I feel the dampness coming in my bones." His grandmother settled her purse on her lap. As Colin pulled into the road, she glanced toward the window of her whitewashed croft cottage.

Jamie scowled back at them.

Colin refused to be bothered by his granddad's attitude, but it upset him that he couldn't say the same for his grandmother. Dressed in her golf sweater and wearing a brimmed cap over her white curls, Jessie twisted her hands in her lap—she obviously was affected by her husband's disapproval.

Colin had heard them talking last night—Jamie wanted her to discuss tomorrow's funeral with him. *Forget it.* Colin had nothing to say about it—to anyone. He figured they had all day tomorrow to deal with that baggage, and then Colin was heading back to Texas right afterward.

"We're gonna have a good day together, you and I," he said to Jessie. "Rain or no rain."

She gave him a brave smile. "Mind that you don't forget to fetch Molly."

Ah, Scotland. A country where dogs were welcome on the golf course. Colin felt himself smiling as he made the turn past the guard gate and then down the gravel drive toward the castle.

Paul the butler waited for them by the front door. Molly, ever obedient, sat patiently with her leash.

"She seems very excited," his grandmother said. "The laird takes his dog golfing every Saturday morning. I'm sure Molly has missed him."

Yes, bringing Molly was a harmless kindness for them to do, and as a bonus Colin got the opportunity to see Rhiannon again.

"I'll be right back," Colin said. While Paul opened the back door for Molly to leap inside the car, Colin left the engine idling and loped toward the castle—he walked in just as had been his habit as a kid, striding through the front rooms in search of Rhiannon.

He found her in the kitchen up to her elbows in flour and other baking implements. Her hair was tied back and her arms were bare. She looked good enough to eat. He paused, enjoying himself.

She gave a small gasp when she saw him. "Colin!" The flush to her cheeks that he liked so much rose and spread. "What are you doing here?"

"We're picking up Molly. Remember?" He'd already phoned her this morning, taking full advantage of the phone number she'd given him. He'd caught her early enough that her voice sounded rough, as if she'd just awoken and hadn't yet spoken to anyone else but him.

"Right! Well...thank you again," Rhiannon said, obviously flustered. He noted that she was still flushed, not looking at him.

Was she thinking about their kiss? He had been...most of the night.

She darted a glance at him and blushed all over again.

He gave her a meaningful look, liking this new direction of their relationship. "Do you want to come with us?"

"Quite funny, Colin. You could be a comedian."

She'd seemed okay with her agoraphobia at the picnic yesterday, so he didn't see where encouraging her a little would hurt. He smiled at her. "Can't blame a guy for trying."

"Right." She wiped the flour off her hands and comically rolled her eyes at him.

He glanced at the mixing bowl on the counter. "What are you making?"

"Cupcakes for Jessie. I thought..." Rhiannon sighed, helplessly shrugging her shoulders. "I wanted to do something kind for your family. It seems so trivial now, doesn't it?"

"She'll appreciate your support. It's not trivial at all."

"Oh, Colin." Rhiannon reached for his hands, grabbed them and held them. She seemed more fiercely upset about the funeral than he'd expected. "Call me today when you have a moment, *please*."

"Of course," he said, though her plea shocked him. Her hands were so soft, and she was trembling with her emotion. He couldn't help it, he ran his fingers up her bare arm.

She watched him do it, her lips slightly parted. There was something about her—a yearning in her—that made him want to stay in Scotland and watch her break free from her shell. He had no doubt in his mind that someday she would.

He interlaced his fingers with hers. And pulled her closer... Closer to him. He felt her body heat. The life force of her breathing.

"Pardon me." A discreet cough came from Paul, standing in the entry to the kitchen. "The engine is running outside, and Jessie asked me to remind you, sir, that the two of you have a very strict tee time."

Colin reluctantly dropped Rhiannon's hands. "I'm sorry. I do have to go."

Rhiannon rubbed her arms as if saddened. He made a note to be more careful with her.

His conscience prickling him, he smiled gently, affecting that old laid-back attitude. "Have a good day with your painting, Rhi," he said as he turned away.

"Go easy on Jessie," she called to him.

He chuckled and kept walking. "Don't worry, I won't outscore her too badly."

"I wouldn't be so cocky if I were you!"

Still smiling, he jogged outside across the gravel and then swung into the car. Molly was sitting in the backseat, perfectly behaved as if she were human, albeit a human who breathed with her mouth open and drooled somewhat.

His grandmother turned in her seat. "And how is Rhiannon?"

He hadn't told his grandmother that was why he was going inside. He darted a glance at her. "Uh...she's good."

His grandmother seemed pleased. "Sorry to rush you, but we're on a tight schedule."

"I understand." He adjusted the mirror and backed the car out, wondering if she would bring up the funeral again. He debated internally whether to have a preemptive conversation with her about his preference for living in the present.

In the end, though, he didn't need to. Jessie spent the drive chatting about her golf club, discussing the sights they passed on their route and "talking" with Molly.

His grandmother was so much like him, it was scary. When they arrived at the car park, he helped her and Molly out, changed his shoes and set up the golf bags—attaching his to a hand-powered trolley and Jessie's to a one-person golf cart that closely resembled a motorized scooter but which she called a buggy. To Colin it looked hilarious, especially when Molly trotted faithfully alongside, her tail wagging with joy.

The course starter greeted both Colin's grandmother and the dog. "How is the laird?" he asked Jessie while petting the golden retriever's coat.

"He's quite well, thank you," Jessie replied. "I'd like to you to meet my grandson, Colin."

"Ah, Colin. To be sure, we know Colin." The starter tipped his cap to Colin, then checked them off on his electronic score-card. "The lads are waiting for you by the first tee."

Jessie smiled, obviously pleased.

"The *lads?*" Colin murmured to her as they walked across the grass, not as manicured as the courses were in the States, but appealing to him nonetheless.

Laughing, she hit him lightly on the arm. "We're playing a four-ball match with two gents who are club members of mine."

*Four-ball match* meant a regular foursome, in Colin's terminology.

He nodded, grateful that there was to be no talk of funerals, and amused that he would be golfing with the geriatric squad, judging by the grizzled beards and graying hair he saw on the men waiting for them by the first tee.

*Ah, well, Mack won't mind so much that I'm golfing without him,* Colin thought.

But if Colin expected an easy, poky game with old codgers, he was sadly mistaken. The other two men in their group were pros as well. One currently played on the tour for golfers over the age of fifty, and the other was a club professional who coached two of their successful junior golfers.

And they *moved.* Unaccustomed to their rapid pace, Colin hustled to keep up. It was the fastest he'd played eighteen holes, ever, and that included time helping his grandmother off and on her buggy. Their play was deadly serious and both men carried their own bags, which were half-full, meaning they contained half the range of clubs by Colin's standards. This lightened their load and seemed to give them more endurance.

Rhiannon had been right. To Colin's utter shock, he *didn't* win the match. He tied the senior player, who had a superior short game—especially with chipping and bump-and-runs. His course management was better, too, but that was a given, since he was familiar with the turf and Colin wasn't.

Still, it gave Colin a reality check. Pensive, he nursed a beer in the club lounge afterward and greeted his grandmother's friends with only part of his normal humility and good cheer.

"I do see his resemblance to Dougie," one woman who'd joined them remarked, peering at him closely around the eyes.

Involuntarily, he stiffened. But his grandmother discreetly *shushed* the lady.

Colin put his beer bottle down on the table. "I promised I'd call Rhiannon."

"Oh, but it's forbidden to use mobile phones in the clubhouse," his grandmother said.

"How about in the parking lot?"

"Eh?"

"The car park," he corrected.

"That's fine, dear."

"Great. I'll come find you when I'm finished."

Colin left the lounge through the clubhouse—the opposite door that they'd entered by—and immediately found himself in the pro shop, filled with racks of golfing merchandise: balls, shoes, clubs, clothing.

He remembered his promise to his grandmother, and searched out the rain suits. They did have some good brands that weren't readily available in the States. Colin detoured to the rack that held his size...and when he glanced up, he was shocked to be staring at a huge, poster-sized picture of himself on the wall.

His jaw dropped. That was him—or a younger version of him—when he'd won the US Collegiate Open. In the photo his head was down and his club was lifted nearly vertically behind him in a classic backswing pose.

He'd never seen this shot. The bronze plaque beneath the poster was inscribed:

Colin Walker
Kildrammond, His First Home Club.

Beneath that were his years on the US professional tour. The ending year was left blank.

He shook his head. Just the fact that they claimed him here, that they honored him...it seemed to hit him right in the solar plexus. He'd never even known.

The rest of the wall appeared to be a trophy wall, photos of all club members in the past and present who'd ever received major golfing honors. Sure enough, the two men he'd golfed with were on the wall, as well.

He threw back his head and laughed.

"He's a right ugly bugger, that one, isn't he?" a voice behind

Colin said. A gruff guy, middle-aged, barrel-chested and with a twinkle in his eye, pointed at the poster of Colin.

"Better-looking than you, old man," Colin said cheerfully. After golfing all morning, he was getting used to the Scottish humor.

"It took you long enough to wander in."

"Maybe if you'd told me I have a position of honor in your pro shop, I'd have stopped by earlier."

"Aye. Your granny had it done."

*My nana,* Colin thought. "I was eight years old the last time I played here. My woods were too big for me, and all I cared about was manhandling them to get more juice in my drive."

The man held out his hand. "McGuff," he said, shaking Colin's hand. "If you stay with us long enough, Mr. Walker, maybe we'll form a local order of Colin's Crew."

Colin laughed. "I'd rather not encourage that, thanks."

McGuff threaded his way back behind the cash register to ring up somebody's purchase. Colin found a rain jacket in his size, tried it on to check that it fit and then brought it over to McGuff.

"If you're ever looking for a place to stay, we have room for you here, laddie," McGuff remarked, ignoring the jacket that Colin had set on the counter.

Colin raised his brow at him. "Thanks, but I have a home."

"It would be a seasonal visit. Come in August for a few weeks. Your granny said that used to be your habit."

"A long time ago." Colin fiddled with a ball washer that was on the counter and imagined the life of being a local club pro, giving stance, grip and swing lessons.

He shuddered.

"You and I have something in common," McGuff said as he rang up the purchase of another lady who came in behind Colin.

"Do we, now?" This guy was a certifiable character. Colin picked up an open bottle of the local whisky, marked Complimentary, and poured himself half a shot into a little plastic cup. The pro shop doubled as a gift shop, and the area did get a lot of tourists visiting the Highlands, so this must've been standard practice. "Is it our love of whisky?" Colin asked with a wink.

"Nah, laddie." McGuff leaned forward. "Somer Grinks."

Colin froze in the midst of downing the dram. He coughed, the whisky burning his lungs.

McGuff slapped him on the back. "Aye. I trained with him, too. No nonsense, the man is."

Somer Grinks led a clinic in Arizona—a boot camp for golfers. It was the worst experience of Colin's career. Grinks had hated him. Barked at him constantly. Told Colin he had talent but no drive.

"We notice you don't train with a swing coach," McGuff remarked. "And you've got a tournament in two weeks?"

Colin smiled politely, not willing to get into this conversation with someone he didn't even know. "Were you ever on tour?" Colin asked instead.

"Aye. The European Tour." McGuff pointed to the posters on the far wall.

"What ended it for you?"

McGuff stepped out from behind the counter. He lifted the leg of his khaki chinos and showed Colin.

From the knee down, McGuff wore a prosthetic limb. Not a high-tech metal one like some athletes had, but a limb made from a material that looked like plastic, with a Scottish blue-and-white flag decal.

"What happened?" Colin asked.

"Motorbike accident," McGuff explained, matter-of-factly.

A purely physical reason—an obstacle that couldn't be

denied. Colin shook his head, not knowing what to say, just feeling sick for him.

"You seem like a good lad," McGuff said to Colin. "I watched you with the McLeod couple after you came in from the eighteenth. You were kind to them. If you want, I'll make a call to Grinks on your behalf."

Colin knew that McGuff was referring to his fall in the rankings, but in a kindly way. "Thanks, but Grinks isn't one of my biggest fans."

"What happened?"

Maybe it was because McGuff had just shown him his prosthetic leg, and he wasn't crying about it, or defiant about it, or ashamed about it, or upset about it. To McGuff...it just *was*. And it was that kind of acceptance that encouraged Colin to tell him the simple truth.

"He kicked me out."

"Why?"

"Maybe he just didn't like me."

"Nah, laddie. He must not have liked your level of commitment. Two very different things."

"But I was a junior golfer."

McGuff patted his phone. "I'll call him for you."

"You don't have to do that."

"I don't have to give you this, either, but I am." From behind the counter, he handed Colin a waterproof jacket, the same brand that Colin had been about to buy. When Colin took the jacket, he saw that it was embroidered "Kildrammond," the name of the golf club.

"Thanks," Colin said. It was a nice gesture on McGuff's part.

"You're one of us." McGuff thumped his chest with his fist. "You learned here, in our club."

Yes, he had. Colin's heart was tight. "How much do I owe you?"

"Put your wallet away." McGuff gave him a look of outrage. "It's a gift from me."

Colin nodded.

"Just remember to come back and see your granny now and then," McGuff said. "Come in August. She gets particularly sad when it's August."

Colin couldn't speak.

McGuff pulled a silver flask from his pocket and poured some amber-colored liquid into two of the little plastic cups from the whisky display Colin had tried. "Try this instead. We don't let the tourists drink it, but you're not a tourist."

He raised his cup, winking solemnly at Colin. "To Kildrammond."

Colin repeated the toast. The fire from the whisky instantly warmed him.

"That has a nice kick," Colin said.

"You're not really a whisky drinker?"

"Not really."

"We do need to get you back in Scotland more often."

*Sure. I have Jessie to visit,* he automatically thought. *Rhiannon, too.*

He wished she was here. "I, uh, need to make a phone call. Thanks for everything." Colin said his goodbye to McGuff, then pulled out his cell phone and headed to the parking lot.

Raindrops spit on his head, so he opened the shopping bag and put on the waterproof jacket McGuff had given him. It fit perfectly.

Then he unlocked the car and got in, but when he bent to push the seat lever back, giving him extra room to breathe, he bumped his hand, which caused his phone to fly across the car, bouncing against the seat and landing on the floor.

Colin leaned over, but he didn't see his phone anywhere. His grandmother's huge purse was in the way; his phone was probably behind it.

He nudged her purse aside and in the process, saw that it was open. Colin couldn't help seeing his name on what looked to be a packet of papers.

He leaned over the seat, perspiring. Should he take a look? Should he snoop inside someone else's personal papers?

But his name was on it. That meant it was his business.

Colin quickly plunged his hand inside the purse, grabbed the packet and then leaned back on the cushions. He was suffocating, so he opened the window, letting in the cool wind, the dampness and a smattering of raindrops.

They were letters. A dozen letters or more—all addressed to him on the envelope, the contents sealed. What the hell? Curious, he flipped through them.

The earliest ones were postmarked Airmail, delivered and then returned. They were addressed to his childhood home in Texas, the place where he'd lived with both parents before the divorce.

Daisie Lee might never have seen the letters.

Maybe she had. What difference did it make now?

He leaned his head back on the seat. He just felt regret. Sad and angry for the missed opportunities with his grandmother.

Why couldn't the adults have figured it out among them? Why had they dragged him through this crap, at eight, when he was powerless to help himself? To protect himself?

The longer he spent in his grandmother's company, the more he was realizing what he'd missed out on.

He dialed Rhiannon's phone number. It rang once, and she picked up. "Hello? Colin?"

Just hearing his name spoken in her kind voice gave him relief. It made him feel as though he'd come home, to a good place, a place that had never left him.

"Rhiannon, do you have a minute?"

———

"COLIN? I'M GLAD you called." Rhiannon's heart was pounding. She clutched her mobile phone and silently excused herself from her discussion with Jamie. They'd been sitting in the back kitchen with Paul. Rhiannon didn't want to talk in front of them.

"Wait a moment," she said to Colin. "I'm heading outside, so I'll need to put the phone down. Hopefully, it's not too windy. Is it raining there? It's raining here."

Oh, wasn't she babbling? But she was obviously nervous. She hurried to the back door, not sure yet how she would handle this situation.

What did Colin know? Her original plan had been to avoid him until she was sure Jessie had told him the truth. Rhiannon was keenly aware that she'd promised him honesty, but still, her first loyalty did go to her life and her people at the castle. It wasn't as if Colin would ever be an everyday part of that. Really, he was likely to leave as soon as he learned the truth.

Standing outside, she put the phone to her ear. "Colin, I'm back."

"Yeah, it's raining here, too," Colin said over the line. "I thought it was a short squall, but it seems to be getting worse."

"Sorry about that. Um, can you wait another minute, please?" She'd forgotten her coat. Crouching and covering her head with her hand, Rhiannon ran toward the formal yew maze behind her art studio. Her family hired gardeners to care for the extensive landscape, but there was one walled garden that Rhiannon alone had the key to. She always kept it with her, tucked into a pocket.

She went inside and quickly shut the door. *Her secret garden.* There was an old tree swing under a canopy of leaves, and she sat on that, the phone to her ear again. "I'm back. Colin, how did it go?"

She heard rain in the background. Loud rain, pattering on a roof or a window. Much harder and more furious than the rain at the castle. "Where are you?" she asked.

"In the car." Colin paused. "I'm wondering if you'll go to the funeral with me."

Rhiannon tried not to groan aloud. Jessie hadn't told him yet. "Oh, Colin," she murmured.

He laughed without mirth. "Sorry. I meant...would you go with me over the videophone? The way that you went to Malcolm's wedding last summer?"

She squeezed the phone tighter in her hand. Emotions warred within her. She wished Jessie had told him the truth, and she was sorry she hadn't—sorry for Colin most of all. He was going to be so angry when he found out. And now, if she agreed to his request, it would be tantamount to lying to his face.

"Rhiannon, are you there?" he asked, his voice sounding fainter.

"I am," she whispered.

He sighed. "Look, I know we're just getting to know each other again. I know it's a lot for me to ask. But..." He paused. "I'm in the car and I noticed that Jessie had a bunch of letters in her purse, all addressed to me. They look like letters she wrote when I was...uh, hell," he muttered.

"What?"

"Some of these are postmarked just before my birthday." He cursed softly.

"Isn't that a good thing?"

"I don't know. I just want to...start again where we all are now, and go forward from there. I don't want to think about the old times. I don't want to think about what-ifs, or who was wrong or right."

"I'm sure it's difficult for them, too, Colin."

"I need *someone* on my side, Rhiannon." His voice had an edge to it.

She recoiled. Physically bent her head over her knees and stared at the ground.

But he was silent, waiting, so she found herself speaking the truth. "Until you showed up this week, hitting your golf balls, I rarely saw Jessie or Jamie. Maybe five or six times a year, Colin, and mostly, it was when they came to watch you on the telly here at the castle for a particularly big match. And I sat in with them—which was rare for me to sit with a group of visitors to the castle. But I did so only because I was curious about seeing you."

"So you've thought of me, then?" he asked in a low voice.

"All the ever-loving time!" she nearly shouted.

He exhaled. "I'm messed up, Rhiannon. You know how we said we'd be honest with each other? Well, honestly, I am messed up. I didn't expect to find these letters or to feel so bad about the funeral. And you're the only person I can tell."

The threat of tears burned at the edges of her eyes. *Oh, Colin,* she thought. "Please drive home. I'll meet you at the gate."

"I will. I'm waiting for Jessie to get back. I just...can't stand the thought of looking at *him* in a casket tomorrow. I came here expecting to piss on his grave, but now that I'm here, and I've met Jessie again...that's not going to happen. I have to be stoic for her tomorrow, and I'm not sure I can do that. Plus, Daisie Lee, she's...well, let's just say I'm responsible for her, too. You know?"

Rhiannon knew. She remembered. "I'm on your side, too, Colin."

There was a short silence. "Thank you," he said quietly.

Her heart was breaking. "I have to be honest with you. I never saw your father again—I don't think he's ever come back to visit." She bit her tongue. Should she tell him what she knew about his dad? She couldn't divulge what Jessie had pledged she would do, but Rhiannon could share this truth. "Do you want to know where your father lived the last I heard, Colin?"

Another silence. "It doesn't matter to me. But, coming from you, yeah... Just tell me what I need to know for the funeral tomorrow. I trust you, Rhiannon."

She squeezed her eyes shut. *May he please forgive me if he ever finds out.* "Well, your father was living in Italy. For how long, I don't know. He married..."

"That woman?" Colin asked harshly.

"Yes, I believe so. But then, I'm sure I don't know everything," she added quickly.

"Children?"

"I...don't think so. Not his own, anyway."

"That makes sense. Otherwise, there would be no inheritance for me."

Oh, hell's bells! She'd forgotten that Jamie had mentioned an inheritance. "Is it...substantial?" she asked carefully.

"Oh, yeah. A million bucks."

Rhiannon put the phone down, knocking her forehead against her knee. Jessie had really stepped in it, hadn't she?

Rhiannon took a breath to compose herself. "Is that why you came to Scotland?"

"It's why Daisie Lee wanted me to come." Colin sighed again. "She has it in her head that I might not last on the pro tour much longer, and that I need to think of the future. And I'll be honest with you: she also looked into your brother's company and how they endorse professional athletes. I want you to hear this from me, in case you hear through the grapevine that it's my reason for being here. Because it's not. I'm not looking for anything from you or your family. I'd rather not even accept my father's inheritance if I didn't need it as a backup to help pay my team members' salaries, to tell you the truth."

Rhiannon waited. She sensed he was going to tell her what he did want, and she was immensely interested in that.

"I just want some kind of harmony," Colin said. "But I'm not likely to get it unless I make a few decisions."

She exhaled.

"Rhiannon, are you there?"

She nodded, but he couldn't hear that, so she squeaked, "Yes."

"What do *you* want, Rhiannon?"

Peace. On her estate.

And Colin there sometimes to be with her, too.

But she couldn't say that aloud to anybody—especially the second part, which was still in the realm of fantasy. And the longer she kept the truth from him, the less likely that fantasy was becoming. "I want to help you in whatever way I can, truly, Colin."

"I told you, just by being yourself, you already do." He cleared his throat, murmuring to someone beside him. "Rhiannon? I have to go, Jessie is here."

*Please, Jessie, tell him what you did.*

"Yes," Rhiannon said. "Goodbye, then."

She ended the call, her head in her hands.

She was involved now. Really and truly involved. She'd been somewhat involved last evening when Jamie told her, and somehow she'd remained quiet about her knowledge to Colin, but now it was worse. He had asked her to go to the funeral and she'd said nothing. She had listened to him speak about his father and she'd said nothing still.

She headed back to the kitchen, where Jamie sat at the side table, nursing a cup of tea.

"Jessie hasn't told Colin yet," Rhiannon announced.

"Aye," Jamie said grimly. He pointed to his own phone, set on the table beside him. "I called her, and she said that she cannot do it. She wants you to help her tell Colin."

"What! Me?"

"She says that you and Colin have a special bond, and that it will go better coming from you, lass."

"But that's not fair!" she blurted.

Jamie shifted uncomfortably. He and Paul glanced at each other.

*They're doubting me. They're doubting my fitness because of my agoraphobia.*

What else could it be?

Rhiannon took a deep breath, and then sat at the table with her hands folded before her. If her parents had been present, Rhiannon had no doubt that one of them would accompany Jessie to speak with Colin. This was exactly the type of drama and stickiness that her mother, in particular, dealt with nearly every month of the year —from the workers they periodically hired to the villagers and their committees to the church community they were part of.

At the end of the day, if Rhiannon didn't handle it, then Paul would bring Malcolm in. That was the reality. And she still had a chance to fight against it, to change it and take charge of her world—and bring on the future she *did* want.

She cleared her throat. She'd just take it step by step—she could do this. "Tell me everything you know, Jamie. Start from the beginning. Why did Jessie make up this horrible story?"

Jamie sighed and gazed at his hands. "Simply put, she wants to bring her family together before it's too late."

"Before it's too..." Rhiannon suddenly thought of Jessie's lost weight. Her tired eyes. The lines in her face. It all made sense. "Is she unwell, Jamie?"

He stared into his teacup, looking terrible. "My wife is ill, Miss MacDowall. That's all I'll say about it."

*Oh, no.* "Has the doctor been seen?"

Jamie nodded miserably. "Aye. We went to the clinic last week. Her heart isn't working properly." He suddenly glared. "It's why I didn't want her to have the excitement, didn't want her to golf today. But she refuses to allow Colin to know. And him so careless and flippant with us."

Rhiannon understood the source of Jamie's anger and frustration. So much more was clearer now. She peered at him. "You do know it's not fair to blame Colin for his parents' decisions? He was caught in the middle when they divorced. He was just a boy—it wasn't his fault."

"Aye. But that was then. He's been of age for years now, and could have called to check on her." He suddenly turned and glared. "I'm angry, lass. It eats me to see how hard my wife has tried over the years and always been rebuffed. She tried to stay in touch with Colin, but her letters were returned unopened and her phone calls unanswered."

He sighed. "All she wants is for her only grandson to know he has people in Scotland who support him and love him. It's why I didn't make a fuss when she first made that phone call.

"But now, lass, I don't know what to do. It's true, my temper flared when Colin arrived smelling of drink and laughing in the wee hours, disrespecting his grandmother. I wanted him to face the pain, so I didn't disavow the ruse that his father was dead, just so Colin would 'go stew in it.' But he's like his grandmother. He avoids painful things.

"And now everything has mushroomed," Jamie continued. "Colin trusts in his grandmother again, and Jessie is beating herself up with remorse, trying to see how to break the truth to him gently so he won't hold it against her."

"Jessie *has* to face it."

"But she's not, lass," Jamie hissed. "The so-called funeral is tomorrow. When Colin finds out she lied, he'll be furious. She'll be more upset than ever. It's a disaster."

It *was* a disaster.

"Colin mentioned the inheritance," Rhiannon said.

Jamie coughed. "My wife told Colin's mother..." He frowned again. "...on the telephone that not only was there to be a funeral, but an inheritance. An *inheritance!* As if Dougie, that charming layabout, had a pound to his name!"

"So...there's no inheritance at all?" Rhiannon asked carefully. "Just to clarify things."

"No, miss. No inheritance. That was a ruse to get Daisie Lee to return her call. You see, even the people in Colin's management company didn't forward on her calls. She didn't have his personal phone numbers. She had to rely on the old number, from Daisie Lee. And the only way Jessie could get that woman to talk to her was to dangle the promise of an inheritance."

"Did Jessie ever think of visiting Colin?" Rhiannon asked.

"Yes, but she has a terrible fear of flying. Surely you can understand."

"I do," Rhiannon said softly. She more than anyone could understand what it was like to be physically unable to do something because of fear.

Jamie shook his head. "She's been waiting for years for Colin to play a tournament in Scotland, or anywhere on the British Isles where she could take a train or a ferry to. But it appears he's been avoiding us. We fear his mother poisoned him against us."

"I don't have harsh thoughts for Daisie Lee. I was young then, but I remember the night she came with Colin in tow. The night they decided to divorce."

"Aye. That was terrible. The worst day of my life." Jamie's voice had turned soft, and he gazed into his cup.

He said nothing more.

Rhiannon felt deeply moved. Jamie was right—she had to do what she could to help mediate. Both for the sake of her own goals and for the past connection she'd had to Colin and his family.

For certain, Jamie wasn't the right person to tell Colin—they were already having difficulty getting along. And Jessie just seemed unable to disappoint her grandson.

"All right," Rhiannon said. "I'll do it."

Jamie's face brightened. "You will?"

"Yes." She drew herself up. She needed to be strong, whether she felt it or not.

She turned to face Jamie. "All I ask is that you please be kind to Colin tonight. No talk of Dougie or the anger over what you think Colin may have done wrong. Promise you'll be supportive of both Jessie *and* Colin. Can you do that?"

Jamie scowled at her.

"Can you at least *try* to fake your support for him?"

"Oh, aye," Jamie grumbled. "But I don't see where he cares for me. It's Jessie who has my worry."

"Then for Jessie's sake, let's hope Colin doesn't get angry and leave Scotland forever."

"For Jessie's sake," Jamie softly repeated.

But it was for Rhiannon's sake, too. And she didn't see how Colin could *not* be angry.

For her own sake, she would try her hardest to resolve this issue.

## CHAPTER EIGHT

RHIANNON PUT ON HER COAT and wellies and trudged to the top of the drive to meet Colin when he returned home. She'd nearly reached Jamie's guard shack when Colin rounded the corner in his sporty car.

Coming to a stop, the engine idling, he leaned over and opened the passenger door for her. "Were you waiting for me?" he called.

"Yes."

He grinned, and it struck her anew at how the sight of his handsome face made her feel—she was all fluttery inside.

"Where's Jessie?" she asked.

"I dropped her off." He smiled sadly at her. "Hop in."

Her heart beating quicker, she stepped inside to the smell of new leather and wet dog. Molly put her front paws on the back of Rhiannon's seat as a greeting and licked her hair, but even that friendliness didn't ease the shakiness Rhiannon felt.

"I need to talk to you," she said to Colin.

"Okay." He glanced at her sideways. "Before I forget, though, I have something to give you."

He passed her a postal package. "It was waiting for me when

I got to Jessie's cottage. It's my way of saying sorry about your broken camera. I tried to replace it exactly, but that model isn't manufactured anymore. This is the best I could do."

She didn't need to open the cardboard box to know that he'd brought her a beautiful and improved replacement camera.

"Thank you," she said. "That was quite fast."

"Overnight shipping, and I apologize again." He looked at her with that charm she loved so much, and then he drove them down the driveway to the castle. The rain squall had passed and small puddles dotted the parking area beside the drawbridge. This was her turf, familiar and safe.

But she couldn't remember a time when she'd had to deliver such bad news. In her carefully constructed life—never. She clutched the box in her lap, wondering how to begin.

If she were Colin, she would want the news delivered gently.

She cleared her throat as Colin parked near the front door. "Did Jessie manage to talk with you about the letters you found in her purse?"

He frowned and stepped out of the car, dodging a rain puddle in the gravel drive. "No."

"Did you tell her that you found them?" she asked through the open door.

"No. I can't talk to her like I can you." He leaned into the back to let Molly out, but the dog put her paws on the back of Rhiannon's seat and barked.

Colin chuckled at the dog and turned to Rhiannon with a comical raised brow. "Will you help me with this pooch of yours?"

"Of course." Colin wasn't making this easy for her, but Rhiannon nodded, doing what it took to marshal the excited canine into the castle and back to Paul, who cooed over her as if she were a long-lost child.

Smiling weakly despite her task at hand—because the sight

of her proper English-trained butler in his suit and tie down on all fours cavorting with an excited golden retriever was just so silly and incongruent—Rhiannon felt some of the tension drain from her shoulders.

"May I see your art studio?" Colin asked, shocking her to her toes.

"My...art studio?"

"Yeah. I'm interested in your paintings. I tried to find some of them on the internet, but I gather they're all in private collections."

"Yes," she said quietly, "they are."

"Is...that a problem?" he asked, some of the smile draining from his face.

"No," she said quickly, aware of Paul's presence and his quiet observation of them while he played with Molly. "You're right," Rhiannon said to Colin. "We should go to my art studio."

It *was* a more appropriate place to have her heart-to-heart with Colin. And she felt relaxed there.

As a rule, though, she kept her workspace private. She could think of only six people in the past year she'd allowed inside her painting studio, and they were all family. Except Jacob—though in a sense, he would soon be family, too, because her cousin Isabel had just announced their marriage date.

"Follow me," she said hesitantly to Colin. "I warn you, though, it's messy."

Paul had stopped making any pretense of playing with Molly and was now staring outright at her.

Rhiannon lifted her chin and with as much calm as she could muster, led Colin out the back way and across the court-yard to the outbuilding that housed not only her studio on the second storey, but also guest rooms on the first floor. She took him up the creaky staircase and into the atelier workshop that she'd fashioned for herself shortly after she'd returned home as a girl.

She stood aside and watched Colin's reaction to her private world.

He seemed to drink it all in, marveling at every detail.

The tall windows placed to overlook the yew garden and the Highland scenery outside, and to let in sunlight so it flooded the surface of her work. Her easel, set with the overlarge landscape she was currently creating, still unfinished. The walls, lined with other landscapes showing the glens and burns of her beloved estate. Even the floor, dappled with painted whimsy, a woodland scene she'd fancied when she was a child and had kept there even now.

Painting had begun as her therapy, her way of healing after the childhood trauma. Over the years she'd developed her kernel of natural talent into a skill that produced beauty. To her, expressing herself through paint was at heart an act of joy, accessible to her only through a place where she allowed herself to be a trusting, carefree child again.

"Rhiannon, this is..." Colin just shook his head. But the look on his face said everything.

"After I was rescued when I was a girl, I had trouble feeling safe again. One of my doctors suggested that I write as part of my therapy, but I preferred to stay in my room and paint. My mother helped me by bringing in tutors and supplies, and all these years later, I still want to paint. It's become more than just therapy for me. It's...turned into the contribution I want to make with my life. People, collectors—they purchase my work for enjoyment and..."

While she was talking, Colin had been nodding, moving from painting to painting, tilting his head and admiring her pieces. But now he'd stopped at her worktable and was staring down at it in stillness.

*The sketch I made of him!*

Rhiannon ran over to it, embarrassment flooding her. She hadn't meant for anybody to see that drawing, least of all Colin.

He picked up the pencil drawing and gazed at it wonderingly. A smile curved his face and lit up his handsome features. Part of Rhiannon's heart seemed to break, for what she still had to tell him.

He held it to the light. "You have an amazing talent."

"I...oh, you weren't meant to see that! I'm terrible with portraits."

"No. You're not," he said, acting miffed at her for saying that about herself.

She snatched the drawing back. "You don't understand—there's a spirit to you that I'm not expressing properly in the lines. But I don't have a lot of experience with sketching people, so I don't know how to do it well and it's frustrating me."

He glanced about the room, a confused look on his face. Certainly, he was comprehending that his was the only portrait in her studio. She felt that she had to explain.

She *wanted* to explain.

"Colin, I..." She swallowed. She didn't like to speak about herself. But she wanted him to know the truth. Her truth.

"Drawing was how I survived the kidnapping, really. The men who took me didn't know what to do with me. They'd transported us to a large warehouse in the countryside and separated me and Malcolm. I was locked in a cellarlike room with nothing inside but blankets on the floor. One of them must have taken pity, because he tossed in a children's coloring book and some pencils. I drew to pass the time. I'd always liked to sketch, even before..."

Colin was nodding sympathetically, listening intently, so she kept going, licking her lips. "Anyway, it's what I did. I hid my drawings under the blanket when they came in the room, which wasn't often. Sometimes they took me out of the cell. But it was a large place we were held in—it was dark and scary, and I always longed for my little cell back."

She rubbed her arms. "And then...well, once we were rescued, I drew sketches of the kidnappers for the police..." She rubbed her arms some more. "So many people died that night, during the rescue. One of the police officers died beside me and I... Well, he was a good man, and so I drew him, too. That was the last portrait I did. I didn't ever want to draw *people* again, because it made me remember that horrible time."

Colin was gazing at her, silently. He was always so talkative, but now he just looked quietly pained.

She lowered her head. It had been a long time since she spoke to anyone about the horror she'd gone through and the feelings her sketches had given her. Maybe not since the days of her therapy. In any event, she didn't use therapists anymore. She really didn't need that kind of help. She'd been in a comfortable stasis about everything in her life for so long.

She looked into his eyes. "But then you showed up on the estate, and now everything is changing. I felt inspired to draw a sketch of you so I wouldn't forget you. That's why it's there..."

"Rhiannon," he said, his voice husky, and he touched the back of his knuckles to her cheek.

She closed her eyes, letting his hand rest there. Barely daring to breathe, she leaned her cheek closer to him, the way Colin the cat rubbed against her hand when she held it out to him.

"I'm glad I came back," he said.

"I am, too," she whispered.

Sighing deeply, he drew her to him.

The intimacy of it made her freeze, at first. But then, gradually, she relaxed her body against his. His hands rested lightly on her back, as if letting her know that she was safe, and free, and not constrained by his embrace.

She pressed her cheek against his; it was warm and scratchy and male. She'd never felt such human closeness before. Her breathing fell into sync with his, and that felt strange at first—the newness of it. She really could imagine that their hearts were beating together, that their blood flowed at the same pace.

"Thank you for telling me," he said, his lips brushing against her hair. "You're the bravest person I know."

"No. I'm just me," she whispered.

"That's what I love about you."

*Love.* He'd said that word.

Surprise filled her, but a different kind. A happy, blissful, light-as-air feeling. She put her arms about Colin and hugged him closer, feeling her breasts flatten against his chest, her thighs press between his strong legs.

"Rhiannon," he murmured. She felt his emotion like a current against her bones.

And then his hand was at the back of her head, cupping her, gently tilting her mouth to his.

He was going to kiss her. *Really* kiss her. As two passionate adults—two people who could potentially embark on a real relationship, as she'd never felt possible for herself.

He kissed her leisurely, sweetly at first, and then deeply. She moved with him as if in a dream, her lips responsive to his and participating fully, learning the shape and movement of his lips, the feel of his mouth. He tasted sweet, like the icing on the cupcakes she'd made. An everyday person, not foreign or unwelcome.

She wanted more of him. Her Colin.

"You're beautiful, Rhiannon." He pulled back and gazed at her. "I wish I didn't have to leave tomorrow."

The reminder that he was not a permanent fixture here was like a bucket of cold water thrown on her chest.

"I really do hope you'll come back to visit," she said.

"Absolutely." He gave her that crooked smile, but it was with a tinge of sadness this time. "It's too bad it took a funeral to get us together."

*Oh, no.* She stepped back, pushing her hands through her hair. For these few moments while they were kissing, she'd completely forgotten about what it was she was supposed to be doing. She'd made a terrible mess of this.

"Colin, I need to tell you something." She looked into his beautiful blue eyes, so happy with her now. But in a moment that would change. "Please don't be mad at me for what I have say."

He laughed at her. "That's impossible, Rhiannon."

"But you haven't heard it yet!"

He shrugged, still smiling slightly, as if indulgent with her. "You don't have to explain any more if you don't want to."

Did he think she was talking about the kidnapping? "No, Colin, it's about you."

"Me?" His smile drained.

"Jessie wanted to tell you today. She really did. But she couldn't, so Jamie asked me to tell you instead."

A crease formed in his forehead. "What do they have to do with us?"

"Nothing. Everything. But this isn't about us!" she said, exasperated and not quite sure how to continue. "Please don't blame them. You have to understand that all these years while you were away, it was torture for them. Especially with you being a public figure and seeing you on the telly, on the sports channels during the big events..."

"Rhiannon, if you have something to tell me, spit it out."

"There is no funeral!" she said all at once.

He tilted his head, looking confused. "What are you talking about?"

"Your dad isn't dead." She weakly smiled at him, hoping he

would be pleased and thankful, but he just stared at her disbelievingly, likely in shock.

"Yes, it's true. He's still alive. That's good news, right?" She nodded, but that just seemed to make him angry.

"Was there a mistake made?" he said between clenched teeth. "Because I was told he died of a heart attack."

"What? Colin...no. Though I don't agree with her methods, Jessie was desperate. All she wanted was to get you here, to bring you into her life again. That was always her intent."

"So it's all been a hoax." A sudden deadly calm seemed to spread over him.

"Please don't look at it that way." Her voice faltered. "Your grandmother didn't intend for it to go on so long—not that that's an excuse," she hastened to add.

Shocked, he was staring at her. "You were in on it, too? You scammed me, too, Rhiannon?"

"No! I didn't even know about it until yesterday."

His eyes widened.

"Please, Colin," she whispered.

But he stepped away from her, shook his head and faced one of her landscapes. He bowed his head, put his hand on his forehead. She'd never seen anyone look so betrayed, as if he couldn't believe what she'd told him. Her heart was breaking and she knew how it must seem from his point of view, that they'd all manipulated him and he'd swallowed it whole, and now he was hurt and angry and embarrassed.

And even this—their visit to her studio, and drawing him, and confiding in him, and *kissing* him with such passion—could be misconstrued as her trying to manipulate him. It was the furthest thing from the truth, and it made her feel flustered...

She wrung her hands. She'd truly started to care for Colin again. And by bringing him to her studio, she'd wanted to make this situation better for him—more personal between them, closer—not further apart. She wanted him to feel *good* about her.

He turned and stared dully at her. "Exactly how long have you known that my father is still alive?"

"Since last night, like I told you," she said miserably.

"Last night before or after we talked about honesty?" There was anger in his voice.

She winced. "I didn't know when I promised you that. Jamie told me on our walk back to the castle."

"So you knew all night after that," he said quietly. "And you knew this morning when I came and held your hand. And you especially knew this afternoon when I called and spilled my guts to you about the letters I'd found—you knew then, as well."

"I'm *sorry!*" She hated how this was turning around on her.

"You should have told me as soon as you knew, Rhiannon. I wouldn't have betrayed you to them." His eyes bored into hers. "You asked me to be honest with you. You even brought my *childhood* into it—talking about my reaction to my parents' divorce." His eyes showed all of his pain.

"I wanted you to know!" she said. "But they asked me not to tell you. Jessie promised Jamie she would tell you today, but then when she couldn't... Jamie asked me to do it. Colin, I'm sorry— this wasn't my choice. There's never been a good time to talk to you about this until now."

"Sure there were. There have been plenty of great times. How about when I asked you to metaphorically hold my hand through the funeral service?" he said, his voice wavering. "That would have been a particularly good time, Jessie and Jamie be damned."

"Don't say that! Please just know that it wasn't my story to tell. I just... I just want peace," she said helplessly. "Like you want harmony in your family? I want healing—for you and for me, for all of us. I have to stay here in this castle, and you'll be leaving again tomorrow for all your adventures. I *have* to make my life here. With the people here."

"You know what, Rhiannon?" He glanced at the door. "I'm sorry, but I've got no peace to give anyone. Not you. Not Jessie. Not now." He turned to leave.

"Wait, Colin!"

But he kept walking. And when he was gone, she sank to the floor, her head in her hands.

She had failed, miserably.

She'd made it worse, not only for her and for Colin, but for Jessie and Jamie, as well.

———

IN HIS LIFE, Colin did everything he could to avoid pain, but Rhiannon had delivered a wallop. The lie had completely blindsided him, to the point that he didn't even have the heart to attempt to turn it around into a good joke. It was too damn personal.

Colin didn't want to examine the whys too closely right now. He just needed to get out of here and breathe some air away from the sting of betrayal.

In the driveway, in the confines of his rental car, Colin laid his forehead against the steering wheel. He didn't want to drive in this mood, but it wasn't far to his grandparents' cottage. He made the short run and parked the car. Gazing up at the white-washed doorway, the garden outside clipped and tidy, he knew he wouldn't go inside. Not yet, anyway.

Instead he dialed Mack's phone number. Colin's caddie picked up on the first ring and agreed to meet Colin where he was.

Mack blew in a few minutes later driving Bonnie's car,

cracking jokes about being on the wrong side of the road and nearly crashing into ditches on the roundabouts.

Colin got into the passenger side and said nothing. He rolled down the window and laid his head back on the seat, letting the cool country air wash over him as they drove the narrow, rural roads.

Mack turned the radio up loud. It was an opportunity for Colin not to speak until they reached that familiar pub on the main street in town.

"Did you get any more news about your inheritance?" Mack asked as he parked Bonnie's car in an on-street spot behind the pub.

"Inheritance?" Colin nearly laughed aloud. He'd completely forgotten about that. He supposed that was another lie.

"Yeah. I don't mean to bring it up, but we're flying home tomorrow." Mack glanced sideways at Colin. "Do you still want to do the pissing-on-the-grave thing?"

Colin got out of the car. "No," he said flatly, "I don't."

He just wanted to get a drink and not think about anything.

"That's cool," Mack said. "It might be a late night. That band from Wednesday night is here again. Remember them?"

Wednesday seemed like ages ago. Colin shook his head. But there would probably be a cover charge, so he reached for his wallet.

"Damn," he muttered, smacking his empty back pocket. "I think I left my wallet in the trunk of the rental car."

"No worries. Bonnie's working the tap tonight."

"How *old* are we?" Colin said aloud. Chatting up barmaids and snagging complimentary drinks—these were stunts they'd pulled back when they were irresponsible kids. He and Mack were in their thirties now.

But Mack had headed inside the pub and was kissing his sweetheart-for-the-weekend on her cheek. Colin found an empty chair and sat with his head in his hands. On principle, he wasn't drinking anything.

One of the golfers he'd met at his grandmother's club stopped by and said hello. Because Colin respected the man, he raised his head and did his best to interact in a normal conversation, as if nothing was wrong.

Music started playing in another room. A group of Saturday night revelers streamed in from the street. Mack returned with a lager for him in a tall pint glass.

Usually, the busy pub would have been Colin's kind of scene, but he wasn't in the mood for a beer. He shook his head to the dark Scottish brew that Mack offered him.

Colin had no taste for it anymore. Not any of it. The realization was hitting him hard—all week, his grandparents had been playing him for a joker, but maybe that was because he'd been acting like a joker.

There was no inheritance, obviously. There would be no pissing on graves—indeed, his father wouldn't even show up. Or call Colin. Or care. That was just the way it was, and not even sweet-hearted Rhiannon-who-wanted-peace could fix that. Colin didn't want her to fix anything for him. He'd thought that she genuinely cared for him. That she saw beyond the surface of his laid-back act to the man he was beneath.

The man he wanted to be.

Colin closed his eyes and thought of their kiss. The way she'd felt in his arms. The way she'd looked at him, as if he'd actually meant something to her.

In that moment, that she—or anybody else—had been lying to him had been the last thought on his mind.

He watched Mack flirting with Bonnie behind the beer tap. Bonnie tossing her red hair back, laughing, probably not knowing that Mack wouldn't ever return for her, wouldn't ever answer her calls again after this weekend. Colin was loyal to his friend—Mack had stuck with him from the beginning, before Colin had become semifamous, and that alone was something important and rare. But Colin didn't want to be irresponsible like him anymore. What had used to seem laid-back and *light* now just seemed like a cop-out.

What Colin really wanted was to reclaim some self-respect. Get back on the tour and kick some ass. Play to win and grab hold of a real life, one where he could go all out, commit to what he wanted and not be waylaid by what-ifs or past failures.

His timing sucked, however. He was one misstep away from having to give up his dream of a real life on the tour. He could easily end up like McGuff, ringing up purchases in a pro shop, and that was not where Colin wanted to be. Not yet, anyway. He hadn't truly applied himself yet, hadn't made his best shot.

If he was honest, all these years he'd been giving it a half-assed effort, getting by on charm and good words. He'd been born gifted with talents—more talents than he probably even knew—and in effect, he'd been squandering them.

For what? A life with no fear? He could pretend that he wasn't enough, because once, a long time ago, the man who'd been his father, in a fit of pique, had said just as much.

*Enough,* Colin thought. *No more.*

No more betrayals. No more lies. No more running.

He stood up from the bar stool. Found Mack and patted him on the back, because none of this was Mack's fault. He'd been a loyal friend, a good guy, ever since Colin first moved to Central Texas. Through high school together and on to university on a golf scholarship, and then to life on the tour as Colin's caddie. Colin would never blame Mack for his own shortcomings. He blamed himself.

Mack blinked at him. "Are you okay? If you need to lie down, I can give you the key to Bonnie's place upstairs. She won't mind. She's a good kid."

"A place upstairs?" Colin repeated.

"Yeah, she lives above the pub."

Something in Colin seemed to snap. A room above a pub? It was so typical of them. And he was tired of it. Tired of being a party guy, and tired of being an underperforming slacker.

He'd learned some positive things on this trip to Scotland. He'd seen a new perspective. Met new role models. Been reintroduced to the grandparents, who, despite their dysfunctional way of showing it, really did appear to care about him.

And there had been the surprise of Rhiannon's influence. Just watching her open up to him, fight against her agoraphobia from the kidnapping, was making him think. Waking him up. He could still respect her, even though he may have trouble trusting her for a while.

He felt as though he was at a crossroads. Stay the way he'd always been, with Mack, drifting from place to place and bumping into the Bonnies of the world. Never daring to push himself. Always wondering *What if?*

Or he could man up and accept the challenge.

"Mack," he said, "I've decided to stay and train in Scotland for the week. You're welcome to stay with me if you want, but if you don't, I'll understand."

Mack set his beer on the bar. "Colin, you can't do that."

"Actually," he said calmly, "I can."

"But what about the tour?"

"I'm still on the pro tour—I'm not out yet. And there's no rule that says I can't train from here for the New York Cup."

Mack shook his head, looking stunned. With a laugh, he appealed to Colin. "What brought this on?"

Colin explained it in terms that his caddie could understand. "I met a couple guys at Kildrammond who I think will make good swing coaches. You know I need to make a change there."

Mack blew out a breath, nodding, his gaze darting toward

the table where Bonnie was delivering a tray of drinks. "Okay, but what about Daisie Lee?"

Colin gritted his teeth, but honestly, he couldn't blame Mack too much for bringing her up. So much of Colin's life at home had revolved around taking care of his mother. Being available when she needed him, more out of guilt and old wounds than because he really wanted to.

"You let me worry about her," he said.

Mack let out a sigh. Colin got the feeling there was more to Mack's reluctance to staying in Scotland than he was letting Colin see. But Colin could guess. *Bonnie.*

"So you don't care if I don't train with you?" Mack demanded. "Come on, Colin. Shouldn't I be worried about that?"

"No, it's not that I don't care." Now that he considered it, though, he did prefer to make this a fresh start, on his own. Mack could be a bad influence—he was too much like the way Colin had been, and Colin didn't want that anymore.

"You know what? On second thought, I do want you to go home, Mack. Take a week's vacation—I'm paying. You're still my caddie, so you don't have to worry about losing your job. You just don't want to be here in Scotland much longer, am I right?"

"Scotland's great," Mack said, rolling a cardboard beer coaster down the polished bar. He glanced at Colin. "It's just Bonnie—if I stay much longer, she'll get the wrong idea."

"Yeah." Colin nodded, watching Bonnie anxiously gazing over at them. She seemed to be what Mack referred to as a *clinger.* Mack liked to be free above all.

"I already told her I'm leaving tomorrow, and that I'm not coming back. If I stay, it will make things complicated."

Colin nodded, feeling sorry for Mack and Bonnie both. "I understand." He slapped his friend on the shoulder. "Take Doc's jet home tomorrow, have a good time on your week off, okay? We'll keep in touch until the tournament."

"You sure we're good?" Mack asked anxiously.

"Always," Colin said. "I take care of my people."

———

STONE-COLD SOBER, Colin took the key his nana had given him and let himself inside her cottage.

"Colin?" Jessie met him at the door. Her eyes were red and swollen as if she'd been crying. "Rhiannon rang us. We were worried you weren't coming back."

He nodded briskly to his grandmother and gave her a smile. Then he figured *what the hell?* and curled his arm around her and gave her shoulder a squeeze. He didn't want her to cry. He felt as though he was the adult now, and he would have to show her the way. "Let's go in the kitchen and talk."

She gave him a look of relief. But this was different from the way Colin had used to cheer his mother up when she was upset. He wasn't going to do that anymore—wasn't going to minimize himself. He wasn't going to let her off the hook for what she'd done. But he wasn't going to blame her, either. How could he? When it came right down to it, after the initial shock of the betrayal, he felt compassion for the situation they'd all found themselves in.

He led her to the table and pulled out a chair for her. Jessie —his nana—really was frailer than he'd realized. He'd had hints that she'd been feeling weak during their golf game, but she'd been wearing her bulky rain clothing and that had hidden her size. Now she wore a thin pajama top, and he could see the weight and vitality she'd lost since she was in the prime that he remembered.

He set his key on the table and sat straight-backed in the

chair opposite from her. Even Jamie came into the kitchen wearing slippers and a bathrobe. Colin nodded at him, too. "I've decided to stay and train at Kildrammond for the next week. Is it okay with you both if I stay here while I do?"

Jamie's mouth fell open. He swiveled to stare at his wife, but Jessie was clasping Colin's hand, nodding, tears leaking from her eyes. "I prayed this would happen."

Colin put his other hand on her thin ones, but he gave her a stern look, too. "This situation will work out for the best—don't you worry about that. But I'm asking you to never lie to me again. Are we clear?"

"Y-yes. Of course."

"Good." He nodded. "If that's the case, then we'll get past this."

Jamie pulled out a chair and sat, too. He seemed to be struggling to say something.

Colin caught his gaze and held it. "Look, I know I was wrong, too. I'm sorry for my behavior when I first landed in Scotland. There won't be any more late nights. I'll call you if what I'm doing might mean a disruption to your schedule."

"You never disrupt us," Jessie insisted.

"Do we have an agreement?" Colin asked Jamie.

Jamie pressed his lips together. He was still struggling with what he had to say.

"I know the years haven't been easy for us," Colin said. "I wish my parents had been able to figure out how to stay together and make it work between them, but they couldn't, and nothing we do can go back and change that."

He made sure to smile at his grandmother so she didn't feel too badly. "I noticed the birthday cards in your purse, Nana. I saw how often you thought of me. I thought of you, too." He nodded to Jamie and addressed him next. "And, yes, I've considered what Rhiannon said to me tonight, and I've decided I want to work on getting past it. Do you want to do the same?"

For a long moment Jamie was silent, he just sat with those pressed-together lips. Then, with a jerk against his seat, and the scrape of chair legs being violently pushed back, he rose and enveloped Colin in a bear hug.

Colin took that as a yes. "Okay, then."

Jamie withdrew, still with that solemn, fierce look on his face. "We took too long. But it's better late than not."

Colin nodded.

"The best day I ever knew," Jessie said, "was the day you came back to Scotland."

"Well, keep that in mind when I'm up at the crack of dawn for my daily tee time."

"Oh, that won't be a problem." She winked at him. "You can start the breakfast for us."

He laughed, his load feeling lighter. He still had to phone Daisie Lee, of course, but he had an idea how he would handle that.

He pushed up from the table and glanced at the time. Nine o'clock, still early, but he was exhausted. "Great. I'm going to bed now."

Jessie followed him to the stairway. When she was out of earshot from Jamie, she said, "I'm sorry for the terrible lie about your father. Would you like to talk with him? I can ring him up right now."

Colin froze. He hadn't anticipated that happening. Not at all. "I don't think so, Nana."

"Colin, you're our family. That will always mean something to us."

His words came out with difficulty. "What's he doing now?"

"Dougie lives in Italy."

Yes, that was what Rhiannon had said.

"With the woman he left my mother for?"

"Oh, no," Jessie said gently. "This is another woman. She...has a young son."

Jessie seemed awkward discussing it with him, as well. He couldn't imagine this was any easier for her than it was for him.

He felt the lump in his throat. Colin had to ask because he had to know. "Does he have any other children besides me? Do I have blood siblings?"

"No, Colin. Just you."

And yet his father had never sought out Colin, not once.

"I'll ring him up," Jessie said. "It will take just a minute."

Colin ground his teeth. But Jessie was gazing at him with such pain and longing that he knew he needed to allow it, for the sake of peace with her. He knew better than to expect anything good to come of it, though.

"Go ahead," Colin said. "Make the call." He'd talk to his father now, do it fast, like ripping off a bandage. Then, afterward, he'd go upstairs and take a long, hot shower. Try and sleep off one of the longest days he'd ever experienced.

Jessie's face lit up with joy at his response, and it made him feel good that at least she was happy. She found her cell phone, an ancient model, and with her brow concentrating, squinting into her glasses, she tapped at a single button. Direct dial.

Colin crossed his arms and leaned against the banister, bracing himself.

Rhiannon's haunting landscape was on the far wall, so he stared at it, jarred at first, because he wasn't yet sure how he was going to deal with her. In the scene she'd painted, a light fog was coming off the grass, and it gave him the feeling of being in a dream. As if none of this were really happening.

Growing up in Texas, in that tin corrugated trailer, he'd dreamed of this moment. Of hearing his father's voice again. Of hearing him say that everything would be okay, that he would come back and fix things and return their lives to normal. After all, Colin's mom had never remarried.

"That's strange," Jessie murmured in disappointment, covering the mouthpiece of her phone and gazing at Colin with a perplexed look on her face. "He's not connecting."

Colin closed his eyes. Felt the disappointment fill him, that old, leftover boyhood feeling of hurt. Maybe it was time to accept that his father would always be this way. Maybe he should just feel grateful that his father was showing him how Colin *didn't* want to be.

Jessie held up a finger to him and then cleared her throat. She was leaving a message on the voice mail. "Hello, Dougie, this is Mother. Please call me as soon as you can."

She ended the call and smiled gamely at Colin. "He will ring back, Colin. Perhaps we can get him to pay us a visit while you're here."

Colin wasn't that delusional. He pushed away from the banister and thought longingly of the upstairs room with the bed and the door. "I'll see you early tomorrow for breakfast, Nana."

"You'll see Rhiannon in the morning as well, won't you?"

Colin paused, his weight creaking on the stair tread. He must have had a pained look on his face, because Jessie walked over and patted him on the hand again.

"You don't blame her, do you? We asked her to help us tell you. Please, it's not her fault."

He gave her a tight smile. "I know all that."

Jessie shook her head. "I'm not sure you understand. Colin, you don't know how Rhiannon was before you arrived. She never would have walked over for dinner to a join a group of our size. Or told Paul to treat her as lady of the manor. Or come out of her studio to make an appearance in her kitchen while Jamie visited with Paul."

"Wait a minute, back up. What do you mean *treat her as lady of the manor?*"

"Rhiannon's mother is lady of the manor," Jessie explained patiently. "Perhaps that's left over from the old ways, but when the lady is here, she represents the castle and its interests to the community."

"Can she really do that, with her agoraphobia?"

"Well, she's making a start. It's precisely why Jamie included her in my..." Jessie gazed at her hands. "...my situation."

By having Rhiannon tell *him* what Jessie and Jamie couldn't. Colin got it now.

He squeezed his grip around the ancient, rustic banister. He could admire Rhiannon for taking steps and being braver. But he couldn't say that he was thrilled with how she'd prioritized being honest toward him as less important than following her protocol and representing her estate.

Especially after she'd made a personal appeal to *him* to be honest with *her.*

And he had been. Brutally, embarrassingly so.

Jessie made a clucking noise at him. "Please give Rhiannon another chance. Don't give up, Colin."

He smiled wanly. He didn't see how anyone in his situation wouldn't be wary of Rhiannon now.

Jessie fanned at her face suddenly, the blood draining from her cheeks. She sat down hard on a tufted chair.

Colin rushed to her side. "Nana? Are you okay?"

"Oh, I'm fine." She took a few deep breaths and then smiled at him. "Sometimes this happens. Nothing to worry about, dear."

He realized maybe there was more to her sudden urge of getting him back to the Highlands than he'd known.

CHAPTER NINE

O N SUNDAY EVENING, Rhiannon sat inside her secret garden. This was her sanctuary. When she was upset or stressed, it was the walled hideaway where she went to try and figure herself out again.

It had been years since she'd spent so many hours sitting beneath the tree, her arms around her knees and her shawl wrapped around her shoulders. She'd thought she'd made progress. She had dared to expand her boundaries and try something new, but that failure had shaken her more than she'd realized.

Colin had left without saying goodbye. Not even Jessie had rung her.

The wisest thing to do would be to go back to the more cloistered life she'd been living. Give up her silly dream of being the lady of the manor. But earlier, while she'd sat at her easel, she realized she couldn't do it—she couldn't pretend that nothing had happened. She couldn't go back to her old life and still be happy.

A spark of hope had been lit inside her—that life could be

different—and now that spark wouldn't extinguish. And yet she couldn't see the path to move forward, either.

She closed her eyes and took several deep breaths. She was fairly certain that Paul would call Malcolm soon, to tell him what had happened with Colin. She was still upset with the way he'd abruptly left her. She didn't know how to process this.

Her mobile rang. *Paul.* With foreboding, Rhiannon answered her phone. "Yes?"

"I received a call from the front gate. Colin has been spotted on the cameras."

She pressed a hand to her head. "But... I thought he was headed home to Texas?"

"Evidently not, miss. At present he's standing beside your studio door. I believe he's knocking."

Rhiannon jumped to her feet, wiping the grass from her skirt.

"I'm on my way," she said into the phone.

"A reminder, miss—we have a landscaping crew on the grounds today."

"Yes. Thank you, Paul." *Drat.* Of course they did.

As fast as she could, she pocketed her phone and rushed to the garden door, carefully relocking it behind her. Peering around the corner with stealth and care, she spotted Colin at the end of the walkway, knocking on the door leading up to her studio.

Her heart did a crazy Highland fling in her chest. Colin looked wonderful, dressed in a casual suit. He was clean-shaven and his eyes a bright blue. She gazed at him longer than she should have.

*No.* No more schoolgirl-with-a-crush behavior. Her best course of action would be to appear perfectly composed, serene, diplomatic—everything she should have been from the first moment she'd bumped into him on the estate. She could do that now—she'd had more practice interacting with him since then.

Backtracking quietly, she managed to make it seem as if she'd just come from inside the yew maze. Without warning, she stood behind him, her hands clasped. "Hello, Colin."

He jumped, then turned. "Hello." He stepped back, not meeting her gaze. "I hope I haven't disturbed you."

Right away, Rhiannon saw that he was being overly formal. The distance he kept from her and the attention he seemed to avoid settling on her face told her that he didn't want to get too close, either.

"No, you haven't disturbed me," she said, equally polite. "How are your grandparents?"

"They're fine." He shifted a rucksack he wore over his shoulder. "You should know I'm staying for one more week to get to know them, and also to train at Kildrammond for my upcoming tournament."

Her mouth opened. If he'd told her he was leaving to join the circus, she couldn't have been more surprised.

"My grandmother explained to me why you did what you did, Rhiannon."

Her heart slowed. "Oh?"

"Yes. I understand you'd like to act as the lady of the manor."

She felt her lips pressing together. "Is *that* what Jessie said?" Her voice was a bit cooler than she would've liked.

He looked at her, this time meeting her eyes. "I don't want anger between us, please."

"Of course not," she agreed.

"I was in the village with Jessie today. We saw the bagpipers practicing their marching drills, and Jessie told me about the gathering on Saturday. She told me about the lady's duties— greeting the bagpipers and visitors in the front grounds before they march off to the fairgrounds. You're going to do all that, I assume?"

"No." Involuntarily she shuddered.

He glanced at her, surprised. "Why not?"

*Because it's too much for me. Because I've already failed at my attempts to be lady of the castle, numerous times.*

He tilted his head. "Rhiannon? Are you giving up? Don't give up on my account."

"On *your*—?"

Just then, the sounds of two other people holding a conversation drifted toward them—the landscaping crew, most likely. Adrenaline filled her—that old fear. She didn't want to be seen, especially by strangers.

"Come inside," she whispered, gesturing to Colin. "Just inside the entryway. Quickly."

But Colin misunderstood her. With an easy gait, he stepped inside the open door and then loped up the staircase before she could stop him.

Her shoulders tensed. She had no choice but to follow him upstairs.

Once inside her studio, he set down his rucksack. He was staring at the small blank canvases she'd prepared earlier this morning, and it embarrassed her. She wrapped the edges of her shawl more tightly around herself.

"What are these for?" He pointed to the canvases.

Striding forward, she began to stack them into a pile. "Nothing," she murmured. "I've changed my mind."

It had been a silly idea, really. She would take the canvases outside and destroy them later.

"They're portrait size." Colin's voice held surprise. "It looks like you're going to paint people."

"No," she admitted, "just my cat. Maybe Molly, too."

"That's interesting. I think you should do it."

She peered at him, because his tone wasn't so blandly formal anymore. He was a bit livelier. Friendlier toward her.

"Thank you," she said hesitantly.

He crossed his arms. "So. Will you attend the gathering Saturday?"

He wasn't about to give up. Sighing, she walked over to the high windows. "Actually, Kristin is going to represent us."

"Malcolm's wife?" His jaw tightened. "Why not you?"

She kept silent. She really didn't want to reveal to Colin her thoughts of inadequacy.

He crossed the room to stand beside her. "Since I'll be here, I was planning on attending the gathering, too. With Jessie, I mean."

So matter-of-fact. No hint or intimation of the kisses, the confidences they'd shared.

"You're welcome to go with us if you'd like, Rhiannon." He stared down at his feet. Maybe he felt guilty over making her upset. Maybe he felt sorry for her.

"No, thank you." Her pride was too strong to be a charity case for anybody, even for him.

He nodded and gathered up his rucksack, preparing to leave.

She was sad that the closeness they'd been building with each other was gone. She supposed it was a casualty of her loyalty to Jessie and the estate. She'd hurt her relationship with Colin by prioritizing this over her honesty to *him*.

"Rhiannon?" He turned to face her. "Why do I get the feeling that if I'd asked you yesterday, you'd have considered it?"

"Because..." She stood there, blinking at him. How could she tell him that she'd been developing feelings for him? That she couldn't forget their kiss?

"If Malcolm doesn't want you to go," Colin said, misunderstanding her, "then he's wrong. You're strong enough to do it on your own. Look what you dared to do for Jessie." He gave her a half smile, not at all ironic. "Five minutes, that's all you need to stand there and show your brother. Like the queen standing on the balcony and making her appearance, just give them all a big wave, then declare victory."

She laughed in spite of herself.

"Do it," he urged.

"You're really not angry at me? Because... I thought you were upset over my hurting you. Or guilty. Or irritated. Or all of the above."

"No, Rhiannon," he said quietly. "I understand why you did what you did, and I'm not angry now. I don't blame you."

But he didn't completely trust her, not as he had before. That was what she read in his face. "Why do you want to help me with the gathering? Did Jessie encourage you?"

"No. But I do want to make her happy."

"And helping me go to the gathering will accomplish this?"

"Let's just say that I'm being a responsible citizen," he said carefully.

"You want to be responsible now?"

"I want to *win,*" he emphasized. He stared directly into her eyes. "Don't you?"

She had her dreams, too, if that's what he meant. "I can last five minutes at the gathering," she said defiantly.

"Yes, I know you can."

"But I don't need you to stand with me," she clarified.

"Fine." He shrugged. "I'll be there to watch anyway. The golf course will be empty. McGuff said that the club will be closed next Saturday because they're all participating in the Highland Games."

There was something about his mannerisms, the way he spoke to her, the smile he used, that just made her heart want to be with him. Even when *he* didn't want *her.*

"Well," she said, "if you can promise to come back and see

Jessie, at least by Christmas or New Year's, then I suppose I could allow you to be my escort at the gathering."

His mouth curved in a smirk. "Is that a dare, Rhiannon?"

Not particularly. She was trying to be polite and aloof with him, even though inside she felt like crying. "Always," she murmured.

"I'm not scheduled for anything over the holidays. I guess I can arrange a visit to Scotland."

He stepped toward her and she held her breath, but just as quickly he backed away, hands clasped behind his back.

"I'll see what intelligence I can pick up for you during my days in the village," he said politely. "If I hear any news of the gathering, I'll let you know."

She could only nod. He spoke as if she mattered no more to him than an acquaintance or a mate from the pub. She supposed this was the price she had to pay to be *lady of the manor*. And if she couldn't have a normal life, like other people, then she should at least try to fight for control of her domain.

It wasn't as if she would ever be leaving.

---

AFTER COLIN HAD LEFT, Rhiannon realized the ramifications of what she'd agreed to do. Making the call quickly, before she changed her mind, she picked up her mobile phone and rang her sister-in-law's number.

Kristin answered immediately. "Hi, Rhiannon. How are you?"

*In over my head.* She felt as if she'd chosen an art project she could never complete. No, worse than that.

"I, er, have something to ask you. Do you have a minute?"

"Of course!" Kristin's voice registered surprise. "Honestly, I'm glad you called. I'm just relaxing at home with Malcolm right now."

It was Sunday, after all. That was a downside of Rhiannon's never leaving the estate. Sometimes she forgot what day it was.

Rhiannon swallowed. She had six days to come to terms with attending the gathering and actually facing all those people.

"Next weekend..." she said hesitantly, "...Saturday, is the annual gathering at the castle. Malcolm mentioned that he was going to ask you to act as lady of the castle and be hostess, but, well..." Rhiannon's voice faltered. "...would you mind terribly if I did the honor? At least at first, I mean. Perhaps you could step in if I find myself failing at the role? Like a backup?"

Rhiannon closed her eyes and cringed. A *cop-out,* she could imagine Colin remarking, if he'd heard that last bit. She was starting to believe she might be insane for agreeing she would do this with him.

"Yes, I'm in," Kristin said quickly, "I think it's a great idea."

"You do?"

She heard someone else whispering in the background.

"Rhiannon?" Kristin asked. "Can you hold on a minute? Malcolm wants to talk to you. I'll call you back tomorrow during my lunch hour."

Meaning, when Malcolm wasn't there listening over her shoulder.

Rhiannon sighed. "Yes. That's fine." She didn't know why she was surprised they'd been sitting so closely. Malcolm and Kristin were the perfect communicative couple—they seemed to tell each other everything and kept nothing back. Complete and total honesty.

"Rhi?" Malcolm came on the line. "How are you? You never called me back to tell me about the funeral."

She'd forgotten about that. But she didn't want to be egged

into a discussion about Jamie and Jessie and Colin. "Long story short, everything is taken care of. No need to worry on this end."

"Is Colin still there? Or has he gone home now?"

"He's training at Kildrammond for the week," she said carefully.

There was a pause on the line. "Why?" Malcolm's tone was cooler than Rhiannon cared for.

"Because, Malcolm, he's getting to know his grandparents again. Please don't think harshly of him."

"Rhi, I've looked him up. Did you know he's on the cusp of being kicked back to the lower-level tour, the one with a lot less money?"

She rubbed her forehead. She wasn't clear on the intricacies of professional golf, but Colin *had* told her that Daisie Lee was worried about him losing his pro tour card and having money problems because of it.

"That isn't our business." Maybe it would be, if she were involved with Colin romantically. But it was clear he didn't think of her in that way anymore.

She sighed again. It *still* hurt. She wished she could have both things: lady of the manor and Colin. In a perfect world she could.

"Rhi, I'm just suggesting you face the possibility that maybe he stayed because he hopes to get one of our company's athlete sponsorships."

She already knew that wasn't Colin's intention.

"You don't need to worry about me, Malcolm. I can handle myself."

"Promise me you'll be careful of Colin's motives."

She was always careful. Careful was her life.

"I'll see you both next week at the gathering," she said to her brother. "Goodbye for now."

———

BACKPACK STILL ON his shoulders, Colin headed toward the rear of the castle.

He'd gone to see Rhiannon intent on doing what was right without getting too close to her, and he'd accomplished his aim. The part about standing with her at the gathering wasn't exactly planned, but it was responsible and good. There was no denying that.

Now he had a few more responsible steps to take.

Colin glanced inside the castle window at Paul, who appeared to be washing his hands in a utility sink in the break-fast area. Colin rapped lightly on the glass to gain his attention.

Paul straightened, tugging on his suit jacket. He opened the side door, frowning somewhat. "Can I help you, sir?"

"Do you mind if I come in?" Colin patted his backpack. "I have something to give you."

Paul's forehead furrowed. He looked as though he was about to say no, so Colin added, "I'm staying at the cottage for the next week. You'll likely be seeing me around the estate."

Tilting his head slightly, Paul stood aside and let Colin pass.

"Do you live here all the time?" Colin asked, taking note of the familiar dining room setup, the side table with stacked dishes and serving plates, and that ever-present tea tray.

"I do, sir," Paul answered crisply.

"No time off?"

"No, sir." A frostier tone. "Since the laird and lady are away, I have volunteered to stay at the castle with Rhiannon for the duration."

"Good to know," Colin replied, nodding. "What are your preparations for the gathering on Saturday?"

Paul stiffened. He darted a glance toward the old-fashioned telephone on the wall.

"You don't have to call Malcolm on me." Colin smiled at him. "I'm asking because I'll be helping Rhiannon at the gathering. She wants to, uh, do whatever it is her mother usually does for the hosting duties. I want us all to be prepared."

Paul blinked, taken aback. Definitely, a crack appeared in his professional butler's composure. "I'll speak to Rhiannon about it."

"Great. Just let me know whatever you need help with."

Paul cleared his throat. "Sir, is there anything else?"

"Yes. Call me Colin, please."

"Very well." Paul swallowed, as if the word didn't come out easily. "Colin."

Colin opened his backpack and took out the plate that had held the cupcakes Rhiannon had made for Jessie. "I'm returning this from my grandmother."

"Ah. Yes. Thank you, Colin."

Colin's phone vibrated in his pocket. He'd left a message with the head pro at Kildrammond Golf Club—hopefully this was him texting him back.

Colin popped the backpack over his shoulder. "Great to see you, Paul. We'll talk tomorrow night. I'm going to stop by after my workout, just so you know."

Paul opened his mouth and closed it. He seemed confused.

Colin gave him another smile. "I'll go out the back way, if you don't mind. It's a shorter walk back to the cottage."

"Very good, sir. *Colin,*" Paul corrected himself.

Outside in the walkway, Colin paused to check his phone. The incoming text message had come from Leonard, his accountant back in Texas.

We've lost the Dry-line clothing endorsement. What do you want to do?

Colin closed his eyes for the briefest of moments. Okay, so he'd known this might happen. How he dealt with it was what mattered most.

He sat on the bench nearby and phoned his accountant. "Hi, Leonard," he announced when the man picked up. "I'm calling from Scotland. I got your text."

"I'm sorry to forward the news to you at this difficult time," Leonard said in a somber tone.

Colin had forgotten that everybody at home still assumed he was dealing with death and a funeral. "It's all right," he replied quietly. "Thank you for your concern." But he plowed onward. "Listen, I've got news. I'm staying here for another week to prepare for the New York Cup. Mack is headed home, so don't be alarmed if you see him at the club without me. Everything else is proceeding as planned. And don't worry about Dry-line. Send them a standard thank-you letter from me. Update the website—take down their logo. If you get any press or communication of note from the website, let me know, and we'll handle it as it comes. I'll check in every day that I'm gone, at about this time. How does that sound?"

There was a slight pause on the line. "Uh... That sounds very good." Leonard had a note of surprise in his voice.

*Get used to it,* Colin thought. *Things have changed.* "Anything else I need to deal with?"

"Uh, I'll need your signature on a financial document."

"What for?"

Another uncomfortable pause. "We need to tap into the trust that I set up for you."

"For?"

"Everyday expenses."

*That's bad.* Colin stood and paced for a moment. "Okay," he said calmly. "Email me the financial spreadsheets you've been keeping for me. You can overnight the document I need to sign, care of a golf club here. I'll text that address to you."

Another silence.

"Leonard, are you there?"

"Yes, Colin. Sorry, I'm just surprised that you're taking an interest in the numbers." It sounded like Leonard wore a smile as he spoke. "I'll get right on those items for you."

"Great. And if Daisie Lee contacts you, please send her to me. In fact, I'm going to call her right now."

"Colin, she's asking about the inheritance you're due to receive."

No surprise there. "Thank you for letting me know. I'll handle it."

They said their goodbyes, and Colin hung up the phone, still pacing.

*Oh, Mom,* he thought. This wasn't going to be an easy phone call to make, but he had to do it.

Facing Rhiannon's yew maze, he punched in the number.

"Colin!" his mother said. "How was the funeral?"

"Fine," he said shortly, not wanting to get into any of that right now.

"How are your grandparents?" Her tone was biting.

"They're fine, too," he said. Because really, this was a negative topic with his mom, and his relationship with them wasn't her concern. "I'm just checking in to let you know that I'm good, and that I love you."

She paused. He didn't usually tell her outright that he loved her. Usually, he made light of things. Made her laugh. Told her funny stories.

"Were any of Dougie's friends at the funeral? Did the new wife come?"

"No." Colin refused to take the bait. "When I get home, we'll talk more. For now, I'm just checking in to let you know that I'm okay. I'll be away for a couple weeks training. If you need anything, I'm reachable by phone. You don't need to call Leonard."

"Do you want me to drive over and check on your mail? The property tax bills came this week. Mine was in the mail box yesterday. I'm going to go down to city hall and—"

"Mom," he said patiently, "you don't need to worry about money anymore. Your house is paid for free and clear, and you won't be evicted. I'm taking care of it."

"But there are expenses, Colin. Did you talk to the Sages about a sponsorship?"

"I don't need a sponsorship from the Sage family," he said as clearly as he could. *I'm going to win a purse at the New York Cup.*

"So you got the inheritance, then? What did the lawyers say?"

"I'll tell you all about it when I get back," he said firmly. "I'm on the road right now and working with some swing coaches, getting ready for the tournament." He phrased it that way because he knew she was on board with that goal.

"That's...wonderful."

"Yes. Don't worry about me. I just need you to sit back and let go so I can focus on my job. It's do-or-die time for me. I can't be disturbed. Do you understand?"

She sighed. "I know. You're right. I just...worry."

"Please don't. It shows you have no faith in me."

"I'm sorry." She sighed again. "I love you, baby."

To her, he would always be her baby, no matter what his age. That was fine, but he had boundaries he needed to strengthen with her. "We'll talk again in a week."

"Can't you keep in touch more often than that?"

"No, and it's not personal." He paused. "If there's a real emergency, then do call me. Otherwise I need to concentrate."

He hung up and turned, only to see Paul standing there,

Molly on her leash sitting quietly by his side, her tongue hanging out.

"Hi," Colin said. How much had Paul heard? "Can I help you with something?"

"No, sir." Paul bent over and unhooked the leash from Molly's collar. The golden retriever took that as an okay to bound over to Colin, leaping up at him, her front paws against his chest.

"Whoa there," Colin said, laughing.

But when he glanced up, he caught Paul looking at him strangely.

Once Molly calmed down and was back beside Paul, Colin wiped off his hands and picked up his backpack. "Have a good walk, you two," he said to Paul. "I'll see you tomorrow."

He couldn't help feeling that he was in a fight for his life, carving out the space that was his.

## CHAPTER TEN

OVER THE NEXT FEW DAYS, heeding her brother's advice to be careful, Rhiannon read everything she could find online about Colin. She found no gossip about his love life, or unseemly behavior off the fairways. That pleased her.

What she did see were sports columns about his shaky-of-late golf career, just as Malcolm had warned.

But Colin had been up front with her about that, so she wasn't suspicious about him the way Malcolm was. If anything, Colin's difficulties made her more sympathetic to helping him with his goals—especially since he was encouraging hers, as well.

He stopped by the castle to visit her once or twice per day, though most of his time was taken up with training. He seemed determined to turn around his career—laying out an extensive practice schedule and plan for each day.

After having coffee with her and Paul and then taking a morning walk over the grounds, he practiced at Jessie's golf club. During his lunch hour, his routine was to eat at a small, local restaurant, before he spent the rest of the afternoon on fitness exercises—running, weights and stretching. He usually shared dinner with Jessie and Jamie in the evenings—though once with her—and then would go back to the practice range while it was still light outside.

She had an inkling it was the most Colin had buckled down and applied himself in a while. He seemed to be enjoying his new life. From what he'd told her, the golf professionals he worked with treated him well. Rhiannon had even become acquainted with one of them—McGuff, the man who ran the pro shop at the club. Twice, Colin had left his phone on the table while they ate lunch, and she and McGuff had video-chatted over the internet connection. A huge step for her.

Today when Colin phoned her during his lunch break, he'd just finished sharing a meal with Jessie. Leaning against his rental car, he dipped the phone outward so she could see a ridge of spectacular scenery. Rhiannon was particularly keen on the loch view, given that their estate had no water frontage.

"What do you think?" Colin asked, turning the phone back toward himself. He wore his golf clothes, a collared shirt and short sleeves that showed his tanned muscles.

*I think you look beautiful.* Swallowing hard, she glanced away from him. Sometimes it bothered her that Colin wasn't interested in her in that way anymore. It was sad, but he'd made it clear, and she didn't know what to do about it. He seemed determined to remain platonic friends, strictly at arms' length.

"What are you looking at?" Colin asked. "Is someone there with you?"

"Oh, no." She gazed back into the phone, carefully smiling at him, keeping her voice light so as not to embarrass herself. "Did I tell you I've been painting Colin the cat today?"

"Really?" Colin's eyes widened. But then he remembered himself and gave her a cheery smile. "Is my namesake getting the portrait treatment?"

"He's resisting it. The wee beastie keeps turning his head away from me and showing his bottom instead. I've tried bribing him with cream, but apparently it's not fresh enough."

Colin laughed. "Is that what he told you?" he teased.

"Of course," she teased back. "Let me walk over and you can hear him squawking about it yourself."

Rhiannon let her phone drop to her hip as she walked back to her garden. Beneath her own cheery surface, her spirits drooped.

Yet again, she and Colin were ignoring that proverbial elephant-in-the-room. Their conversation was always easy now, optimistic and pleasant, but never reaching the depths of honesty they'd once enjoyed. She wasn't surprised—she'd let Colin down. And even if he did decide to trust her again, she knew he could never promise to commit to visiting her beyond once or twice a year at best.

This surface cheeriness was the closest they could come to a real relationship.

She hated that.

Trying not to cry, she opened the gate and stood in her garden. Her secret garden. Only three other people—her parents and Paul—knew about it. Yet even they didn't know everything that it was to her.

Colin certainly didn't need to know the significance of her location. Exhaling a clearing breath, she pointed her phone toward her easel, set up under the tree in the corner, her palette and paints on a table beside it. She'd placed the cat's pedestal beside a wild catmint plant that he particularly enjoyed, and had poured a spot of cream on his favorite china plate.

Rhiannon pointed her phone camera at Colin the cat and his private bliss. No panoramic shots of her garden. "As you can see, my cat is spoiled rotten."

"You're painting outside?" Colin asked. "Where? I don't remember that tree."

Because he'd never been back here, not even when they'd been young. Her locked, walled-off garden was her secret—in later years she'd found it, explored it, built it back up from ancient ruins and encroaching heather.

"We're behind my art studio," she hedged.

"I can't visualize where you are. Will you show me tonight?"

She dragged her bare toe in the grass. She was thinking of a way to tactfully tell him no, when on the screen, she saw Colin's face turn away. Jessie's voice was muffled in the background, and she appeared to have distracted him.

When he turned back to Rhiannon, he looked bothered. "Excuse me, Rhi."

He fidgeted with the buttons on the phone, and the picture Rhiannon was seeing dipped sideways, dropping to a view that showed the side of Colin's trouser leg and the door of his rental car.

If he thought he'd muted the phone in addition to blocking her view, then he was wrong, because Rhiannon could clearly hear their conversation.

"That was my father who called you just now, wasn't it?" Colin was asking.

Jessie made a sympathetic cluck. "He isn't able to talk to you yet, but I'll work on him, dear."

"I'm fine without talking to him," Colin said tersely. "You don't have to worry about me."

"I know I don't have to worry about you. You were a fine, braw wee lad, and now you've grown into a fine, braw man."

"Then why don't we just leave it alone? I don't care that he doesn't want to talk to me."

But even Rhiannon, muffled as the conversation was, heard

the pain in Colin's voice. She imagined the crushed expression in his eyes.

And then the camera moved, and Rhiannon saw his face again. Hard. Closed. He'd retreated into anger. This was the first truly honest emotion she'd seen from him in days.

*Oh, Colin.* Without realizing it, she made a small noise of sympathy in her throat.

*He's wrong, you're worthy,* she ached to tell him.

He frowned at her. "I hope you didn't hear any of that."

"I did, actually. Sorry." Her instincts were to offer to walk with him around the grounds when he returned, and try to lift his spirits, but this didn't fit with their new, less-trusting relationship.

She wiped her eyes. Unexpectedly, her own phone beeped. The message flashed clearly across her screen that her uncle John was ringing her.

"Excuse me," Rhiannon said as cheerily as she could. "I have another call. May I talk to you in a bit?"

"Sure," Colin said. He ran his hand over his face, but even that didn't erase the look of pain.

"I'll ring you in a few minutes," she promised.

He nodded, and she switched to her uncle's call, finally able to draw a deep breath...

"Hello, Uncle John."

"Hello, Rhiannon. I've just left my office. I should be at the castle by four o'clock, in order to pick up your painting."

*I can't believe I forgot!*

"Er, certainly, Uncle," she said, "my landscape is ready. I'll just bring it downstairs for you."

"Very good." He cleared his throat. "I have another commission for you, and it comes with special instructions."

She chewed on her lip, not sure that another landscape commission was what she wanted just now.

"We'll discuss your security plan for the gathering, as well," he said.

More issues that had defined her before Colin had returned to Scotland. She swallowed. "We'll talk when you arrive."

"Very good, Rhiannon. I'll see you soon." He hung up.

Suddenly a thought came to her—the athlete endorsement that Sage Family Products sponsored! Maybe this would be something she could give that would help Colin.

She connected her mobile phone with Colin's number, again using the video option. He picked up immediately. She saw that the lines of his mouth were still grim.

"Colin," she said softly. "My uncle is stopping by this afternoon to pick up my landscape for the buyer who commissioned it. Would you like to meet him?"

"Your CEO uncle?" Colin's face clouded even further. "What, do you think I can't win a tournament purse myself?" Clearly, he'd forgotten his cheery falseness, too. "Do you think I need an endorsement for when I fail?"

"Possibly," she said, sighing.

His eyes widened. She was being brutally honest with him, and it had obviously shocked him.

What would be the harm if her uncle included Colin in the local athletes' endorsement program? Besides, she was showing Colin that she trusted him. To be introduced to her obscenely wealthy and powerful uncle was a bit like being introduced to the legendary Wizard of Oz. For an athlete who needed an endorsement, it was a special gift.

"If you don't mind, Colin, I'd like to introduce you to him as my good friend."

"Why?" he demanded.

*Because you're important to me.*

"My uncle is important to me," she said instead. "He takes special interest in me. He runs my business affairs. He even spends most Christmases with me and my parents. But I warn you, he can be intimidating."

"I'm not intimidated by him, Rhi."

That meant he was coming. Inwardly, she smiled, though she tried not to show it.

"Keep in mind that he's always surrounded by bodyguards," she warned. "My uncle is inaccessible, he doesn't meet with media and he rarely speaks publicly. Outside of people in his upper echelons, he doesn't socialize."

"I'm a pro golfer, remember? I'm around business types like him all the time." Colin shook his head. "I may not be A League yet, but most CEOs are golf fans, and golf fans know my name."

"Then impress him for me. Show him how well I'm progressing."

Colin seemed to be thinking. "When is he coming?"

"In three hours."

"Fine," Colin said. "I'll be there."

———

RHIANNON PACED BEFORE the fireplace to calm her jittery nerves.

She wanted to help Colin arrange an endorsement, but her invitation had been impulsive and off-the-cuff, not well thought out. And now that she'd had time to consider what she was doing, she saw the danger.

If he received an endorsement, bringing Colin into the fold of her family's business would only entangle him more deeply in her life. It would be emotionally harder for her when he finally left.

She heard the sound of tires on the drive. Uncle John had arrived in a black town car. Behind him was a second vehicle, a van large enough to accommodate the immense size of her painting.

Rhiannon swallowed. There was no going back now. Colin was on his way, too.

She rubbed her arms and observed her uncle's entourage.

As the men emerged from the town car, she noted a driver and an assistant in the front seat, and a guard beside her uncle in back. Two guards in the van stayed seated.

Her uncle valued loyalty. He was CEO of their family's business, and he'd built it up from nothing. Rhiannon's mother was a Sage, one of five siblings, and the only girl. John was her mother's older brother. He'd taken Rhiannon's brother, Malcolm, under his wing after the kidnapping, and Malcolm was currently president. But Uncle John didn't show any signs of slowing down or letting go of company control anytime soon.

Rhiannon let the curtain drop and went to sit on the couch before the fireplace. She smoothed her dress and folded her hands in her lap.

When the bell rang, Paul quietly nodded to her and opened the door.

Just as she was about to rise, Colin the cat wandered across the rug toward her. Chuckling inside, she picked him up and settled him on the couch beside her.

As her uncle came into the room behind Paul, Rhiannon rose. Uncle John had come in alone, without his guards or assistant.

She smiled as he approached and greeted her with a kiss on the cheek.

"Good afternoon, Uncle."

"Hello, Rhiannon. How are you?"

"Well." She had much she wanted to tell him, but he'd already stepped to her painting, which leaned against the side of the couch. He reached for the packing cloth that covered it.

"May I?" he asked, even as he lifted the cloth.

She didn't answer.

"This is b—" *Beautiful,* he was starting to say, because that was what he always said to her about her paintings, ever since she was a girl.

But this time he stood back and tilted his head, staring at her newest work.

This wasn't the first time she'd worked with such a large—six feet by four feet—canvas. The painting was so unwieldy she hadn't been able to carry it downstairs herself. Paul had bundled and moved it with the help of a local man who Paul sometimes hired for laboring jobs.

"You've done something different with this work," her uncle said.

Rhiannon inclined her head. "Yes, the painting called for it."

"That's a lovely crofter's cottage."

"It is."

He remained silent, his head still tilted.

Rhiannon waited. Thus far, the works she'd created were strictly nature landscapes, all of the Highlands. A few were painted as gifts for friends and family, but most were sold to wealthy contemporaries of her uncle's, people who'd purchased them on commission after seeing his private piece.

This commission, as Rhiannon understood it, was for a wealthy industrialist who lived somewhere in Asia.

"This is the guard's cottage at the far end of the property," her uncle noted, "on the border where James Walker and his wife live, is it not?"

"It is."

"Did you paint it from memory?"

He was asking her if she'd walked to the edge of the property to sketch it. "No, I painted it from a photograph I took of the actual cottage."

"Why, that's..." His face registered a struggle to control his emotion. "...that's wonderful, Rhiannon."

"Thank you. I walked Molly there one morning this week, just to see if I could do it."

He broke into a smile—her hardened, business-toughened uncle.

Relieved, she sank onto the couch. "Will you have some tea, Uncle? There are a few things I'd like to discuss with you."

At her signal, Paul stepped forward and poured their tea from the presented service.

When Paul had discreetly withdrawn, Rhiannon settled Colin the cat in her lap. First, they would mention niceties. Then, she planned to initiate a discussion regarding her next commission. Lastly, she'd introduce Colin.

Uncle John sipped his tea, then placed it precisely in its china saucer and went straight to his point—apparently skipping the niceties. "I'd like to discuss the gathering on Saturday. I've arranged for two bodyguards to keep watch outside your studio for the duration of the event. You needn't worry about being bothered by stragglers on the grounds."

She stiffened her spine. "I won't be staying in the studio this year."

Uncle John paused with the rim of the cup midway to his lips. "Oh?" he asked, once again placing the cup inside the saucer.

She looked him square in the eye. "I'm prepared to fill my mother's traditional role, at least for the initial greeting."

A nerve of concern ticked over his left eye. "That isn't necessary, Rhiannon."

"I've thought about it, Uncle. This year, that's the role I prefer to take."

"What's brought this on?"

"My parents are gone, Malcolm is married, Isabel is getting married soon and I'm looking to the future."

He nodded silently, considering her. "Do you think you can handle it?"

She didn't know. She desperately hoped so. She was trying not to think about it too much, to tell the truth. "If I'm to live in this castle, I want to live as lady, and not just a painting recluse."

"If you're worried about the financial aspects of your future, you needn't be," he said gently. "Your money has been set up in trusts, and even if you never sell another painting, you've enough funds to stay in the castle without danger of being evicted." He cleared his throat. "And that leads me to the second order of business." He smiled. "I'm pleased to say that I've secured another commission for you. An important collector has expressed interest in you, Rhiannon."

He was figuratively patting her on the head, as if she were a sheltered naïf who was too delicate to make her own plans.

She'd never looked at it from this perspective before, until Colin had challenged her.

"This collector of yours," she asked, "is he buying my painting because he appreciates the work, or because of the notoriety of the name Rhiannon MacDowall?"

Uncle John's face clouded. She'd stepped into delicate territory.

"Rhiannon, your name is on your paintings, that's true. They're there because they're yours, you've created them, and you're a world-class talent."

"Maybe." She'd trained, heavens how she'd trained—out of love and the desire to lose herself in something meaningful that took all her focus and energy. It had been healing for her, but now she was restless. She was changing. Her world wasn't frozen, suspended in time any longer. It was marching on. People were marrying.

*Old loves come home to visit.*

"Uncle, I do love my landscapes. They're special, they're beautiful...and they play an important part in earning money to live on, as well. But I'm making some decisions about a change in my artistic direction, and I'd like to know, what have we been charging for price?"

He shook his head. "You don't need to worry about that, Rhiannon. Ever."

"I want to know because it's my business." She touched his hand. "Please."

He seemed to think for a moment. Her uncle was nothing if not a businessman. Finally, he inclined his head. "I'll take that under advisement."

"What does that mean?"

"I consult with art experts. I hand-choose your buyers. They've signed written pledges with me to keep your works off the market during your lifetime."

"So...in effect, you're running my business?" She'd never thought of it this way. She contrasted herself with Colin, who was his own man.

"Rhiannon, while there is breath in my body I will not allow you to be used or hurt because of the notoriety of your kidnapping. I *will not* allow it." His voice rose and then turned to ice.

Her heart pounded. She and her uncle had a close, loving relationship. They'd never quarreled, much as she and Malcolm had never quarreled.

Nobody quarreled with her, really. Nobody upset or challenged or questioned her.

Until Colin's arrival.

She stood. There was much she needed to fix, and she was shaking just thinking about it.

"You look pale, Rhiannon. Please sit."

"I prefer not to."

"May I call the doctor?"

"No."

"I don't think—"

"She knows what she wants, sir," said a curt voice.

*Colin.* She felt a smile spread over her face.

She turned, and he looked like heaven to her. Familiar, kind, always her champion. And for this meeting with her uncle, he'd changed into business clothes, his hair combed back and his face clean-shaven.

Uncle John's face was as stony as the side of a rock cliff. He was obviously displeased with Colin's presence.

Colin strolled into the room with his easy gait. Without waiting for an introduction, he sat, picking up the cat and tucking him onto his lap. The cat purred and stretched the white underside of his furry neck toward Colin, for unfettered access to one of Colin's scratching sessions.

"How did you get past my bodyguards?" Uncle John demanded of Colin.

"I didn't see any bodyguards." Colin hooked a thumb over his shoulder. "I came in from the back."

"Isn't that door always locked?" Uncle asked Rhiannon. "And isn't the guard on the monitor? Those are our express instructions."

"The guard is my grandfather," Colin said. "He knows my intentions are good."

Her uncle's voice was ice. "Did James Walker let you in?"

"No, I let myself in. I'm Rhiannon's friend."

Just by walking in like this, and displeasing her uncle, he'd surely canceled any possibility of an endorsement. But he'd spoken up for her because he believed in her.

She looked at Colin, grateful, and he winked back at her. That same old insouciant charm that sent shudders through her.

The dimple in his cheek. The spark in his eye. She couldn't help smiling at him. A teary-eyed, happy smile.

No matter what she did or didn't do, nothing would wipe from his mind the adventurous, happy, outgoing person she'd been before she was hurt. There was comfort in that. She could fall in love with that.

"How long were you listening to us?" her uncle asked Colin.

"Since the part where Rhiannon said she preferred not to sit."

Her uncle glared, and Colin gave him a small, apologetic shrug. "Sorry. I forgot to introduce myself. My name is Colin Walker, and I'm a longtime friend of the family."

"Is that so?" her uncle said coldly. "Then why have I never heard of you before this week?"

———

COLIN HAD SAT with titans of industry. With CEOs. With wealthy investors. With celebrities and with top athletes from various sports.

John Sage didn't make him nervous. He was just another man, same as him. Colin did, however, feel hot under the collar that Rhiannon's uncle was obviously trying to influence her into doing something that she didn't want to do.

But that was Rhiannon's battle to fight. He forced himself to relax, to offer an easy smile to John Sage.

"I met you once," Colin remarked. "During one of the family weddings at the castle, years ago."

"Is that so?"

"Uncle," Rhiannon interjected, "I asked Colin to stop by because I wanted you to meet him. He's an old friend from when I was young."

"Have you kept in touch?" Sage asked mildly, crossing his

legs and looking at Colin as if he should think carefully about his answer.

Colin smiled tightly. "My parents got divorced, and then I stopped coming to Scotland for summers."

"Why are you here now? What do you want?"

Colin absently ran his fingers through the thick fur coat of Rhiannon's cat. The tabby cat easily purred and stretched as Colin scratched the animal's ears.

He glanced up to see Sage staring him with a face like a guard dog's, massively protective of Rhiannon. It seemed to Colin that he wanted to stifle her, and that made him angry.

"What do I want?" Colin repeated. "A sunny day, a kick in my clubs and my friends around me. And if I could permanently remove that slice I sometimes get in my long drives, that would be good, too."

"You're a golfer?" Sage asked.

"Yes, sir. I learned to play at Kildrammond. My grandmother took Rhiannon and me there when we were young."

"So you're a local sportsman."

"I'm on the pro tour."

"The American tour?"

"Yes."

"Ah."

From the third degree he'd just given him, Colin knew full well that Sage would further check him out later. Fine with him —he didn't want or expect anything from John Sage.

Sage stood. "Well, I'll take the painting to the car. Colin, will you assist me?"

"Absolutely."

"Uncle," Rhiannon said.

They both turned.

"I can vouch for Colin."

Colin had expected her to remain silent, to slide out of the room silent as a ghost, as she often did.

"You're vouching for his character?" Sage asked, amused.

"Yes, I am. He's worthy of our endorsement. Colin's a local golfer, so I suggest we consider him for one of our athlete sponsorships. It would please me very much."

"My niece is gentle-hearted," Sage said to Colin.

"Not really," Rhiannon said softly. "I'm practical. Colin is an excellent candidate to represent our family company. As for myself, I'm reconsidering my future, and I don't think I'll be taking on any commissions for landscapes for a while. Artistically, I'm in the midst of a change in direction."

Colin found himself staring, slack-jawed.

Sage seemed stunned, as well. But then he recovered, wiping his hands on his pants. "I'll stop back to have dinner with you soon, Rhiannon."

Colin stood also. "I'll walk outside with you."

Sage gave him a curt nod.

Colin carried the painting, somewhat awkwardly because of its bulk, through the door and across the gravel lot toward an idling black van.

In silence, the two men carefully stowed it in the back. Colin waited, because he knew Sage wanted words in private with him. Colin didn't mind—he had a few words to say, himself.

Once the van with the painting drove off, and Sage's bodyguards were inside his car with windows closed, Sage motioned Colin aside.

In a low, crisp voice, Sage said, "My niece is special to me. Some may think she's handicapped behind her castle walls, but she's really quite remarkable. I watch her do her best to make the world a better place from her position within the estate. I've seen her nurse birds with broken wings that others told her to give up on.

She doesn't. She's gentle, and I fear that you're a project of hers." Sage looked meaningfully at Colin. "And most especially I fear that you don't feel the same way about her that she feels about you."

Sage was dead wrong. To Colin's view, *he* was the one who didn't think she was handicapped. While everybody else tiptoed around her, he took her as she was.

She was beautiful. Strong. Colin hated that Sage assumed she was weak. That was like people who assumed Colin was weak because he was easygoing.

"You don't have to worry about how I treat her," he said.

He watched as Sage got into his black town car, and it wound back up the long driveway. Then, because something very important had shifted inside him, he strode back inside to find Rhiannon.

Paul was clearing away the teacups using his butler's cart. But the door was open, and he gazed at Colin as if he'd been listening to his and Sage's conversation.

"Where is she?" Colin asked.

Paul's lips pressed together, and he glanced down. Colin waited.

"In her garden," Paul finally said.

"Her yew maze?"

"No. It's a secret garden."

"A secret garden?"

"Yes, that's what she calls it." Paul looked at Colin. "You should let her alone there for a while. That's what we do."

It was impossible for him. Colin had been fighting his feelings all week, doing his damnedest to remain aloof, putting on an act of indifference that he just couldn't fake anymore. "I won't hurt her, I promise you."

Colin went out the back. He wasn't sure where her secret garden was, but he could guess. He walked the length of the walkway before the yew maze, all the way to the gray stone wall at the edge.

Colin the cat sat like the king of the jungle, in a patch of sun beside a wooden door.

Colin knelt and petted him. "Where's your mistress, sweet boy?" he whispered.

The cat gazed at him with calm green eyes. Then he turned his head toward the wooden door.

Colin pushed it open and walked inside. He'd expected this to be just another entrance to the yew maze, but it wasn't. This was a small walled garden, completely enclosed. It smelled of loam and plants. Prickly rosebushes, climbing green vines, and a riot of flowers. Around the perimeter was a footpath lined with crushed white stone pebbles.

"Rhiannon?" He followed the path. And found her in a grotto in the middle of it all. He sat down beside her.

"That went well," she said in a lighthearted voice.

He laughed drily. "Yeah, splendid."

"How did you find me?"

"Colin told me where you were."

"That cat." She smirked. "It figures."

He glanced around. "What is this place?" He gazed at her, kneeling, as if she were meditating. Or praying. "Is this where you come to recharge?"

"Interesting that you say it like that."

"As opposed to?"

She frowned. "That I'm hiding in here."

"I don't think that at all. Maybe you just need to center yourself." He lay back on his elbows. "I center myself at the driving range. Or by walking a few miles before breakfast." He glanced at the blue sky, the cloud formation that looked like a sword. "That takes me through the day, usually."

"My secret garden," she murmured. "Don't know what I'd do

without it." She smiled and lifted the tarpaulin off one of the small canvases she'd made. On it was a half-painted portrait of Colin the cat.

He laughed. "He's a handsome bugger."

"I don't usually paint outdoors. I also don't usually do portraits, and yet here I am. Stretching myself."

"Are you really going to refuse the commission your uncle offered you? Don't you need the money?"

"Technically, I don't *need* money. I'll always be taken care of through family trusts." Her voice was steady and Colin knew she was covering for emotions that he wanted to understand.

"But that locks you in, doesn't it?" he asked. "It takes away your freedom."

She was silent, but he could tell that she was thinking. A line appeared in her smooth forehead.

"He feels responsible for me. He feels guilty over what happened."

"You mean with the kidnapping?"

"Yes." She pinched her lips together. "Malcolm and I were kidnapped by a group of young men who thought they'd get a large ransom. Sage Family Products was beginning to be well-known in Britain and Europe, and the assumption was that we were rolling in cash."

She sighed. "But we weren't. And straightaway, when the ransom demand came in, my uncle refused to pay. Uncle John was then, and is now, the head of the family, so he made the decision to involve the police. Of course, it went badly." She was silent. "Afterward, when so many people were killed, and I...preferred not to leave home, he took on the burden of believing it was his fault. It isn't, of course."

"So tell him you don't want him to manage your business anymore. Do it yourself. You can, you know."

"And you think that everything can turn around so quickly?"

she asked teasingly. "I'm handling these changes in my life, Colin, but I'm handling them my way."

"Okay." If she didn't want his opinion, then there was nothing he could do about it.

A long silence stretched between them.

She drew in her breath. "I invited you to meet my uncle because I was hoping that you'd get to know him and have the opportunity to talk with him about an athlete sponsorship."

"Why?" he asked.

"Selfish reasons, mostly." She gave him a wry smile.

He sat up on one elbow, wanting to hear those selfish reasons.

"Truthfully, I'm half in love with you, Colin." She shrugged sheepishly. "I think I have been since the moment I saw you again, even in the mud with my broken camera. No." She shook her head. "It was before that, when we were children." She wrung her hands. "But to love you now, as an adult, I need to venture out on my own more. And the first step is running my estate. I've *had* to make that my priority."

"I thought you wanted peace?" he asked, dumbfounded by her words and her honesty.

"I thought so, too. But if I really wanted peace, would I be going to the gathering? Or antagonizing my uncle? Or..." She glanced at her easel. "Attempting to paint a portrait of a cat?"

He laughed. *I really do adore this woman.*

They were silent again for a moment. *Damn.* He couldn't fake it anymore. "Would you like to go to the gathering as my date?"

She gazed at him with lowered eyes. "Why?"

"Because I like you, Rhiannon. I like hanging out with you. And not...just as friends."

Her eyes widened and she sat back.

"I've been avoiding it, thinking about the day I have to leave, but I can't hold back anymore," he said. "And...whatever other complications we have—your agoraphobia, my travel schedule—that's not important so long as we trust each other." He looked at her. "Do you trust me?"

Slowly, she nodded.

"Do you trust me enough to go as my date?"

She frowned at him, blinking.

"What?" he asked.

Then she smiled shyly. Not that fake-cheery smile they'd been flashing back and forth all week, but a real one. "Actually, you'd be *my* date. And in that case, you'd have to wear a kilt for me."

"A...kilt?"

"Aye. A true Scotsman's kilt," she insisted stubbornly.

Why? Because she was attracted to him and thought that kilts were sexy, as a lot of women did, or because she simply liked the old traditions?

Either way, he had a feeling he would enjoy finding out.

## CHAPTER ELEVEN

"THE GATHERING" was a yearly celebration organized by Rhiannon's family.

Every June, members of local pipe bands met on the moor in front of their castle. After a greeting and short reception hosted by Rhiannon's parents, a parade march then wound for several miles through back roads and culminated at fairgrounds outside the village. There, the Highland Games commenced.

Rhiannon hadn't been to a Highland Games since she was a wee lass, but she remembered the pipe band competitions, sheepdog trials, Highland fling contests and, of course, all the feats of strength and endurance such as the caber toss and tugs-of-war.

Malcolm returned home each year for the gathering, as did their extended family members. For days beforehand, the castle was turned upside down with preparations. Rhiannon's mother, assisted by Paul and a group of caterers from town, always planned a buffet menu for the participating pipers, their friends and family and all the various Sage aunts, uncles and cousins.

Since Rhiannon's parents would be absent this year, Paul and her mother had prearranged for caterers to take charge of the menu. Paul had volunteered to organize the setup of folding tables and chairs, as well as a small portable tent in case of rain.

Besides the food—and drink—a major tradition was the greeting by the laird and lady. Malcolm had volunteered to give the laird's welcome speech this year. The lady's role, traditionally, was to stand in the refreshment tent and greet the villagers by name. Rhiannon's mother had prided herself that she remembered every last one.

Rhiannon would never perfectly fill her mother's place, but she desperately hoped she could last the five minutes that Colin had challenged her with completing. If she could do that, maybe she could show him that her agoraphobia wasn't such an obstacle.

She stood at the full-length mirror in her bedroom that Saturday morning, her fingers shaking as she fastened her silver brooch. She hadn't dressed for such an event since she was a child.

That was another time-honored practice—the traditional clothing. Rhiannon modified it somewhat to match her offbeat and eclectic taste. She wore a short blue jersey-knit dress with a light tartan stole over her shoulders.

While her brother would wear his MacDowall kilt, she'd decided on Black Watch. Jessie had confided to Rhiannon that Colin's kilt would be in that tartan. Jamie was a World War II veteran and had fought in the Black Watch Regiment, so it was an ode to him. Jessie had been kind enough to loan the Black Watch stole to Rhiannon.

She'd spent a fair effort drying and smoothing her hair with a flatiron and applying cosmetics. Typically she was far more casual with her appearance, but she wanted to put forth her best effort.

Rhiannon imagined there would be a fair amount of curiosity about her. The mass of pipers and the crowds who followed them was quite large, and Rhiannon knew her emergence would be a spectacle. Not many of the villagers had seen her since she was a child. Even if work crews came to the castle, Rhiannon stayed out of view. The few people she did visit with typically came from the town of Inverness or beyond, such as Dr. McLean, her family doctor, her painting tutors and any other trusted specialists whose services she needed.

She'd thought about each moment of the day at length. Hopefully, she'd found a strategy to cope that would work for her.

Selecting some drop sapphire earrings that matched her eye color and then slipping her feet into a pair of short boots, she was ready—armored and prepared for battle. She took one last appraising glance in the mirror. This would be the closest she came to fancy dress, and her heart was feeling skittish.

*Colin is my date today,* she reminded herself for the hundredth time this morning. *Don't chicken out!*

The pleasure she would have of being with him and watching his reactions to the fanfare was a great incentive. He'd never been to the castle in June before, had never witnessed the excitement that *was* the gathering. She would urge him to go on to the Highland Games afterward—he would enjoy that.

Downstairs, Rhiannon greeted Paul. Bustling about the kitchen, ordering the caterers about, he was in his officious glory. When he saw Rhiannon, he shooed away the workers and stepped into the sitting room with her.

"You look beautiful, miss."

"Do you think I can do this?"

"How do you feel?"

She took a shaky breath. "As if I'm taking a small step that I'm jittery about, but ready to do."

"I'm pleased to hear it. You can count on me to help."

"Thank you, Paul," she said gratefully.

He beamed at her. "Now, we have thirty minutes until the family arrives, then another hour until the bagpipers."

At the word *bagpipers*, he made a face showing his distaste.

A remembrance of mirth bubbled within her. "Poor Paul, you never liked the pipers, did you?"

"The dreadful caterwauling," he confided behind the back of his hand. "Please don't tell your mother I said so."

Three weeks apart from her gently formal mother, and Paul, their proper English butler, was subtly transforming. Rhiannon winked at him. She rather liked that he was confiding in her.

"So, is our plan ready to be executed?" she asked.

"Yes. Molly is fed and brushed. She'll be standing beside you in the refreshment tent."

"Excellent."

"Malcolm should be arriving shortly. He's prepared a short speech as stand-in for the laird. Kristin will be with him, as well."

"Ah." Apprehension swirled in Rhiannon's stomach. She hoped Kristin really would be okay with the news that Rhiannon definitely planned to greet the villagers as lady of the castle. No backup was needed, or at least, she hoped so.

Rhiannon checked her mobile phone—no messages. "Paul, have you seen Colin?"

"Ten minutes ago he knocked at the door for you, but I told him you weren't ready for visitors."

"Do you know where he is now?"

"He said he would find you, miss."

If she didn't find him first. "I'll be back in a few minutes, Paul."

He nodded, and Rhiannon headed for the back garden, her secret garden. Her boots made a solid clunking noise on the paving stones leading to the wooden door. Just a few, quiet moments of peace and then she would be ready.

She must have forgotten to lock it, because the door was unlocked and inside Colin was sitting at her tree swing, absently lounging in thought. When he heard her approach, he turned his head and stood, smiling lazily at her.

The sight of his familiar face made her knees weak, her palms damp. But it was the kilt he wore that had her swallowing with an unexpected lust that hit her to her core.

The black kilt jacket fit him smartly about his broad shoulders. Silver buttons in a row down his chest. A Black Watch kilt with sporran in front, and from his knees down, she admired his muscular legs with a smattering of dark brown hair.

He wore rough boots and short socks—not the long kilt socks and formal polished shoes that were customary. Like her, he was not so traditional. She covered her mouth and held back a smile.

"Rhiannon..." He spoke in that low voice that echoed to her bones and drew shivers from her. "You look great."

"And you...fill out a kilt quite well," she said, breathless.

His gaze lazily traveled over her. Somehow, everything between them had changed. He met her eyes in a direct, knowing stare.

She placed her hand on her chest, her heart pounding.

"Will you sit with me for a moment, before everybody arrives?"

She found herself nodding, unable to speak.

He shrugged out of his jacket and spread it on the grass for her to sit upon. As she walked to him, he took her hand in his and helped her down. His hands were large, rough and calloused from his life outside. Hers were soft from all the lavender hand cream she applied—the chemicals from her oil paints and other solutions were terrible for skin.

But he didn't mind her hands—he gently let go of them as she settled into a reclining position, her stole on the ground beneath her elbows, her boots crossed at the ankle and the skirt of her dress stretched as close to her knees as the thin material would go. He sat cross-legged beside her, and his bare knee brushed against her leg.

All week, in an unspoken pact, they'd been so careful not to touch each other. Ever since they'd kissed in her studio all those days ago, it was as if they'd agreed never to mention it or approach that possibility again. He was preparing to leave the castle and Scotland. She had to stay, obviously. For them to have a physical relationship wasn't wise.

But now, in the peace and serenity of her garden, with no sound but the whisper of wind in the trees and the occasional song of a skylark calling to his mate, it was easy to forget those differences.

She sat up, leaning her weight on the heels of her palms and dropping back her head to gaze at him. He'd missed a small spot of shaving cream—she reached out and dabbed it away with her finger.

He smiled directly into her eyes. "You're relaxed already. You don't need to meditate in your garden."

"No," she said, surprised. "I guess not."

"How do you want me to stand beside you today, Rhiannon? Close by, or with plenty of space?"

"Like we are now is nice." She gave him a long look, replete with a meaningful smile. She was fine, comfortable with Colin just the way he was with her. But if he wanted, she was willing for so much more.

She ran her fingers lightly over his hand. A lock of hair dropped over his eyes, but she could see the longing and the need in him, too.

"You can hold my hand," she whispered, "if you'd like. It might help me get past the initial fear."

"I'll be by your side as long as you want. You can count on it."

Her heart filled with happiness. She stretched her fingers so they were intertwined with his. He had done this with her in the kitchen that first Saturday and she'd been shocked by it. Now she yearned for more.

He brought her hand to his mouth and kissed it. Each knuckle. Each fingertip. It was as if a gate had been lifted between them, and the emotions were flooding out.

And then a succession of car horns sounded from the direction of the castle's front entrance.

They each looked at one another. Their bubble was broken.

Rhiannon sighed, lowering her hand. "That's probably my cousin Gerry."

"Sounds like a convoy. How many relatives will be here, exactly?"

"Well, you know Malcolm, plus his wife, Kristin. I'm not sure which of my aunts and uncles will be present—Paul has been tracking that—but I talked with my cousin Isabel, so I know she's coming. And Gerry, of course." She rolled her eyes. "He never misses a party. He's one of the boisterous ones."

"You'll have to introduce me to everybody," Colin said, smiling.

"Yes, and you may run screaming, but I warn you, they'll forever count on you to be a part of our gatherings if you're seen with me today."

Colin nodded, eyes twinkling. "That was the lecture Jamie gave me, in essence."

"So you're prepared for that?" Rhiannon was saying it lightly, but she was aware how meaningful the sentiment between the testing, jokey words was.

Could she *really* count on Colin to understand the extent of her fear? And to come back for her if she failed?

"Watch me and see." Colin winked at her, then got up, brushed off his kilt and held out a hand to her.

She clasped it and he hoisted her up, playfully.

And yet...he faced her in all seriousness, holding both her hands in his. "I have faith in you. In us. We'll make this work."

She swallowed. He really did believe in her. That made all the difference in the world. "Thank you for suggesting this to me in the first place," she said quietly. "I mean it." She was proud of herself just for making the attempt, and that was a big change for her.

Suddenly, Molly bounded toward them, barking. Rhiannon had left the door open, and when she went and checked the pathway outside, she saw that Malcolm and Kristin were down the lane, knocking on the door to her art studio.

Motioning Colin outside, she quickly closed and locked the garden door.

"We'll be right there!" Rhiannon called to them.

"Hi, Rhiannon!" Kristin waved happily. Rhiannon's sister-in-law wore a long MacDowall tartan skirt and a frilly white blouse. She had taken her promise to assist Rhiannon quite seriously.

Behind her, Colin made a small noise in his throat. "She's dressed just like your mother used to, for all the big castle functions," he murmured.

"Yes. Kristin's ready to step in for me, in case I back out. I hope you don't mind, but I'd like to talk with her privately."

"Sure." He looked at her carefully, as if he was going to say something, but then decided against it. "I'll, uh, do some advance work on the reception setup with Malcolm."

She gave Colin a relieved smile. "Thank you."

"We're okay, Rhiannon. If things get crazy, we'll just...remember our time in the garden this morning. That'll get us through."

She nodded. Colin was eyeing the pathway as Malcolm

advanced toward them, glowering questionably. Her brother looked like a mean, fierce Highlander in his kilt.

"Is that, uh, a dagger in his sock?" Colin asked.

"Technically, it's called a *sgian-dubh*." She pronounced it *skean-doo.*

"Yeah, I sort of remember that. It's all coming back to me now." He scratched his head. "It's a ceremonial knife, right? Not sharp or anything."

"In Malcolm's case, I'm afraid, that's a real blade." With a wry smile, she shrugged at Colin. "If you'd like one, too, I can raid our castle stores so you'll be evenly matched with him."

"Yeah, you guys always had a lot of weapons lying around, I remember that, too."

She laughed.

But she'd noticed that Colin wasn't in a hurry to leave her. He kept his hand protectively on the curve of her back. Malcolm hadn't scared him off.

She was glad. She enjoyed the feeling it gave her, of proprietary warmth, as if they belonged together and had a future as a couple.

Her brother and his wife stopped before them. "Hello, Malcolm. Hi, Kristin." Rhiannon gave them a huge smile. "This is Colin Walker—he's my escort today. Colin, you know my brother. And this is Kristin, his wife."

They all exchanged greetings. Kristin was her usual self, chatty and friendly. Shorter than Rhiannon, she had beautiful curly blond hair and sparkling green eyes. In Rhiannon's opinion, her brother had found the perfect match for him.

"May I speak to you in private?" Rhiannon murmured to her sister-in-law.

"Of course! Let's go up to your room," she said, dragging Rhiannon away.

They headed inside the castle. Upstairs in her bedroom,

Rhiannon sat on the window cushion and Kristin relaxed on the bed.

"You look wonderful," Rhiannon said. "I hope you're not disappointed that I'm making the traditional greeting today."

"Are you kidding?" Kristin sat up, her eyes bright. "I think it's great. I'd hoped you would, but I came prepared anyway, as you can see." She indicated her long skirt, rolling her eyes. "This is what Malcolm recommended I wear, though it does seem kind of hot outside for it. Am I overdressed?"

"No, you're perfect. You know my brother, always the traditionalist."

Kristin smiled. "Actually, I'm thankful you're doing the ceremonial honors. I'd rather just sit back and watch everything."

"It's your first time at a gathering, isn't it?" Rhiannon paused. "Will *Malcolm* be upset if you don't do the honors?"

"Jeez, no, don't worry about him—he'll be really happy that you want to do it."

"I do." Rhiannon felt relieved. "I really do."

"We're completely supportive of you." Kristin put her hand to her head, groaning slightly. "Honestly, I'm feeling kind of sick, anyway."

"Can I get you something for it?"

"No." Kristin glanced at her sideways and smiled shyly. "Actually, I have something to tell you. You're like a vault, Rhiannon—we can trust you with anything."

"What is it?" Rhiannon asked quietly.

"Well, Malcolm and I haven't told anyone yet, because it's still very early days, but..." She grinned at Rhiannon. "We're going to have a baby."

"That's...wonderful," Rhiannon whispered.

"We don't know if it's a boy or girl yet, but the stick was pink, so I'm pregnant for sure. I have a doctor's visit scheduled for next week."

Rhiannon walked over and hugged Kristin somberly. "You'll be brilliant parents."

"I think that's the first time you've hugged me." Kristin looked thoughtfully at Rhiannon. "Do you remember when we first met and you thought I was Malcolm's fiancée? He'd said the only way he'd ever bring anybody home is if he was engaged, and you mistakenly thought it was so?"

"Yes. And look how brilliantly it's turned out."

"What's happening, Rhiannon? You have a *date* today. Is he the Colin who was working in the guard booth last year?"

"No. This is the original Colin, my childhood friend. Colin the cat's namesake."

"Why didn't you tell me about him when I called?"

Rhiannon felt her cheeks growing warm. "You know me, Kristy." She didn't talk about her private life, even to Kristin or Isabel. Not that she usually had much news to tell.

"Yes," Kristin said, "I do know you." She stared at Rhiannon long and hard. Then with a devilish look, she tugged Rhiannon's hand. "Follow me!"

"Where? I have to find a *sgian-dubh* for Colin."

"We'll get one of those, too. Just come with me."

Out of curiosity, Rhiannon allowed Kristin to lead her into Malcolm's old bedroom, where he and Kristin stayed whenever they were overnight in the castle. Rhiannon never ventured inside their private space—that door was usually shut, and Paul was the one who supervised the housekeeper who'd prepared for their visit.

Rhiannon waited awkwardly while Kristin fished through a chest of drawers and finally handed her a *sgian-dubh*. "Here it is. I knew I saw one somewhere." Then she motioned Rhiannon into the en suite bathroom, where Rhiannon saw towels, toiletries and a leather travel case set on the glass shelves over the sink.

Kristin opened a lower cabinet and reached into the back.

"Here." She drew out a bundle and pressed it into Rhiannon's hand, closing her palm around it. "I know this is totally presumptuous on my part, but I also know that you're not likely to leave the castle, and this is just in case an emergency happens and you need it. Better prepared than not, right?"

Rhiannon opened her hand. "Condoms!" she said, her cheeks blazing.

"I'm sorry, was that too forward of me? Maybe I shouldn't have been so impulsive."

Rhiannon wasn't a modern woman in that way at all. She wasn't used to talking about sex...she didn't have close girlfriends for that. She had Kristin and her cousin Isabel to chat with, but they didn't talk about her confidences, and certainly not Rhiannon's love life, or lack thereof.

"You two must think I'm hopelessly naive."

"No! Not at all. And this isn't Malcolm speaking, this is me. Just...know that the condoms are here if you need them."

"You won't tell Malcolm about it?"

"Jeez, no! This is girl talk, Rhiannon. Okay?" Kristin covered her mouth and smiled, the way she so often did when Rhiannon saw her with Isabel these days.

Downstairs, Colin waited for her in the great room. Apparently, a few more people had arrived at the castle. But the only person she saw was Colin. Holding her breath, Rhiannon descended, feeling strangely as if he could read her mind. His gaze never left hers.

In her small dress pocket, she'd carefully tucked away the stash of three condoms.

*Ye gads.*

She was so worked up over her conversation with Kristin that she hadn't noticed how everyone in the room had gathered around, staring soberly at her.

She jerked her gaze back to Colin. He shook his head lightly and pointed to his eyes with two fingers. *Look at me,* he was telling her.

*Yes,* she thought, feeling giddy, *I'm standing here thinking of making love to you.*

And enjoying it very much.

———

COLIN WATCHED RHIANNON descend the stairs, proud to be with her. If she felt nervous about mingling with the public outside, she wasn't showing it.

Through the windows, he'd seen cars and trucks pulling up, and he'd watched marchers wearing kilts and carrying bagpipes assemble on the grassy moor. Jamie had told Colin that the laird had arranged for extra security, but that roadblock seemed to have caused a backup at the gate. For now, it was mainly Rhiannon's family in the great room, greeting each other and sharing laughter.

But a hush had come over the room when people noticed Rhiannon descending the stairs. Colin felt himself gritting his teeth. He wished they hadn't done that. The last thing Rhiannon needed was to feel spooked. He believed in her; why couldn't they?

*Look at me.*

He gave her an encouraging signal, and she returned a silly grin.

She went to him and took his hand. He imagined that everyone in the room observed her touch him and then lean so close that anyone might think they were intimate with each other.

*Whoa.* His body reacted instantly.

"That was interesting," she whispered in his ear.

"Uh, what was?"

"What happened upstairs. I'll tell you about it later." She grinned and held out a dagger sheathed in a worn brown leather case. "Here. This *sgian-dubh* belonged to my late grandfather. It's Malcolm's now, but Kristin said he wouldn't mind you using it today."

*Sure* he wouldn't mind. Colin hefted the weapon. "Is it sharpened? I'll need to defend your honor if anyone gets out of hand."

She laughed. "My protector. Actually you and Molly will be flanking me on either side. I plan to have Molly on her leash. She's a good attack dog when she needs to be."

"So, what's our plan for the day?" he asked seriously. "Is it a receiving line you have to stand in?"

She shivered, and he regretted asking the question. "Never mind, Rhiannon. How about if we stand by the drawbridge and you can wave at the crowd as if you're Queen of Scotland?"

She laughed again, thankfully. "There is no Queen of Scotland. But you've brought up a good point."

She brought him to the window and pointed to the gathering scene. "Traditionally, when the pipers are warmed up and are dressed in their parade clothing, they assemble into a band and perform for us. Then Malcolm will make a short welcome speech, offering our hospitality. The caterers will mingle with trays of food, and I'll stand in the tent and greet whoever wishes to say hello."

She exhaled. "Five minutes, that's my goal you said, right? If I can last long enough to greet the first group of people, then I'll declare victory."

"Five minutes." He'd chosen that short bar because he'd known she could do it.

"Oh, look who's here." Rhiannon fixed her attention on a couple who was approaching. The woman appeared to be related to Rhiannon; they had the same build, but the woman's hair was a vivid blond, to match her vibrant personality. The man at her arm was more taciturn, with a guarded expression. He had a close-cropped military haircut and he kept his back to the wall, his gaze sweeping over every detail in the castle as if checking for snipers.

"Colin," Rhiannon said, turning to him, "that's my cousin Isabel Sage. She's getting married in Edinburgh later this year. Jacob Ross is her fiancé." Rhiannon leaned closer and murmured, "Jacob is a US Secret Service agent."

"Seriously?" Colin murmured back. While Isabel and Rhiannon happily greeted each other, Colin tucked the sharp dagger—*skean-doo*—into his sock, and glanced warily at the Secret Service agent, who, judging by the bulge under his jacket, was packing heat.

Rhiannon introduced him. "Isabel, Jacob—this is my date for the afternoon, Colin Walker."

Isabel inclined her head with a smile. "I'm pleased to meet you, Colin."

Jacob, the Secret Service agent, just grunted.

"It's nice to meet you both, as well," Colin said.

Isabel murmured something in Rhiannon's ear. Rhiannon smiled and nodded at her.

"We'll be back in five minutes," Isabel said to Colin and Jacob. "Girl stuff."

"Sure," Colin agreed.

He and Jacob watched the two women head for the staircase.

"They'll be in the bathroom talking about us, right?" Colin asked, hoping to lighten the mood.

"How long have you known Rhiannon?" Jacob said in response. Colin could see right away that this was an interrogation, not a friendly bull session.

"Uh, since we were both eight years old."

Jacob grunted. By the nod he gave, Colin knew he'd given an acceptable answer.

"So, what's the plan?" Jacob stared out the window. "The security staff seems to be doing a good job on the perimeter. Where's Rhiannon going to be holed up once everything gets started?"

Colin shifted. "Actually, Rhiannon will be participating today. I'll be standing beside her while she's greeting the locals under that yellow awning over there." He pointed.

Jacob stared at him. Then he cracked a smile. "That's a good one."

"I'm not kidding."

Jacob shook his head, flabbergasted. "What brought this about? Rhiannon doesn't greet the public."

Colin glanced out the window at the moor, bustling with the activity of arriving vehicles and assembling pipe bands, and sighed to himself. He was starting to understand that no one in Rhiannon's family had any faith in her. "Evidently, she's changed her mind."

"Wish I'd known that," Jacob griped. "I could've helped prepare security. I do that every day for a living."

Before Colin could reply, he spotted a familiar-looking redhead wandering the grounds and staring intently at the castle.

*Oh, hell,* it was Bonnie. Mack's friend was craning her neck, probably searching for any sign of Rhiannon. Colin remembered that she'd had a curiosity about her.

"What is it?" Jacob was instantly on alert, catching Colin's expression and then scanning the grounds with eagle eyes.

"Nothing dangerous. I'm just thinking there are locals who are going to be interested in meeting Rhiannon for the first time. From what I've heard around town, they call her 'the recluse in the castle.' I'm worried there might be a gawking factor at play."

Jacob frowned. "That's not good."

"Yeah, I know." Colin had an idea. "Why don't you and I work in tandem? We'll set up a receiving line of sorts—you'll manage it at one end, and I'll watch the other. Make sure Rhiannon doesn't get too crowded."

Jacob nodded. "That'll make me breathe easier."

Colin noticed that Bonnie had followed behind a group of Rhiannon's cousins, heading for the drawbridge.

"If you'll excuse me," Colin said to Jacob, "I need to talk to someone. I'll be back in a minute."

"Just make sure you're here when Rhiannon gets back," Jacob ordered.

"Yeah. Thanks, I'll be sure to do that."

He wasn't sure why Rhiannon's cousin's fiancé was so interested in *his* date, but Colin would deal with that later. For now, he needed to intercept Bonnie before she stumbled into Rhiannon.

He caught up to her outside on the drawbridge. "Hey, Bonnie."

Her face brightened. "Colin! How's Mack?"

"Uh, I don't know, I haven't seen him lately." Colin hadn't talked with his friend since he left for Texas. Knowing Mack, he'd taken him up on that vacation offer and was probably waterskiing somewhere. Colin would give him a call from the airport before he left on Monday.

"Well, will you tell him I said hello?" Bonnie asked hopefully. "Maybe if I had a pen, I could write my phone number for you to give him?"

Colin was pretty sure she'd probably already given her number to Mack. He felt sorry for her. Mack wasn't ever going to call her; in fact, if he recognized her number on his phone, he wouldn't pick up. That was how Mack rolled.

"If you don't hear from him, don't take it personally, Bonnie. It's not about you."

"How could I not take it personally?" Bonnie demanded, her voice somewhat shrill. "Who else would it be about?"

"I'm sorry," Colin said quietly. He really was.

But Bonnie seemed so dejected that Colin made her an offer he might not have made otherwise. "If you'd still like to meet Rhiannon MacDowall, then come over to the awning when you see me standing there. She'll be greeting people in her mother's place, but only for a few minutes. Get in front of the line. I'll make sure you're escorted in."

"Thanks, Colin." Bonnie sighed. "I wish I'd met you before I met Mack."

"No. You don't." Colin glanced behind him at the castle, wondering if Rhiannon was back yet.

"Your heart is with her, isn't it?" Bonnie asked.

"Look, Mack's a great guy. He's just not ready to settle down and commit, if you know what I mean."

"He sure gave a good impression of it," Bonnie said mournfully. "We were inseparable while he was here."

*While he was here* being the key words. But Bonnie didn't see that, and Mack wasn't going to point it out.

"Colin, lad?" Colin's friend from the Kildrammond pro shop was in his kilt, the prosthetic leg with the blue-and-white Saint Andrew's Cross displayed proudly. McGuff slapped Colin's arm, then caught him up in one of his bear hugs. "I didn't expect to see your ugly mug here today." McGuff set Colin down and glanced at Bonnie with interest. "Who's the pretty lassie?"

Colin made the introduction. "Bonnie, this is McGuff."

"Ian McGuff," McGuff corrected.

"Ian McGuff," Colin repeated. "He's a stand-up guy."

"That I am." McGuff made an emphatic stomp with his prosthetic leg. Bonnie's mouth dropped open.

"Seriously," Colin said, trying not to smirk. "Ian is the most *committed* person I know." There was a good fifteen-year age difference between Bonnie and McGuff, but if that was Bonnie's cup of tea and commitment was what she preferred over Mack's playing-the-field attitude, then Colin wasn't about to discourage it.

"Aye." McGuff slapped Colin on the arm. "You be at the practice range tomorrow morning at eight o'clock. I'll meet you there."

Colin didn't know how McGuff managed to get up so early on a Sunday morning after spending Saturday night celebrating.

"I'll be there," Colin promised. It was to be their last full day of training before Colin flew home to the States.

Colin's tournament began on Thursday. He'd fly home Monday, recuperate Tuesday, fly the short hop to New York on Wednesday morning and then prepare for the first round of play on Thursday morning.

"Well," McGuff said, "they're lining up the pipers. I need to be getting back." To Bonnie he directed, "I'll buy you a drink later, lass."

"The drinks are free," Bonnie pointed out.

"So they are. But did I mention that I give personal table service?" He winked at her.

Colin noticed that a smile had settled on Bonnie's face. She was considering McGuff's offer.

Colin said his goodbyes and headed inside the castle to Rhiannon, just in time to catch her coming down the stairway again. When she saw him, she blushed even more furiously.

He chuckled as he approached her. "Why are you being shy with me? What's going on?"

She pressed her hands to her cheeks. "I'll tell you later."

But whatever she and Isabel had discussed, Rhiannon seemed happy. He just smiled and shook his head. Whatever was going on with her was fine with him. This was a big step for her, and so far, she was handling it like a champ. He felt fiercely proud of her.

Outside, the haunting drone of bagpipes and drums started up. Rhiannon's face brightened.

"Come to the drawbridge!" She nudged Colin, and the two of them were among the first of the Sage family members to head outside to view the presentation of the pipe bands to the laird of the castle.

Colin squeezed Rhiannon's hand, letting her know that she could trust him to be a constant presence. But she seemed immersed in the spectacle. There was something about the pipe bands that was deeply haunting and mystical. The historical ballads, with their proud and sad history, stirred his blood and seemed to resonate with his bones.

When the pipe bands had each marched past Malcolm's chair, and the last band stood in formation, Malcolm rose and delivered the laird's speech. Colin had to admit, Malcolm gave an impression of authority and strength. Colin would never want Rhiannon's brother on his bad side.

And then came Rhiannon's cue. "The lady will greet participants in the refreshment tent," Malcolm declared.

Jacob, the Secret Service agent, gave them a discreet signal. He'd already formed a sort of impromptu rope line, and Jessie and Jamie were at the head of the queue.

"Are you ready?" Colin asked Rhiannon.

"Do you think I can do it?"

"Not a doubt in my mind."

Still, he saw her stiffen. Her breathing accelerated. She was beginning to get that look in her eyes he'd seen the first morning he'd bumped into her behind his grandparents' cottage.

"Hey." He gazed into her eyes. "Do you remember how we

were in the secret garden? Do you remember that feeling when we were sitting on the grass?"

With two pink spots in her cheeks, she nodded.

"Just keep that feeling going, because I'm here with you for this."

"I know." She smiled at him, a trusting smile. Her hand in his squeezed him back, holding him tight.

"Let's go," she said.

It was a short walk to the awning. Rhiannon stood with dignity, her other hand lightly on Molly's head, who sat beside her keeping her guardian's eyes on her mistress's daughter.

"I'm ready," Rhiannon murmured.

Colin nodded to Jacob, who strictly controlled the line. One by one, he began the process of sending people into the tent to see Rhiannon.

Jamie and Jessie set the tone for everyone who would follow. Jamie gave Rhiannon a simple nod. Jessie wished her well. Neither made a move to touch Rhiannon, and from the hushed tone of the audience, Colin decided that they were watching closely and taking note.

The real test began when the first couple of strangers approached them.

"Hello, Rhiannon," the gentleman said politely. He wore a band major's uniformed kilt jacket. "I don't know if you remember me, but I was custodian at your primary school."

Rhiannon smiled gently. "I do, Mr. Foster. Thank you for coming to the gathering."

The Fosters moved on without dawdling. The second couple moved forward. A similar, straightforward greeting and a digni-fied response from Rhiannon.

Colin noticed that she kept her attention on him between the greetings. Sometimes Colin murmured in her ear, or told her light jokes. Jacob helped, too, by giving strict instructions to the people waiting in his queue.

Five more minutes passed, and Rhiannon remained where she stood. "My mother should be careful," she murmured lightly to Colin. "I may decide to take over her job permanently."

"Excellent idea," he replied. "Make sure to warn me so I can reserve my kilt rental in advance."

"With your own *sgian-dubh?*"

"Extra sharp, in case I need to duel."

"You'd need a sword for that."

"Good thing you have an arsenal in your castle."

She smirked, tilting her head to him. "We really are a team, aren't we?"

They were. Oh, hell yeah, they were.

Whoever had first called Rhiannon a recluse was just dead wrong. Her fear reminded him of himself, when he'd begun entering tournaments and he'd had to get used to focusing his nerves and performing under pressure. That was all this really was.

And then a thought caught hold of him. He wanted her to come home with him to Texas. Maybe follow him on the road for a tournament or two.

Why not? He didn't see what everyone else saw. To him, she wasn't a damaged woman who needed to stay within the protective walls of her castle. He *saw* Rhiannon. A living, breathing woman with desires, humor, strength of character. She'd been good for him, and he only hoped he was the man for her. He wanted to be committed to her. He wanted to build something with her.

He wiped his palm on his kilt. Turned around to the table behind them and poured her a drink, a dram of whisky from the laird's private reserve. She stayed for the last of the greeting line; about a half hour total she'd stood in the heated shade.

Even Molly had given up and was lying down, panting.

"We need to fetch her some water," Rhiannon said.

"I'll get it," he answered. The pipe bands were marching up the drive and toward the road that led to the village, a long snaking line. The pipes made their mourning wail and the drums kept time. The spectators who'd accompanied them walked behind; boys and girls scampered alongside, calling out in excitement.

They would all continue their day at the Highland Games, but for Colin and Rhiannon, their roles in the proceedings were finished. Colin breathed a sigh of relief.

He found the dog's bowl in the kitchen, then filled it from the tap and brought it outside. Jessie was seated in a chair in the shade, looking fatigued. "Don't worry about me," Jessie said. "Jamie is bringing round the buggy to ferry me back to the cottage."

"Great," Colin replied. Around them, the lot of relatives was fast emptying out. All the Sage cousins and aunts and uncles were climbing into their luxury cars and mini-SUVs and heading to the fairgrounds. Paul and the caterers were still present somewhere, but they were busy cleaning up after the event.

*We're alone again. We can move forward now.*

Colin felt Rhiannon's presence before she touched him. Her thin, bare arms wrapped around his neck, her soft, warm body pressed to his back. "Please, can we go somewhere and celebrate?" she breathed.

His body reacted instantly. He turned, and she was smiling at him, flushed with her success, her eyes glowing and her lips so damn willing.

Groaning, he cupped the back of her head, intent on showing restraint, being gentle, but she wiggled and pressed closer to him, and he couldn't resist her.

He took her in deep, primal kisses, each one longer and more thrusting and sensual than the last. She was willing and eager and pliant. She wanted him, too. She felt exactly what he felt.

Fumbling in the sporran to be sure he had his car keys, he backed up with her until he felt the handle of the passenger door press into his hip. He wanted to whisk her out of here. From his peripheral vision he saw Paul glancing their way. That was just wrong. They should be alone. They should be out of here, away from the reminder of her old life, the people who thought of her as someone and something that she wasn't, not at heart.

"Colin, I care for you so much," she murmured, a mixture of longing and love mingling in her eyes. It damn near killed him. "I want to get even closer to you. As close as two people can be." She glanced at the car behind him.

"Do you want to get inside?" he asked. "Do you want to drive away with me?"

She sighed at him, her eyes only on him. "I do," she said.

With a nod, he opened the passenger door of his car and waited for her to sit. She was smiling at him, not at all afraid. Before the mood left, he hustled around to the driver's side. Once seated, he took her palm and kissed it. "Are you sure, Rhiannon?" he asked one more time. "You're absolutely sure you'll leave with me?"

"I am," she said. With wonder in her eyes, she ran her fingers over his lips.

What could he do? He kissed her, then started the engine and headed toward the guard booth.

It was a substantial guard booth, with a back room, a kitchenette, a bed, a bathroom. He'd been inside many times before with his grandfather, in his youth. Now, as they zoomed past, Colin caught a glimpse of the guard stationed inside. Not his grandfather. Still, he wanted to get away from anyone who knew them.

He would take her into town, he decided. Check into that romantic boutique hotel where he'd meant to stay in the first place, but had somehow never found the reason to go there. Until now.

Rhiannon's head was flung back on the seat as she stared dreamily at him. One hand was on his kilt—he could practically feel the heat of her hand through the thin scratchy wool...

Suddenly another hired guard—one of her uncle's security team, perhaps—stepped forward in the road directly in front of them, not looking...so careless. Reacting quickly, Colin jerked the steering wheel, thankfully avoiding hitting the young man, but swerving onto the only place he could safely stop, on the shoulder of the one-lane road that led into town.

The near-miss served to jolt Rhiannon. As if waking from a dream, she snapped back her head and then turned to stare behind her, out the back window and toward the castle. It seemed to Colin that her home looked so small from the top of the drive and the boundary they'd just crossed.

A scream came out of Rhiannon's throat, an unholy, unearthly, bloodcurdling scream that scared the bejeezus out of him.

With both hands, Rhiannon twisted and writhed in the seat as though she was trying desperately to escape. But she was secured in place by her seat belt; all she succeeded in doing was choking herself, making it worse. Her screams were like guttural cries.

Colin's heart pumping ferociously, he whipped off his own seat belt and scrambled to get out the door and around toward the back of the car—he wanted to reach her door, open it and free her... The screaming was like nothing he'd ever heard in his life.

His hands on the back fender, he rounded the car, but he slipped on the gravel, losing his balance...

The car started rolling. The automatic transmission... Colin realized too late that he hadn't taken the extra seconds to push the gearshift into Park. Stuck in his off-balance position, Colin couldn't get out of the way in time. The car's rear wheel rolled over his left foot.

He cried out—the pain was excruciating. A torrent of curses rolled out of his mouth. But Rhiannon was still struggling with her seat belt like a woman possessed, and he needed to get to her, get to the car and secure her first.

He put weight on his foot, but it couldn't hold him. And the pain, oh, hell, the pain...

*My golf tournament,* he belatedly remembered. The pro tour. His career. His tour card that if he'd been in danger of losing before, he was even more in danger now.

Everything he'd wanted, he'd worked for, he'd planned for— it was all in jeopardy. The horror of it rushed back and smacked him in the face.

The guard finally made it to the side of their car.

"Put the gear in Park," Colin snapped at him. "And then get Rhiannon out. Get her out. Get her safely out of this car."

"Yes, sir." The young guard opened the door and gently freed Rhiannon, even as she clubbed and smacked him and kicked him in her state of utter panic, utter fear.

"Don't hurt her, for God's sake!" Colin shouted.

Rhiannon was free, on her feet, and her response was to flee, in a blind panic, sprinting past them around the gatehouse and down the drive toward the castle.

Colin put his forehead on the roadway and grimaced in pain. His foot...his frigging, messed-up foot.

"Sir? Can I help you?"

"Do you have a phone?" Colin managed to get out.

"Yes, sir. Right here."

"Do you know Malcolm MacDowall's mobile number?"

"I do, sir."

"Good, phone him up, right now, and tell him to get here as soon as he can. And oh, hell, tell him to bring Ian McGuff with him, too, since I need a ride to the hospital. Will you do that?" he gritted out.

"Yes, sir." The guard bent his head to fumble with his mobile phone.

Colin lay back down. It was obvious that he had to get to a doctor as soon as possible, and if he had to have anyone with him, he would much rather have McGuff than Rhiannon's brother. Besides, Rhiannon needed Malcolm right now.

He didn't even want to think about how Malcolm was going to react when he found out what Colin had done.

## CHAPTER TWELVE

COLIN SAT ON an examination table in the hospital with his left foot elevated, waiting for the results of his X-ray.

Head in his hands, he still felt shell-shocked for all that had happened.

Malcolm had come right away, thankfully for Rhiannon's sake. He'd taken one look at the location outside the estate perimeter where Colin had driven his sister before grimly driving on, toward the castle and Rhiannon, leaving Jacob to pilot Colin and his rental car to the closest emergency room.

On the way, Jacob had received the call that Rhiannon was okay, resting at home with Malcolm. Jacob had quietly informed Colin of that fact, and Colin was filled with relief for it, at least.

He glanced at Jacob, sitting in a plastic chair against the wall with his arms crossed and saying nothing.

Jacob hadn't said much during any of the ordeal.

When they'd arrived at the facility, Jacob had silently walked beside Colin as a nurse wheeled him into a processing area and then, an hour later, into this tiny examination room with a government poster warning about the dangers of gluten allergies and their effect on the stomach.

Colin could definitely see himself developing a stomach ulcer if he waited here long enough.

He looked again at the taciturn Secret Service agent. The man had a talent for sitting as still as a ghost and not making an expression or betraying an emotion.

Secret Service agents were professional bodyguards, after all. He seemed to have his own agenda in accompanying Colin, but Colin wasn't sure what that was.

"You can wait outside if you'd like," Colin said to him.

Jacob stared back. "No, thanks. I'm good."

"I would prefer that you wait outside, actually."

"Sorry." Jacob shrugged, but he didn't look sorry. "I can't do that."

"Why not?"

Jacob stared straight ahead. "Rhiannon's sake."

"Rhiannon?" Jacob had been overly protective of her all during the gathering. "Why Rhiannon?" Colin asked. "What's your allegiance to her?"

Jacob flicked a glance to him but said nothing.

Colin closed his eyes. Jacob was probably present on orders from his fiancée, that was all. Maybe the pain was making him paranoid. The throbbing from his foot and his worry over it healing improperly were messing with his head.

More than anything else, he was racked with guilt over what he'd done to Rhiannon. "I bet the last person she's thinking about right now is me," he muttered.

Jacob grunted. "You're wrong."

Colin shifted, and a fresh bolt of pain shot through his foot. He gritted his teeth. "Why? Have you heard from Rhiannon?"

Despite phones not being allowed in the hospital, Colin had noticed Jacob discreetly glancing at his cell phone's screen and tapping out a message here and there. Colin had assumed that Jacob was checking in with Isabel.

Jacob nodded. "Yes, I've heard."

"And? How is she doing now? What's she saying?"

Jacob fell silent again.

Colin didn't know what to do about Rhiannon. He thought she'd been fine at the gathering. She'd lasted the afternoon greeting everyone who'd wanted to meet her, and then she'd said she wanted to be with Colin. She'd insisted, really. The agoraphobia hadn't seemed like such a problem in those moments.

He stared at his swollen foot, blown up to elephant-man size. He didn't know what was going to happen, with her or with his foot. His plans were upended—he had no idea if he would even be allowed to fly home Monday. Flying was the worst thing for inflamed tissue, and if it was broken, or if he got a cast...

The reality was, he didn't see how he would be playing golf on Thursday. But he had to think positive thoughts, because the alternative—not being able to play, and losing his tour card—was out of the question.

Whatever diagnosis the doctors came back with would tell the tale. Worst-case scenario, he was looking at a career-ending injury.

He felt as if a black gloom was threatening to envelop him.

"What did you expect from Rhiannon, anyway?" Jacob suddenly asked him, disrupting his personal nightmare and contributing more fuel to the fire.

Colin was damned if he'd let anyone question him about his relationship with Rhiannon. She was special to him, and that was private. "Excuse me?" he said coldly.

"Don't you know she's a recluse? Rhiannon can't leave the estate. It gives her panic attacks."

"Yeah, I know about Rhiannon," he said irritably. "Look, she got in the car with me, voluntarily, and asked me to take her away. Not that it's any of your business."

Jacob gazed quietly at him. "Do you know how I first met Rhiannon?"

"No," Colin said flatly.

"My father was one of the police officers who rescued her when she was a girl. He stormed the warehouse she was being held in, but he died in her arms later that night."

*Oh, hell.* Colin hadn't known that.

"Afterward, she drew a sketch of his face," Jacob continued. "A damn good likeness." His voice wavered. "All those years, and she never said anything to anyone about what he said to her that night, until I showed up at the castle just before Christmas last year. She turned my life upside down—set it right, actually—when she told me what he'd said about me before he died."

"I'm sorry about your father," Colin said. He hadn't known any of that.

"Thanks." Jacob was silent for a moment. "I didn't know him. I was young when he left us."

"That doesn't matter. It still sucks."

Jacob nodded curtly. "I'm sorry about your foot. I can't help you with that, though."

"Actually you can. When you were in the village, did you, uh, see a bald guy with a prosthetic leg under his kilt?"

Jacob lifted an eye brow. "Saint Andrew's flag on the leg?"

"That's him."

"Sure. He was marching the fairgrounds with his band and blowing on a bagpipe."

Yeah, that sounded like McGuff. "He's been a good friend, and I really need him here to consult with me about the right sports doctors for my injury. I left him a message earlier, but he didn't pick up."

Jacob nodded. "I'll go outside and try to call him for you."

"Thanks," Colin said. "I appreciate it."

Jacob stood, but before he left, he turned to Colin. "Are you going to end it with Rhiannon after this?"

Colin ran both hands over his face and through his hair. His eyelids felt gritty. "Trust me, after what I just did, I expect her to end it with me."

"She won't do that. She's attached to you. Rhiannon doesn't abandon people she's attached to."

*Was* she attached to him?

She'd said she was half in love with him, but the last time he'd seen her, she'd been screaming. His actions had given her a massive panic attack, and that scared him, frankly.

How could he be sure he wouldn't hurt her again? And how could they be together if she never found it within herself to leave the estate?

Jacob misread Colin's silence. "If you're going to end whatever you've got going with her, then do it now and go easy. She's been through enough."

"Sounds like you would rather I leave her alone."

"I want what's best for her."

"Yeah, I do, too," Colin said, feeling testy. "And, to be honest, this is really none of your business."

Jacob sat again, staring at Colin. "Maybe not. But I've seen the official incident reports about what happened to her during the kidnapping. It took me months of digging around and building relationships with people in Edinburgh, but I finally got my hands on them. I've not shared those reports with anyone, but I will tell you this, Colin—I don't think she remembers everything that happened."

"She does. She's told me."

"No, I don't think so. If she'd told you what I read, then you wouldn't have tried to leave with her like you did."

Colin swallowed. His physical pain and the fate of his tournament play didn't seem so important anymore. "Whatever you're trying to say, just spit it out."

Jacob pulled the plastic chair closer to Colin. Leaned forward and put his hands on his knees. "I won't sugarcoat it. The investigators found rope in her cell—she'd been tied down to hooks on the wall in a cement cell for the better part of eleven days. They think she was molested. But she refused to speak of it to the rescuing officers."

Colin felt sick to his stomach to think of her going through that hell. Jacob stared hard at him. "I know you don't want to hear this," he said evenly. "Nobody does." His jaw worked, as if he was furious inside. "Her connected, wealthy family has put a lot of effort into protecting her from having to discuss anything she doesn't want to talk about. That's what she's used to. My point is, Colin, it's not a good idea for you to expect too much from her."

As Colin saw it, *that* was the problem—people not expecting enough from Rhiannon. "I think differently about her," he said stubbornly. "I believe in her."

"Colin—"

Just then a man appeared in the hallway with a chart in his hand, obviously the results of Colin's X-ray. Pausing, he knocked on the doorjamb. "Colin Walker?"

"Here," Colin said, raising his hand.

"Hi, I'm Nurse Stephens. These are orderlies Jones and Frye." Nurse Stephens gestured toward two other workers who'd entered the room—a middle-aged man and a young woman. They carried supplies—bandages, a medical boot and a pair of metal crutches.

"We've got a caber tosser in the next room with a bloody foot, as well," Nurse Stephens said cheerily, gazing at Colin's kilt. "We can always tell when the Highland Games are in town.

Well, let's uncover his foot and see what we have," he instructed the young woman.

"What exactly are you going to do?" Colin asked.

"Why, we're fitting you with a boot and crutches," Nurse Stephens said. "And the doctor will be along shortly to discuss the results of your X-ray with you." He smiled at Colin. "More important, an aide will be by to give you some pain medication."

"I don't want pain medication." Colin needed to stay alert and coherent so he could deal with the facts and make decisions. He was still reeling over what Jacob had told him. Furious over what Rhiannon had gone through. He shook his head. "Can I speak with a sports doctor, please? I'm a golfer, and I have a tournament next week."

"Yes, sir, we read about your profession on your chart. You gave us the information we needed when you checked in at the triage station."

Colin blew out a breath. "Just tell me—are any of the bones broken?"

"I'm not supposed to—"

"Please," Colin asked.

The nurse imperceptibly shook his head. *No,* he mouthed. *Not broken.*

Colin relaxed. That was one thing in his favor. "How long until I can put weight on it? Tomorrow?"

"Er...everyone is different, sir, but typically it's a matter of weeks."

"I don't *have* a matter of weeks."

"And even then, you'll be needing therapy treatments."

This was more than he'd expected. Colin closed his eyes.

"I'll find your friend," Jacob said quietly to Colin. He held up his phone, earning a scowl from all three hospital workers.

"Thanks," Colin said to Jacob.

With a grim nod in Colin's direction, Jacob left the room.

"Okay," Colin said to Nurse Stephens, "fit me with the boot and crutches. But tell me, if I fly home now, will I do any further damage to my foot?"

"Well, you'll need to keep the swelling down with ice packs, rest and elevation. Before you leave, we'll give you instructions." Nurse Stephens paused. "Is it a short flight?"

"About ten hours."

"Oh," he exclaimed, looking horrified, "I don't know as I would recommend that. But you should check with the doctor."

*Just perfect.* The young aide had him stretch out his foot, and Colin got a fresh look at the injury. Angry, red flesh swollen with fluid.

He groaned.

Colin needed to see a sports doctor—someone who would treat him with the perspective of an athlete who required top performance from his body. And every second was critical. Early treatment was most important to successfully healing.

Colin reached for his phone. Rules or no rules, he needed to talk to McGuff, *now*—

"Laddie, there you are. I came as soon as I heard."

Accompanied by Jacob, McGuff stood in the doorway, still wearing his kilt and his breath smelling as though he'd been celebrating with whisky.

Colin had never been so relieved to see his friend. "You got my message?"

McGuff scowled. "What message? I came because Jessie rang me at the pub. Your friend Rhiannon contacted her, and then she contacted me."

*Oh, Rhiannon.* Even after the way he'd messed things up with her, she still worried about him.

Whatever else happened, whatever Colin lost from his life, if he had to endure pain, he was grateful to be where there were people who cared about him and who looked out for his best interests. And it was becoming clear to him that Scotland might be such a place.

He felt measurably better with his friend's presence. "What do you recommend?" he asked McGuff.

"I'd let the pretty lassie fit you with medical boot. Then take the crutches they give you. I know just the doctor we might be able to see on a Saturday evening if we're nice to him."

"I can be very nice."

"I know you can. Chin up, we'll get you fixed," McGuff said cheerfully as he studied the damage to Colin's foot. "It's still attached to your leg, is it not?"

Colin remembered with shame that McGuff had gone through a far worse accident than he had.

"Sometimes things happen for a reason. This isn't the worst thing in the world, laddie."

"I have to keep my tour card," Colin said quietly. "If at all possible."

McGuff glanced at him. "Do you want it badly enough to work with Somer Grinks again?"

There were drawbacks to that. Grinks's contempt for Colin's work ethic, for one. The lousy way Grinks had made Colin feel when he gave him those withering looks, for another.

"If you'd like, I'll arrange for you to have a conversation with him. And I don't do this lightly," McGuff warned. "Did you know Grinks sits on the board of your American Association? If anyone has sway in easing the path and bending the rules for special cases, it's him."

"I didn't know that." Colin looked at McGuff gratefully. "I'll think about it—thanks."

"Never mind, lad. I'm doing it because you're my friend and you've shown me your character. Now, let's get you fixed up and then brought home to your castle. There's somebody there who's been asking for you."

RHIANNON WAITED FOR Colin in the great room before the stone fireplace. She was watched over by the full contingent of minders: Jessie, Malcolm, Isabel and Kristin, while Paul bustled in and out of the kitchen ferrying sandwich trays and biscuits.

Rhiannon's instincts had been to wait alone, retreating to the quiet of her private world, but a desire to show her family that she was fine—not in need of their solicitousness—had overtaken her and now, here she was.

Isabel and Kristin sat on a corner couch, quietly browsing a stack of Isabel's bridal magazines and commenting on dresses. Malcolm said nothing, just drummed his fingers on his leg, absently watching a football match on the wide screen. Jessie knitted in a chair by the window. Rhiannon simply kept an eye on the front drive.

They'd been waiting for hours. They were rather a subdued lot, likely on her account, Rhiannon supposed.

Today's incident horrified her still.

The thing that most shamed her was that she'd run from Colin. She felt terrible about that. He'd been writhing in pain, and in her panic, she'd been unable to consider staying and helping him—she'd just reacted and bolted from a sense of her own terror. In all her past years of panic attacks, she'd never experienced anything quite like this before.

She hoped Colin came back to them, but she wasn't sure he would. He had a plane ticket home for Texas, scheduled to leave on Monday from Edinburgh. She wouldn't blame him if he picked up his things from the cottage and then drove straight to an airport hotel.

Molly laid her golden retriever's head on Rhiannon's lap and gazed mournfully up at her. Their family pets always seemed to pick up on her mood.

"Poor Molly," Rhiannon murmured, ruffling her fur. "And you did so well today, staying obediently on your leash before all those people." Rhiannon had done well, too. Better than she'd expected.

But it hadn't been enough.

Tears threatened to break through, so she hurriedly brushed them away and then glanced around. She'd been discreet enough that no one had noticed. At least their silence enabled her to pretend she was inside her secret garden. She could close her eyes and quietly move through today's events moment by moment, remembering how she'd felt at each step of the way. Maybe then she could find an answer, because it was unacceptable that her reaction could be so out of hand that it directly resulted in injury to another person.

Especially to *him*.

She swallowed, the tears threatening again. No one else lifted her day like Colin.

More than anything, she'd wanted to be with him. She'd wanted to go where he did, to physically express her love for the man she deeply cared about the same way any other woman would.

The problem was, she hadn't thought it through well enough before the passion overtook her. Rushed away by her hormones and emotions, she'd blithely agreed to hop into that car without really thinking about the ramifications of crossing the boundary line.

Tires sounded on gravel outside, and everyone looked to the window.

Jacob stepped out of the driver's side of the car and then assisted Colin from the passenger's seat. Colin wore a medical boot on his left foot and walked with the aid of crutches.

Rhiannon's heart sank. She'd been nurturing the hope that he would miraculously be without injury.

Jacob carried Colin's sporran, boot and *sgian-dubh* into the great room for him. Both men still wore their kilts, as did Malcolm.

Colin's eyes widened when he saw them all sitting there with her. He seemed shocked by the small crowd of people waiting for him. He gazed questioningly at Rhiannon, and she gave him a tentative smile.

"Are you all right, Colin?" Malcolm spoke first. "What's the diagnosis?"

"McGuff's specialist said it's deep bruising, essentially."

"I'm sorry."

"I'll be fine," Colin said curtly. "Thanks, though."

Jacob set down the clothing items that Colin had been required to jettison at the hospital, and then he took out his own car keys. "Malcolm, Kristin, Isabel—let's get going."

Isabel gave Rhiannon a smile of support. "We'll see you later," she murmured. "Take care."

Kristin scooted off the couch, too, and the two women and Jacob said goodbye to them and then immediately headed off.

Malcolm hesitated. "Are you all right?" he asked Rhiannon. "Really?"

"Yes," she answered, "please do go. Stop worrying about me."

For once, her brother obeyed her.

That left Jessie in the room with them. Colin's nana picked up her knitting and gave him a pat on his broad shoulders. "I'll go have a wee cuppie with Paul in the kitchen. You and I will talk later."

"Thanks, Nana," Colin said.

Now the two of them were completely alone. The room was so silent Rhiannon heard the grandfather clock ticking. Colin remained standing.

"I'm sorry I did that to you," he said in a low voice.

"What? No!" She walked over to him, but he didn't seem to

be welcoming her as usual, so at the last moment she decided to just lean against the back of the couch she'd been sitting on, her fingers gripping the edges. "I'm the one who's sorry. You did nothing wrong. I did, when I ran from you."

A line appeared in Colin's forehead. "Is that because you thought I was kidnapping you?"

"No!" She gave him a look of horror. "I wish I'd acted like that when I *was* kidnapped. Colin, do you realize how many years I've berated myself because I couldn't scream or run from danger?"

He made the closest noise to a laugh that she'd heard since he came into the room. "You sure screamed well today, Rhiannon. Ran the hundred meter dash in close to ten seconds, too."

"Yes," she said lightly, "but don't be signing me up for the Olympics yet."

His smile faded away. They both knew there was no dancing around the subject. They had to address it.

"Rhiannon, I made a mistake inviting you into that car. You told me from the beginning what the rules were, and I should've followed them."

"Actually I'd changed my mind about that." She fingered his *sgian-dubh* on the table. "I was trying to leave the property with you on purpose. You and I did have a whopping success at the gathering today, didn't we?"

"Yeah, we were doing pretty good until it all blew up, weren't we?"

Put that way, it sounded pathetic, even to her. When it came down to it, the way she lived her life wasn't normal or compatible to a man like him. He was a public person; he traveled, he competed, he enjoyed his life on a much bigger canvas than she did.

She'd wanted to share some of that canvas. She'd been

willing to at least try, in a small way, to mesh with the realities of his life.

"My plan was to ask you to go on tour with me," he said. "Just to the first tournament in New York, just to have you there. You know?"

He'd wanted to take their relationship that far? She hadn't realized he felt so strongly about her, too. Rhiannon put her hand to her heart.

But Colin's smile faded as he studied his foot in the medical boot. "I have to withdraw from the New York Cup, Rhiannon."

Her heart cried for him. "There'll be another tournament when you're healed, won't there?"

"Of course." He gave her one of his brilliant smiles, as if everything were fine when they both knew that it wasn't. "My team is looking at the schedule for September."

"So...would you still like to try to be with me?" She held her breath, hanging on his answer. Something about him seemed reluctant, as if he was leery to trust her again.

"Rhiannon, can we sit down a minute? I need to ask you about something."

"Okay." Her heart pounding, she took the smaller couch, where Kristin and Isabel had been looking at bridal dresses. Colin hobbled over on his crutches, and setting them down, took the seat at cross angles to her, their bare knees touching.

But he wasn't paying attention to that right now. He was looking at her very seriously. Was that sorrow in his eyes?

"Were you molested by the kidnappers?" he asked in a low voice.

"What? Colin, who said that about me?"

"I'm sorry to ask. But I want to be clear about what happened so I know the truth of what you went through." His face was deadly serious.

"Does that make a difference to you?" she asked.

"Yeah, I need to understand everything because I don't want to hurt you again. The honesty of it is what makes the most difference. It's important to me that I hear this stuff from you, not other people."

She could understand that. Important people in his life had kept things from him. Things that had eventually blown up and hurt him deeply, like the funeral. Colin had lived with deception for too long.

But her refusal to speak about all the details of her kidnapping wasn't about being deceptive. Her silence was about keeping control of her emotions, about keeping a grip on her sanity and not frightening herself. If she didn't talk about what had happened, then she could forget about it, lock it away and convince herself that everything was okay.

"Honestly I wasn't molested. I wasn't even physically hurt." She indicated the medical boot on his foot. "You were injured today more than I ever was."

His mouth twisted. "What about the ropes they found attached to the wall of the cell?"

"I'm sorry you heard about that. It wasn't as bad as you're probably thinking. They tied me up the first night, but when they realized I was too scared to run, they didn't do it again."

"Did you ever talk about it with anyone?"

She smiled sadly at Colin. It was true that some traumatized women worked with therapists, wrote down their stories, sometimes even went on speaking tours as a way of regaining their power over their abusers. She had the utmost respect for these women, but they weren't her. "It just isn't my way to talk to anyone, Colin. I am who I am."

"Sometimes I wonder about that," Colin said quietly. "I don't want to push you, but wouldn't it be good for you to look into a professional treatment program for your agoraphobia?"

She stiffened. "I went through that when I was young. I know their techniques."

"If you're sure…"

"I am, Colin."

"Okay." He nodded. Blew out a breath. "Well, I'm glad your kidnappers are dead," he muttered.

"Don't say that." She stared at her hands. "To Malcolm those three men were monsters. To me…honestly…" She looked up at Colin, because the only reason she was speaking so frankly was for his sake. She wanted to *try* to be there for him—give him what he needed from her.

Tears welled in her eyes. "The truth is that I felt sorry for them. The youngest one especially. He wasn't…cut out for what the other two had drawn him into. I listened to them at night through the door, and…"

She shook her head. "I prefer to leave it to rest. I always knew that I would tell the policeman's son what he said about him before he died, and I did—I told Jacob Ross when he came to me last year. That was a promise I made to myself long ago. But as for the rest of it…"

She sighed. "The main thing that bothered me, Colin, was that I lost control and panicked. Because of my fear, I didn't speak out or run when we could have. Maybe that's why keeping my emotions steady and calm is so important to me. I find calm here, on the estate. But it's not working for me anymore, because I want to be with you. More than anything, I don't want to lose what we found this week. I want to bring it further. That's what I was trying to do by getting in that car with you."

She gazed at him, pleading and feeling desperate, laying her heart out on the table for him.

The way she saw it, she had two choices. Stay the way she was, safe in her castle and free from fear, or try again to leave so she could build a life with him on his terms. The love she was feeling for him was something she didn't want to risk losing.

Rhiannon took a deep breath. She'd been thinking about this, and it was a big step for her. "You helped me to be lady of the manor this morning, and I still want that, someday, but my mother is coming back in a few weeks. So before she returns, I'd like to take the natural progression and venture off the property. I'd like to try to leave the estate again with you, Colin. Without a car this time."

His jaw appeared to drop in surprise.

"Colin, if you could help me try one more time, if you could be patient with me again, and let me do it consciously, out of love, then that would mean a lot to me."

"I can be patient."

"So...you'll stay in Scotland a while longer, then?"

"Yes. McGuff's specialist thinks it will take two weeks to recover enough that I can play again. Until then, I'll stay here. But after that, I'm spending a month in boot camp with a swing coach, and then some training practice before I head back to the tour."

"Sounds like you'll be busy," she said wistfully.

"I travel, Rhiannon. It's the reality of my life."

She didn't know if she could ever live like that. It was too much for her to even contemplate that lifestyle right now.

Colin obviously saw her reluctance. He nudged her. "The boot camp I'm going to is at a quiet, peaceful location in the Arizona desert near Sedona. Rhiannon, it's a painter's paradise. We could find a private cabin near the golf course where you wouldn't be bothered by outside people. If you could make it there...if I could arrange a private flight for you out of Inverness, I think you'd love it. Really love it."

That was a big step for her. A *huge* step. It was terrifying to think of that unknown.

But she looked at Colin sitting across from her, so relaxed and casual. His top buttons were undone, and his kilt was askew. Whenever she let herself gaze at him for any length of time, she felt herself falling for him a wee bit more. She thought of the condoms upstairs and the way that he'd kissed her.

She *wanted* that closeness with him.

He noticed her looking him up and down, from the edge of his kilt to the chest hair peeking through his shirt, and he gave her one of those knowing smiles, letting his head fall back against the leather couch.

"Rhiannon, do you want to live? Really live with me?"

She was mad with it—the yearning for him, imagining the feel of his hands sliding over her skin, of his hard body close to hers.

"Yes. But I've got to cross the border first." The boundary of her estate to the outside world. She didn't know if she could do it.

"We'll make it happen," he said, rising suddenly.

She drew in her breath, dizzy with the power of his presence —even on one foot and with a pair of metal crutches.

When Colin said he was going to do something, he did it, and with flair that was his alone.

*Two more weeks,* she thought. *I have two more weeks with him.*

Gazing at him, she wondered if what she felt for him was enough motivation for her to actually leave.

## CHAPTER THIRTEEN

BY THE NEXT AFTERNOON, Colin had decided that if he had to be sidelined by an injury, then he was in the best place in the world to recuperate.

Rhiannon fussed over him, moving him into one of the empty ground-level guest rooms in the outbuilding that housed her studio. When he'd returned to his grandmother's cottage after talking to Rhiannon that afternoon, the first thing he'd done was pack his duffel bag and his clubs. With a straight face, he'd told Jessie that the move made sense because he had difficulty climbing her steep staircase with the boot on his foot.

Jessie had only smiled at him. Colin was sure she knew what was up.

He loved being near Rhiannon. When she'd said she wanted to try again to leave the estate and that she wanted him to help her, he'd felt a big "Hell, yeah!" scream inside him. The part about Sedona—about finding a cabin alone in the desert—had been pure spur-of-the-moment thinking on his part.

It made sense, though. Sedona was remote and quiet, similar to her home. He hoped it would be an appropriate first step in helping her experience life beyond the castle.

He stood in the guest room with the windows that looked over the back maze, the morning light warm on his face, and he pulled on his navy T-shirt and a pair of cargo shorts. His grandmother had laundered everything for him, and his clothes smelled like her detergent. He liked it.

Scotland was having a relative heat wave. About time, considering it was almost July. He would miss the barbecues and fireworks of the holiday on the Fourth at home, but it was a small price to pay. Daisie Lee wouldn't be thrilled, but Colin had phoned her before the gathering yesterday, and he didn't owe her a call back for another week. The new boundaries in their mother-son relationship made him breathe easier. He liked not having to worry about her so much.

He was starting to believe that this could happen—that he could have the change he wanted in his life and that Rhiannon could work to leave the estate with him. It still concerned him that she'd refused to bring in a professional to talk with, but if there was anything that Colin knew, it was he couldn't make people do the things they didn't want to do. That was just futile.

He heard music drifting from an open window in Rhiannon's studio above him. The smell of paint and turpentine was heavy in the air. He had appointments to attend—a therapeutic treatment with heated wraps that McGuff had set up, and then a conference call to a tour official in the States—he needed to head out soon to pick up McGuff. He slung his backpack over his shoulder and grabbed his car keys, then hopped over using his good foot and opened the door.

Rhiannon came bounding down the stairs. She wore that halter top that drove him crazy, the one that didn't exactly cover everything. He found himself staring, mesmerized.

She paused when she saw him standing in the open doorway. "Oh! Colin." Her expression was awkward.

"What are you painting today?" he asked.

"*Who.* It's a portrait," she said shyly.

"Someone's posing for you?"

She flushed. "Paul is. He's up in my studio."

Paul wasn't competition to Colin at all. Still... "Don't you want to paint *me?*" he asked, a little bit hurt.

"Yes. Of course." She gave Colin a guilty smile before changing the subject. "How is the room? Are you comfortable there? Did you sleep well?"

"I sure did." She'd fixed up the room nicely for him, even though it didn't have any furniture inside except a mattress and a low table, which amused him. "The bedding and the towels are great. The water isn't working in the shower down the hall, though, so do you mind if I use a shower in the castle?"

"Oh." She fidgeted. "My father shut that water off before he left. I completely forgot." Her tongue came out and licked her lips. "There's a shower in the bathroom attached to my room. You know where my bedroom in the castle is, right?" She was avoiding his eyes.

He knew where her bedroom was, exactly. "Yes."

"Will you, um, be able to walk up the staircase?"

To get to her bedroom? He'd crawl if he had to. "I'll manage," he said, trying not to smile.

She nodded. Her hair was messed up, tousled in the back. He had the urge to run his hand through it and fix it. But Rhiannon was being shy with him, maybe about the painting— maybe about him being in her bedroom—so he didn't push it.

The sharp edges of his car keys dug into his palm. Truthfully he would like to push it, but that wouldn't be wise or right.

She noticed his car keys. "Where are you going?"

"To Inverness to meet McGuff. I should leave now. I'll shower when I get back."

She frowned. "You can drive with your foot like that?"

"It's my left foot, Rhiannon."

"Oh." She nodded. "Right."

"No, left."

She didn't get his small joke. She seemed distracted. She swept her eyes over his torso. Bit her lip. Flicked her gaze up to meet his stare. Blushed and then glanced away again.

He bit back his own smile again. His girl was shy, he knew that. Now would be a good time for him to leave, but he lingered anyway, just watching her. There was something about her that made him want to sit and watch her move all day.

One good thing about the delay in his training—it gave him time to spend with Rhiannon. Now he just had to figure out a way to make her feel better about crossing the estate boundaries again.

The door to her studio creaked open above them, and Paul descended the stairs. "Hello," he said when he saw them. To Rhiannon, he said, "Are we finished, then?"

Colin didn't like the glow that Paul was exuding. He was too damn happy, humming and light in his step. But what man wouldn't be, with all Rhiannon's attention focused on him as she painted?

"Sorry," Rhiannon said to Paul. "I forgot about you up there. Why don't we take a break for a bit?"

She glanced at Colin. "May I carry that for you to the car?" She indicated his backpack.

The backpack was newly important to him—his receptacle because he couldn't carry items *and* use his crutches at the same time. But he wanted to be clear with Rhiannon that he wasn't incapable. "No, thanks, I'm fine."

He resisted the urge to use the crutches and instead, walking slowly, tested the weight on his left foot. The doctor—the sports doctor who McGuff had brought him to—had recommended Colin try this periodically to aid with the healing. It didn't hurt much, to his relief. The foot just felt tender.

Rhiannon ambled along beside him at his snail's pace. He said nothing as he concentrated on his footing. She was quiet with him, too. Hopefully, if Colin did everything right, his injury would heal well.

"What would you like for dinner?" he asked when they finally got to the car. "I'll pick up something for us to share tonight."

She blushed again. "You don't have to do that," she murmured.

"I get hungry, Rhiannon." He'd said it harsher than he'd meant.

"I know you get hungry. I get hungry, too." She stared at the car, trembling.

He could kick himself. He'd forgotten how meaningful this damn car was to them. She'd been inside it when she'd had her panic attack. "Rhiannon, I'm sorry. You don't have to—"

"I *want* to," she insisted.

She gave him a slight nudge, so he did what she was urging him, and sat inside the car.

Rhiannon got in after him. Sitting lightly atop him, straddling him with her knees, she bracketed his face in her hands and kissed him, light kisses that she rained down on him.

"Hey," he said softly, and gently touched her cheek. She looked terrified, frankly. "I know you're worried about something. Please don't be afraid of me."

"I'm not," she whispered.

He kissed her back, slowly and gently. Sifted his hands through her beautiful hair.

She made a small whimper. In her shorts, she rubbed against him, as if making love, but with their clothes on.

He did his damnedest not to squirm. He held her hips lightly, caressing her thighs with his thumb.

In the back of her throat, she moaned. Her skin was warm to

his touch. The air smelled like the intoxicating sweetness of her perfume. He felt himself growing aroused.

Abruptly, she backed away. She seemed filled with emotion, her chest rising and falling and her hands trembling with feeling. "Colin, I *want* to drive with you. I *want* to shop with you for dinner. I want to do everything that other people take for granted."

"We'll do all that," he said, still breathing heavily, not sure where this was going, but wanting to reassure her. "I swear we will."

"I honestly worry," she said in a low voice. "I thought about it last night after we went to bed, walked through it all in my mind, and I think I got scared. That's why I've decided to paint everybody. I'm trying... I want to say goodbye to them that way. I think it will nudge me forward."

"You're not saying goodbye to me, are you?"

"No." She gave him a hesitant smile, but then climbed out of the car and stood on the loose gravel. She rubbed her arms, glancing around, but there wasn't a soul to see them. The guardhouse wasn't visible from this angle and Paul was out back in the kitchen.

"But you're afraid of me, is that it?"

"No. It's just that... I'm not experienced." She looked inside the car at him. At his eyes, then...down at his pants.

He was still aroused. *Damn it.*

He placed his backpack on his lap. "I think I know what we need to do."

*Romance her. Make her a really nice dinner and help her relax.*

"Yes," she interrupted his reverie, "I know what I need to do, too. Please just give me time." She set her chin.

Before he could say a word, she'd turned and walked off in light, quick steps, across the drawbridge before disappearing inside her castle.

He closed his eyes and groaned. He knew better than to chase her. She was skittish, and even contemplating leaving the estate was a huge step for her—he knew that.

*Let her go. You can't change her.*

But it was a good lesson to learn now—if he gave her his heart, he might not get it back. As much as he pretended that wasn't so, it was.

———

FOUR HOURS LATER, Colin returned to the castle from his day in Inverness.

He was hot and irritable. He'd sweated through a workout that involved floor work, stretching, some moves with rubber bands, but nothing that stressed his injured foot. Then he'd had a long talk with McGuff about the upcoming tournament. But it was hard to concentrate on anything else but Rhiannon, especially after what had happened in the car earlier.

Privately, Colin had decided that he wouldn't push her until she was ready. She'd asked for more time and he would give it to her.

He just felt so raw with her. He didn't think he could deal with her not being able to be with him. Not after everything else that had gone wrong in the past weeks—his injury, his break from Mack, his failure with his father.

He'd brought back some dinner, enough for three, so that Paul could join them. Colin would use him as a buffer, at least for now. He'd found some great-looking fish at a stall in town, and together with some local vegetables and a box of pastries, he would assemble an easy meal.

He slung his backpack over his shoulder and hobbled his way toward Paul's kitchen using the crutches. He left the dinner in the refrigerator for now, and then concentrated on his slow, painful course up the long, curved central staircase to the working shower Rhiannon had suggested he use.

Her bedroom was in the same place at the end of the long hall where he remembered it, but that was where the similarity ended. She had a king-size bed now, unmade, and a sitting area off to the side. He felt as though he was intruding, so he didn't look at her things any more than he had to. He just grabbed a clean bath towel from a stack inside the bathroom, took off his medical boot, stripped out of his clothes and turned on the water.

Before he hopped inside the large, tiled space, he shut the door and locked it, too. Just in case she came into her room. He didn't want her embarrassed.

But he'd forgotten to bring his toiletries, so he had to use hers. Her soap. Her shampoo. Now he had the scent of Rhiannon on his skin. Great. Way to drive himself crazy.

Before he got out of the shower, he turned the water to cold. The showerhead was huge and it gave a waterfall rinse, so he just put his whole head under the spray and gritted his teeth, chattering with the chill of it.

He was breathing a whole lot easier when he finally stepped out and toweled himself off. There were a few cubbyholes inside the modern, built-in vanity, so he glanced through them, searching for a comb.

He found one beside a stack of what appeared to be...*condoms.*

What was she doing with condoms? Colin paused. He pulled out the stack. Three of them. Lubricated. Extra large.

O-kay. He wrapped the towel around his waist. Water dripped from his hair and trickled down his chest.

He didn't know what to think.

The doorknob rattled.

Colin sucked in his breath. Without thinking, he unlocked

and opened the door.

"Oh! I'm sorry, Colin! I didn't know you were here." Rhiannon stood with both hands up as if she was coming in to wash them from her painting session.

Colin stepped back so that she could enter. He realized he was still holding the condoms, so he dropped them back in their cubbyhole quickly. "Uh. I was looking for a comb."

But Rhiannon noticed that he'd found her condoms and blushed furiously. Her skin went completely pink.

Yeah, he was embarrassed, too. The water kept dripping down his chest. Down his legs.

Rhiannon backed up against the doorjamb. Her gaze traveled from his face and then down the rest of his body.

He could barely breathe. He'd subjected himself to a frigid shower, but he felt anything but cold now.

"I can't believe this," she murmured, blinking fast. And then her lips started to quiver.

"I was just leaving."

"Don't!" Her eyes rose to meet his. "It's not you. I'm just...sad."

"About what?" he asked softly.

She took the condoms from the cubbyhole and held them out to him. "I didn't tell you, but Kristin gave me these the day of the gathering."

He'd hoped they'd been for him, but he wasn't going to assume anything. He waited for her explanation.

"Colin, since you can't take walks with me in the morning anymore, I walked today by myself. As an experiment, I tried to cross the boundary line." She gazed at her feet, looking so forlorn. "And I still can't do it."

"Is that what you're most worried about? That you won't be able to leave the estate after all?"

She nodded.

"Aw, Rhiannon." He reached out and cupped her cheek. "I thought we were going to do it together."

She looked hesitantly up at him. "Do you think I'm a freak?"

"No. And I never will. No matter what."

———

WITH HIS REASSURANCES, Rhiannon felt some of her misery lift. She'd been wrestling with her failure ever since morning. She'd woken up wondering how she could fulfill what she'd promised him yesterday—to try again to leave the estate. Her bravado had left her, and she was left with an achy feeling inside, and full of doubt. But while she doubted herself, she also longed for Colin.

Now, with his big, calloused hand cupping her cheek and his warm blue eyes smiling down at her, she felt a glimpse of hope that together, maybe they really could handle anything.

She rubbed her fingers against the towel that was slung low around his hips. She touched his flat stomach, the skin so smooth, rippling with muscles underneath. The skin here was paler, not as tanned from the sun as his arms were. A Texan golfer's tan, was what she supposed he had. Oh, how she ached to bring him into her studio.

She ached to do so much more than that to him.

Drawing in her breath, she decided to just come out with it. "Colin, could we please...?"

"Yes, Rhiannon?"

She licked her lips, her mouth feeling so dry.

With one hand he scooped her hair, moved it to her back. His lips brushed against her neck, close to her ear. She shivered.

"Come here," he murmured. "Let me do something for you."

It sounded enticing. And fun. "Wh-what?" she asked, breathless.

"Get your mind out of the gutter," he joked. "Here, stand in front of the sink. I'm going to wash your hands for you. Isn't that what you came in here for?"

It had been. Chuckling at her, he motioned her over to the sink. Turning the water on, he stood behind her, arms around her, and slowly, sensually soaped up her hands. She had blotches of paint all over them, and they smelled of thinner, too. Not so very romantic or sensual of her.

But the way Colin lathered her fingers with soap and rubbed his hands over hers was extremely romantic and sensual. She'd never realized there were so many nerve endings in the hands. She sighed and leaned back against him.

He felt so nice. She just needed to remind herself that of all the people in the world, Colin Walker was the person she most wanted to be with. He had never hurt her and he never would. Over and over, he'd proved that she could trust him.

When her hands were sparkling clean, he turned off the tap. But he wasn't finished with his ministrations yet. He opened a jar of hand cream—part of Malcolm's Born in Vermont brand that her sister-in-law sent her from overseas—and rubbed a generous amount into the tops of her hands, her wrists, between each finger. Colin was thorough. Gentle.

The smell of lavender essential oil filled the tiny bathroom, calming her nerves. Through it all, Colin gazed into her eyes, giving her looks filled with adoration.

"Thank you," she murmured, rubbing her hands together and pressing them to her lips when he was finished. "That feels...really nice."

He inclined his head to her.

Licking her lips again, she glanced at the condoms on the vanity. Then at the cramped room they stood in. She reached out her hand to him. He caught it and kissed her palm.

"Rhiannon, for our first time, I don't want a quickie in the shower before the water goes cold."

She liked how he said *our first time* rather than *your first time.*

"So I have a proposal," he continued. "I'd like to make a nice dinner for us. A date, if you'd like to eat with me in your castle dining room?"

Her heart beat in an excited little staccato. He was going to make this evening beautiful for her. No pressure, no fear, just plenty of romance.

"I would love to, Colin," she breathed.

———

HOURS LATER, AS the gloaming fell across the central Highlands and the night birds began their longing calls to their mates, Rhiannon patted a serviette across her lips, enjoying the dinner Colin had cooked for them.

A light dinner—buttered whitefish with spring asparagus, and big flutes of champagne.

She appreciated the champagne—it left her feeling as if she was glowing and calmed the tiny bit of nerves she felt. Colin was his usual self—charming and a joy to converse with. He seemed carefree, as if they weren't about to take a big step that would change the heart of their relationship forever.

If she went back to his room with him, they never again could go back to being "just friends."

They would be lovers.

She took a sip of champagne, the last of the flute. The last of the bottle.

Colin stood and lifted their dirty plates.

"What are you doing?" She winked at him. "We have Paul for that."

"This is *our* date, Rhiannon."

"He's a butler. He takes pride in his job. If you do it, he'll be angry with me tomorrow."

"Ah." Colin smiled and put the plates down. "The lifestyles of the rich and famous."

She laughed.

He glanced at the clock, then at her. Making a formal bow, he said, "Thank you, my lady. I'll be leaving you now. I trust you can get back safely to your room?"

She frowned at him. "I thought I was going back to your room?"

His lips twisted. She couldn't tell what he was thinking.

Finally, he sat again. "Maybe you'd like to wait for marriage...?"

She stared at him in confusion. He hadn't offered to marry her. She knew this.

"Why?" she asked with a smile. "It's fine, Colin. With you, I would definitely live in sin. At least for tonight."

"You don't have to do that for me."

She wanted to, and not *for* him but for herself. She leaned closer to him. "I know you have a lot of things you're committed to—your career, your life in Texas, your grandparents in Scotland. I won't pretend I'm more important to you than any of that. I have my own...*things,* too."

Her agoraphobia, for one.

Frowning to herself, she pushed away that thought. "Tonight, I want to stay with you. Just...one night." To be a normal person. "Do you want to do that, Colin?"

For a split second he blinked at her, hesitating.

*Don't ask me if I'm sure. I am sure.*

He picked up his crutches and motioned to the door. "My room," he murmured.

"Naturally." She'd preferred it that way. It made her feel as if she was actually being brave and daring. Goodness knew, she needed to be brave and daring about something.

She was quiet as they slowly walked the darkening path that led to her studio outbuilding. To the room he stayed in. The night air was cool, and she held back her hair with one hand in order to feel the breeze brush past her neck. She'd dressed lightly, in barely any clothing. A short, sleeveless dress of thin linen material that rubbed her skin as she moved. The whole thing was closed by a row of buttons that went top to bottom.

Colin had dressed up for her, too.

She glanced at him, so handsome in the moonlight. Her heart beat faster. Desire for him seemed to pool in her belly.

They'd stopped before the door to her outbuilding. He had a key now. She waited for him to unlock it.

"Ah, Rhiannon." He turned to her and gave her a heartfelt sigh. "Nothing about you has been what I expected."

Yes, she was complicated. Weren't most women? "I'm not that pigtailed girl who ran after you through the woods."

"No, you're not." He drew her close and gave her a kiss, full on the mouth. She moaned and leaned into him.

———

"LET'S GET YOU INSIDE." With one hand he led her over the threshold, then down the hall on the first floor to the guest room farthest away.

She'd chosen it for him because she couldn't remember anybody else staying here, ever. The rooms were used as overflow during family weddings and quarterly meetings regarding their trust funds, but this room wasn't typically occupied because it was the only one without furniture. To make up for the lack of furnishings, she'd dragged one of the mattresses inside—the nicest one.

He unlocked and opened the guest-room door for her, too.

Inside, the soft glow from a small lamp flickered on a low

table beside the bed. The room was bare and neat, devoid of anything else but the made-up bedding and two plump pillows.

"If I'd known you were coming, I would have strewn it with rose petals," he said.

She pressed her hands to her lips. "That sounds romantic and lovely."

"You're romantic and lovely."

"Really? I wish I'd known this about myself earlier."

"I knew." He laughed and put his hands around her waist. "I loved you as a boy. I'll love you as a man. And as long as we're true to each other, I'll love you when I'm a worn-out geezer."

She smiled, too, curling into his arms. "You always were a charmer." Cupping his cheek, she pulled him down to kiss her.

Everything turned tender all at once, and the night felt like a dream. He was gentle with her. First, he drew her down with him as they lay across the bed, still dressed in everything but their shoes. With his hand bracing his head, he told her all about his home in Texas.

The lamplight shone across his face as he spoke of his life there. She'd never really asked him about this part of his world before. She wanted to hear about it. She wanted to know everything about him, everything she'd missed—not just what his body would feel like joined to hers, but his dreams, his home, his desires. She was glad he was taking this slow approach with her. She'd decided to let him lead the way—she would follow him wherever he took her.

"Did you ever have horses?" she asked him, lazily stretching her toes, intertwining her legs in his. "I always imagined you back in Texas with horses."

"No, Rhiannon. I never lived on that ranch. Mom and I stayed in a...homey trailer...and got used to living as two people in the family."

He smiled at her. As he spoke, he leisurely unbuttoned her

dress. She took her time unbuttoning his shirt, too. She finished before he did, and she pressed a palm to his warm skin.

"Now I live in a big house," he said, "and it's a lot for just one guy. But I'd always promised myself that after living in a cramped tin can, as soon as I made any money I'd buy my own castle."

She laughed. "*Is* it like a castle?"

He chuckled, too, and as he did, she felt the lifeblood of him moving beneath her palm. His laughter. His heartbeat.

"Yes, Rhiannon, I have a big stone fireplace, and I have a set of crossed swords over it, too."

"Truly?"

"Um-hmm." He'd succeeded in opening her dress, and now he was lightly running his hand over her belly, over her breasts. She sighed and stretched beneath his touch. She'd worn a skimpy white lace bra and panty set that she'd chosen because it reminded her of frilly wedding-night wear. Silly of her, maybe, but that was how she felt with Colin—silly and free.

The lacy bra opened from the front. Colin undid the plastic clasp. Laid aside the scratchy material. Coolness from the night air and the open window brushed over her skin, tightening her nipples.

His caresses—the small circles he drew while he spoke, the languid strokes of his seduction—heated her skin and filled her with unfamiliar, pleasurable sensations.

His hair fell over his eyes, covering them, so she smoothed his hair aside. It was soft and fine beneath her fingers. She adored watching his eyes as the slight glow from the lamp lit his face.

"What else is in your castle?" she asked.

"Hmm. One thing I have that you don't is a pool. Not as cold as a loch in August, but... I'll take you skinny-dipping there sometime by moonlight if you'd like."

"We never did *that* when we were young."

"No, but isn't it high time we did?" His hand lightly stroked over the lace panties.

She groaned and raised her hips to meet his touch.

"Yes. Oh, yes, it is time," she whispered.

He leaned over and kissed her, gently, deeply, thoroughly. His fingertips stroked her breasts, caressed her nipples. He was learning the landscape of her body by gentle exploration.

She had already thoroughly assessed his. The broad chest with the smattering of hair between his breastbone, and then the long line that dipped over his belly button and disappeared under his waistband. As he pressed and stroked against the flimsy white lace of her panties, an urgency, a hunger for him built within her.

"Please," she whispered to him. Her fingers shaky, she unbuttoned and unzipped his trousers.

Without a word, he stripped off the rest of his clothes. She leaned back on one elbow, drinking in his body. In the flickering candlelight, he looked so beautiful. Long, muscular legs. Everything just...perfect. She'd studied figure drawing as a correspondence course, but she'd never...she'd never...

Tentatively, she touched him. Stroked the length of him, ending with her palm on the smooth head, damp with a bead of male fluid. She rubbed her palm over it, and he sucked in his breath.

A look of ecstasy took over his face. She reached below him and gently cupped his testicles.

"Ah, Rhiannon," he breathed. "How did I live without you?"

"Not as well," she said cheerfully.

He laughed and then caught her mouth in his, rolling her over onto her back, drawing up her knees on either side of her, exposing her in a way that was vulnerable.

He drew back, upright on his knees. Reaching for his

discarded trousers, the metal zipper making a clinking noise, he fumbled in the pockets.

"A condom," he said solemnly. "Will you help me?"

Her heart feeling full, she nodded, her head back on the pillows. He guided her hands over his. "Place them on mine," he said. She kept the connection with him, through his eyes, through his hands, through the warmth of his body touching hers.

Gently, the condom was unrolled. Sheathed.

"Rhiannon," he whispered in a shaking voice, "I...don't want to hurt..."

"You won't." But oh, she wanted him. She didn't feel in the least afraid. If she could walk over the estate line with her heart as full and as happy as she felt right now, then they both would be in a fine place, indeed.

Settling in, she raised her hips and guided him in. Slowly, so slowly. She kept her eyes on Colin's, the connection between them a taut, emotional line.

His body, joining hers, filled her. A feeling of fullness, of completion. A tiny bit of pain at first, but it eased as her body stretched and adapted to his.

"Oh, Rhiannon." He kissed her deeply, his arms trembling. He kept still, waiting for her to feel ready. And then the pleasure returned. She moved slowly, then with more urgency, meeting his thrusts. There was more pleasure this time, and she kept going. She took charge, a completion of what they'd started in the car earlier. And once she'd surrendered to it, letting Colin's body bring her to bliss, suffusing over her, it was a thing of beauty.

She sighed. Utterly content, she nestled her cheek against the warmth of his chest.

CHAPTER FOURTEEN

RHIANNON NEVER DID go back to sleeping alone again. For the remainder of their two weeks together, they shared rooms, though she did prefer staying in the little, odd guest room that no one but she and Colin had ever slept inside.

The romance of the new place they'd set up together was what drew her. Bit by bit she fixed it up as if they really were a couple. A silly fantasy—given that she had yet to leave the estate with him. But she pretended that she had. She moved in a small chest of drawers and filled it with some clothes. Turned the bed so that the morning rays woke them through the east-facing window. Colin took the side closest to the door; Rhiannon, to the left of him.

She never tired of falling asleep in his arms. Of discovering the pleasures of becoming physically closer to him. Making love before the dawn when they were both still sleepy. In the shower, while they washed each other and laughed under the spray of her waterfall showerhead.

She felt as if she were in heaven, so content. Inside her heart, she was preparing to leave the estate. She'd completed all eight of the small portraits. And on their last Friday together, she lined them up in her studio and gazed at them.

Colin, her aging cat. Molly, her mother's dog. Both her parents, painted from a digital photograph she kept on her computer. Jamie and Jessie, painted from a studio session, and Paul's portrait completed the same way.

The eighth portrait was of Malcolm, even though technically he didn't live at the castle anymore. Still, he'd been part of her day-to-day life for so long, she felt as if she was finally saying goodbye to him as well.

"Don't make it into too big a deal," Colin warned her. "Don't build *leaving* into so much that it scares you."

"I'm not thinking about the *act* of leaving," she said. "I'm thinking about the *place* I'm leaving—my reclusive refuge." Saying goodbye to the person she'd been for so long—most of her life. "It's going to be a challenge to stay calm when I'm away from my garden."

"All I can offer for advice," Colin said, "is that when I'm at a tournament and I need to stay calm, I keep my thoughts focused on the hole I'm playing. If I thought back to the last hole I'd played or the hole yet to come, then I'd lose my concentration and not be able to play at all."

"Given that analogy, I suppose I'm stuck at the seventeenth hole, unable to move on to the eighteenth."

"That was in the past," Colin said quickly. "This time, we have a plan."

———

THEY DID INDEED have a plan. One that involved whisking Rhiannon to the cabin in the desert without coming into contact with hardly anyone except Colin. They'd thoroughly discussed the logistics. From private car, to plane, to car again—with just the two of them inside.

Colin walked from the outbuilding where he and Rhiannon had been living for the past two weeks. He headed for the rental car they were loading with his and Rhiannon's luggage.

His foot had healed and felt much better now. It still wasn't in top form—and neither was his swing—but he'd arranged a sweet little rental cottage for them in the Sedona Desert of Arizona for the next four weeks while he trained and prepared for his tournament.

Beyond that, who knew? He didn't think of anything past that point. For now, it was enough they were leaving the castle together.

Rhiannon wanted a big ceremony and he'd been unable to talk her out of it. Her thinking was that if everyone was there to see her "succeed," then she would be less apt to lose control and "fail."

Her words, not his. Rhiannon was more conscientious, more black-and-white in her thinking and less carefree than he was, and probably always would be. It was her personality, and he appreciated her for who she was. He didn't argue.

She'd arranged to have the people in her castle life present today to see her off: Jamie and Jessie; Paul the butler. Paul even carried her pets outside. Rhiannon said goodbye to everyone, but she sobbed hardest of all at leaving her aging cat.

It was just impossible to bring him. Even if he survived the trauma of the flight, there were quarantine laws for animals.

Rhiannon's uncle had arranged for Colin and Rhiannon to fly privately on the Sage family's company jet. John Sage still didn't like Colin, but it was clear that Sage would always adore his niece. And when Rhiannon had told her uncle that Colin came as part of her "package," what was Sage to do?

Colin watched Rhiannon as she gently set Colin the cat on

the ground, then wiped her eyes with the back of her hand.

"We'll call him on internet videophone every night," Colin reassured her.

Rhiannon sniffed. "I know."

Molly the dog was next, and Rhiannon gave her a big hug, too.

"Let's go," she said, turning to Colin, "before I change my mind."

They walked over to the rental car, where Jessie and Jamie waited. Jessie was dabbing at her eye with a white handkerchief.

"Come on now," Colin said. "We're visiting again in September, after my first two tournaments are over. We're not leaving forever."

"It's not the same," Jessie cried. She and Rhiannon hugged each other tight.

That was another change in Rhiannon. Colin had never seen her touch anyone much at all when he first arrived at the castle. Now she did it at the drop of a hat.

"It's all those female hormones," Jamie muttered. Stoically, he held out his hand to Colin. "Goodbye, lad. You'll be coming home for Christmas this year, aye?"

"Yeah," Colin said. "Hogmanay, too."

"Of course." Jamie drew himself up in outrage, as if any other option was heresy. He gave Colin a sideways glance. "And what about Daisie Lee?"

Colin sighed. "She's welcome to come with us if she'd like." He planned to make the offer to her—he and his other grandmother were the only two people Daisie Lee had left in her life. "If my mom doesn't want to come, I'll be sorry to spend the holidays without her this year. But that's the way it will have to be."

It was clear he was engaged in a new balancing act. That was the choice he'd made. The life he wanted to commit to.

"Are you ready, Rhiannon?" he called to her.

"In a moment." She trotted over to Jamie, still wiping her eyes.

"Now, Jamie," she began, "you'll be helping Paul with anything that needs doing at the castle? At least until my father returns end of August, I mean."

"Aye," Jamie agreed.

"And you'll remind Jessie to take her medication. You'll drive her to her doctor's visits as scheduled?"

With anyone else, Jamie would have taken offense at the implication that he couldn't see to taking care of his own wife. But Jamie would always have a soft spot in his heart for Rhiannon. "Aye, lass. She'll be fine. Don't worry about her."

Colin glanced back at his nana. Rhiannon had finally gotten Jamie to confess that Jessie was being treated for a heart condition. Colin now knew that this diagnosis had been the initial trigger that had driven her to make up the story about his father in order to get Colin to Scotland in the first place.

Colin shook his head. It seemed so long ago—weeks ago. He'd forgiven all, and in doing so, his life was already better. Everything he wanted was in front of him.

"Ready, Rhiannon?" He had her on his side. Now they were leaving so he could fight his way back into the golf world. He was itching to get started again. He missed it—the tournament play, the competition—with a fierceness that surprised him.

Rhiannon gave him a goofy smile. He shut the trunk of the car. Between the trunk and the backseat, eight small portraits had somehow fit inside, along with four suitcases of clothing, his golf clubs and all of Rhiannon's art supplies so she could paint in the desert.

Rhiannon gave him a long embrace. He closed his eyes and breathing deeply of her scent, sifted her hair in his hands.

He would miss this place, the Shangri-la where he'd spent most of the happiest times of his life. Part of him regretted tearing her from the roots, but Rhiannon wasn't meant to be a recluse. Getting her into the wide world with him really was the best thing for her.

He took her aside so they could speak in private. He meant to give her one last pep talk. All good coaches gave inspirational speeches, and she deserved no less.

Clasping her hand, he faced the top of the long driveway with her.

"We'll walk together up the hill," she said. "Won't we?"

That was the plan. He gazed into her eyes, nodding, and gently squeezed her hand. "Do you remember what we talked about, how you'll be taking your secret garden with you?"

She nodded, too, so he continued in a low voice, as soothing as he could make it. "The whole world can be your secret garden, Rhiannon. Always remember that, and you'll keep the good feeling with you."

The tip of her tongue darted out, licked nervously at her lips. "What if I can't?" she asked. "Will you still accept me as I am?"

*No. Don't go there, Rhiannon. Failure isn't an option.*

But he maintained his smile for her. "I appreciate you for who you are. This mistaken view of yourself as a recluse isn't who you are."

A line grew in her forehead. "Mistaken view? How can you say that?"

Oh, he'd screwed up. But Colin kept up his smile and squeezed her hand again. "Look at me. I've watched a strong woman navigate the thorniest of problems, with friends and strangers alike."

"The panic is real," she whispered.

Yes. He knew that. Though it wasn't the same thing, standing in front of an audience of millions where a putt was do-or-die could be panic-inducing, too.

But he didn't say any of that—wouldn't try to make that

comparison. Instead, he would speak to her from his heart. Put it all out there, feeling as vulnerable and scared as when he'd been that little kid whose dad had left him, on this very same driveway while she'd been there, too.

"Do you love me, Rhiannon? Am I enough for you?" he asked, a catch in his voice.

Her lips quivered. "Oh, Colin." She gazed into his eyes for a long time. "You're more than enough," she said quietly. "You're everything I've dreamed of. You're the reason I'm inspired to leave my estate—so I can be with you."

There was a lump in his throat, the kind you didn't just swallow away quickly. Running his hand through his hair, he nodded to Rhiannon, blinking. His vision was blurry for some strange reason.

"I'm ready," she said gently to him. "Let's walk up the hill together."

She squeezed his hand and started the trek with him.

It was a long walk directly into the setting sun. Like following the rainbow to see what was on the other side, except that rainbows were an illusion and there was never another side. Just bright shiny colors that dazzled and then disappeared into the ether without warning.

But his rainbow hadn't disappeared yet. Maybe this time it wouldn't disappear. Maybe perfect happiness really was possible.

That was what it felt like to Colin. The property line was there, shimmering in the heat ahead of them. They were aiming for it together.

Rhiannon stepped over the border onto the roadway...

Time seemed suspended. A car drove past them. *Whoosh.*

Rhiannon recoiled.

"Look at me," Colin said. "Look into my eyes. Stay with me... We'll be fine, as long as we're together."

Another car drove past them, faster this time. Another *whoosh. What in the hell?* Colin thought.

"Please, Rhiannon."

But it was too late. She'd run back to her side of the castle.

"Don't you give up on us," he called. "Don't you give up!"

She crumpled into a ball, crying and holding her sides. Shaking, as if the fear of a thousand storms were raining down on her.

"Rhiannon!" He shook her, trying to call her out of her trance.

"Colin, that's enough!" Jamie had hastened up the drive, steering Jessie's motorized scooter. "You let Rhiannon be!"

Jamie was right. Colin knelt beside her, holding her in his arms, cradling her. "It's all right," he said. "Shhh, you'll be all right."

He took over the buggy from Jamie and brought Rhiannon back to her castle. Back to her safety and what she needed.

———

MAYBE HER INITIAL BELIEFS had been right all along, Rhiannon decided. She was just too damaged, unable to have the kind of life other people had.

Whoever heard of an agoraphobic out in the world, traveling about with a globe-trotting man, anyway? It was absurd.

Colin left for the airport after he couldn't delay it any longer without risking missing his flight time.

She supported what Colin needed to do for his career. He'd tried everything to keep her with him.

Rhiannon stayed in the castle so she didn't have to see Colin drive away. He'd unpacked the car, and she averted her face as Paul sadly but dutifully carried back her paints, her portraits, her luggage.

That night, Rhiannon moved permanently from the castle to the outbuilding. Up in her art studio, she poured her grief into painting a portrait of Colin. It was the most beautiful work she'd ever done. She needed no camera, no photograph, no sitting. It poured out of her from memory. From love.

That effort took days of blessed concentration and absorption in her work, and when she'd finished, she hung the portrait in the guest room she and Colin had lived in together.

She spent hours curled up on the bed, sleeping with her face pressed to his pillowcase, which she'd refused to wash—she could still smell him on it. Gazing at the portrait of Colin gave her comfort because it helped her to remember what they'd had.

In the end, even though her relationship with Colin had strengthened her by inspiring her to push and expand her boundaries, it had weakened her, too. She felt as though she'd failed. What was the point in going on each day if each day she only failed again?

He did call her once a day, but he seemed exhausted and so far away, not only physically but emotionally. She put on a good front, reassuring him that everything was all right with her. She got the feeling that he did the same for her, too. They both knew there was nothing more they could do for each other. Even his love couldn't change her. Even her willpower couldn't defeat the panic attacks that she'd lived with for so long.

And every day, more of the spark went out of their relationship.

If it went on like this, she feared, there would come a point someday when it would die completely. She knew the risks, but felt powerless to change course.

Paul worried for her. And Rhiannon couldn't lie to him, because he saw her plainly before him each day. At first, she neglected eating. But Paul fed her dutifully, and she tried to take better care of herself, for his sake. Jessie stopped by often with pies and other fattening treats. Jamie brought supplies from town, including frames to make more canvases, but Rhiannon didn't have the heart to start any new projects.

And then one day, Rhiannon's cousin Isabel showed up. Rhiannon was grateful to see her. Isabel Sage had a master talent for putting on a good face. Of all Rhiannon's family and friends, Isabel was the one least likely to chasten Rhiannon, or even show any type of worry or horror over Rhiannon's red eyes or puffy appearance.

"Hi, Rhiannon!" Isabel swept in like a perfect, beautiful, gracious guest. She grinned at Rhiannon, showing her dimples, and then kissed her on each cheek. "I'm sorry I stopped in without warning, but I was in the area and got an idea it would be fun to have an early lunch with you. Here." She opened a bag to reveal two green salads. Rhiannon's stomach seemed to turn over in rebellion, but honestly, a salad would be better for her than forcing down another slice of Jessie's lemon pie.

Isabel sat at a table in the back kitchen and entertained Rhiannon with amusing stories of the office where she and Rhiannon's brother, Malcolm, worked. Isabel was president of the cosmetics division.

"...and I brought you some lipstick samples," Isabel said, digging into her voluminous purse. "We've been doing a whole campaign with new colors for autumn based on the Highlands."

"That's great," Rhiannon murmured, gazing at the sprawl of mini lipstick tubes across her kitchen table.

"This is the color I chose for my wedding dress," Isabel babbled. "And this one complements the bridesmaid dresses I chose." She sighed, gazing at Rhiannon. "With your dark hair, it goes perfectly. It's too bad that—"

Her eyes widening, Isabel caught herself. But without missing a beat, she laughed at herself. "I come here intending to buck you up, but then I do the opposite and stick my foot in it. Never mind me and my wedding. Enough said. In my heart, you're my dear maid of honor, so we'll leave it at that. Tell me about your parents. The summer will be over soon. Are you excited they'll be coming back from their trip?"

"I could still be your maid of honor," Rhiannon said irritably. "I'll be present through videoconferencing at the church. You could put the computer monitor up front with you every bit as easily as you could put it in the back."

Isabel smiled and nodded, but Rhiannon could tell that it was her "agreeable" smile. "There's a lot that goes into it," Isabel said.

"You could phone me up for each part," Rhiannon insisted, feeling stubborn. "Or someone could. I don't see why my agoraphobia has to be...the end of every relationship."

Her voice was sounding shrill. This was nothing like her. Maybe she was waking up. Maybe she was tired of mourning. And maybe she was a wee bit disappointed in Colin, too. He'd known what she was. They could work around this. They could...

Isabel patted Rhiannon's hand, bringing Rhiannon back from her thoughts. Isabel gave Rhiannon a sad but gentle smile.

But Rhiannon felt an insistence that wouldn't be denied. "What does a maid of honor do that I can't with my agoraphobia?"

Isabel waved her hand. "You're right, Rhiannon. It's perfectly silly of me. What does it matter if you're not at the reception to lift my train when I need help going to the toilet? Or hold back my hair in case I need to throw up from nerves?" She giggled lightly as if confiding, whispering behind her hand. "Which I might, because it appears I have a new history of doing that when I'm excited. Throwing up, I mean."

At the mention of "throwing up," Rhiannon had a twinge

that she might vomit, too—the visual of it hit her hard. She groaned and put her hand to her stomach.

"Yes, Rhiannon," Isabel continued, merrily talking away, "I'll put you down in the program as maid of honor. I'll put a screen on the staging beside me, and there you will be. It'll be splendid."

No, it would be ridiculous. Isabel was right. Rhiannon's life was no better than a half-life. Just because she used technology to phone Colin or see him on an internet connection, it wasn't the same as being there with him. She couldn't touch him. She couldn't hold him. She couldn't walk down a church aisle and slide into a pew beside him, or dance with him at a wedding reception.

If she didn't feel so sick to her stomach, she might actually go and do something about it, immediately—if only she knew what to do.

"You look pale as a ghost!" Isabel exclaimed. "And you're sweating. Are you ill?"

"Just...a bit nauseated. I think it's the stress."

Isabel gathered her purse. "I'm sorry. I'll go. I'm disturbing you."

"No..." Rhiannon put her hand on her cousin's sleeve. "Please don't leave. It's just...since Colin has been gone, I'm missing him more than I expected. I dream about him and when I wake up, I don't always feel physically well."

Isabel's eyes narrowed. "Does this happen every morning?"

"Usually," Rhiannon admitted. "Why?"

"Could you be pregnant?"

Rhiannon laughed. That was ridiculous. "Of course not."

"Could you *possibly* be pregnant?"

"We used birth control every time."

"Birth control isn't perfect." Isabel rose to her feet. "Please,

I'd like to run out and pick up a pregnancy test for you. Would you mind?"

But...this couldn't possibly be true! Rhiannon must have given Isabel a look of horror and fear, because Isabel clasped her hand and patted it.

"If it's false, we'll rule it out, won't we?" Isabel gave Rhiannon a gentle smile. "This will just be between you and me. My lips are sealed."

Numbly, Rhiannon tried to wrap her mind around what Isabel was saying. Could it be possible?

Because it was so far-fetched for her—an agoraphobic with a *baby*? She had never really allowed herself to imagine being pregnant. A life, growing inside her, a result of her and Colin's love for one another?

The thought made her weepy.

*Colin would make a great dad. If I could just leave this estate, I'd make a great mum, too.*

Maybe this was a sign.

"Rhiannon?"

She *needed* to change. She *needed* to get off this estate.

"I...think I would like to talk with my doctor, please," she said to Isabel.

"Your family doctor?"

"No. My therapist."

"I didn't know you had one," Isabel said, surprised.

Rhiannon had nothing to lose but her fear and her pride. Maybe Colin had been right. "I want to see the therapist I used to have. My old one, from when I was a child."

The therapist Rhiannon's family had dismissed at her insistence because she'd been so full of fear that she'd convinced herself—and them—that staying calm was the thing she'd needed most.

Turned out it wasn't.

## CHAPTER FIFTEEN

COLIN HAD HATED to leave Rhiannon behind. But he didn't have a choice. He couldn't help her overcome her fear—not even with his love.

Yes, he did believe she'd wanted to leave—she was in tears as the car left without her—but Colin couldn't make the change for her. Couldn't physically force her to cross any line.

It was clear to him that she needed professional treatment, though he hadn't been able to convince her of that while they had their weeks together in Scotland. Whenever he'd brought it up, she'd refused to discuss it.

On the Sage Family jet, her uncle had suggested that Colin face the fact that Rhiannon might never leave the estate.

*"I don't believe that,"* Colin had retorted. *"I have faith in her. She's stronger than she knows. It just isn't her time yet."*

Weeks away from her, he still believed that. But part of strength was admitting when it was time to call in the professionals.

He should know. He'd done it for himself with the coaching boot camp he was enrolled in.

He stood at a driving range on the edge of the lonely desert and toed the bucket of practice balls at his feet. He'd been working on all aspects of his game, and he was seeing results.

In the weeks he'd been away, he'd made real progress with his work. Though the best times were during the day when he was busy and didn't have to think about anything other than the job at hand.

If he hadn't gone to Scotland in the first place, hadn't stayed with his grandparents and met Rhiannon again, then nothing like this would've happened. He wouldn't have had the opportunity—or the necessary change of perspective about himself—to apply himself like he had.

He dropped a practice ball on the mat, drew his club back in an arc and drove the ball in a sweet, powerful swing. One by one he finished driving the rest of the balls, emptying his bucket.

Panting, he tugged off his glove with his teeth and ran his hand through his hair. He'd started work before dawn, stretching his muscles and joints and watching comparative videos of his swings. Now, the sun had barely risen over the top of the far mountains, and he planned to hit many more buckets of balls today, practicing his swing mechanics. His next tournament was in two weeks. That would be the test for him. He couldn't waste the opportunity to prepare.

His coach wanted to meet him for breakfast, so fifteen minutes before their appointment, he packed up his bag. He headed toward the clubhouse, missing the company of Rhiannon and Molly to walk with him in the mornings.

But if there was one thing he'd learned in all those years with his mom, and now, with his grandparents, it was that it was futile to try and force someone else into happiness.

The only *happiness* he was responsible for—and could take steps toward improving—was his own.

———

THE THERAPIST whom Rhiannon had worked with as a child had retired and was no longer living in the country. Not sure what to do, Rhiannon made an appointment with Dr. McLean, their family physician.

As always, he arrived at the castle and saw her in the privacy of her bedroom. After listening to her symptoms and her concerns about having a baby while she still suffered with agoraphobia, he suggested they start with an overall physical checkup. Happily, he declared her generally healthy—pending the results of some laboratory tests. Then he drew blood for a pregnancy test, though there would be a twenty-four-hour wait for the results.

Rhiannon pressed the small bandage on her arm, slightly embarrassed at being in the position of facing an unplanned pregnancy. "We were very careful," she remarked sheepishly. "We're not irresponsible teenagers. We always used birth control."

Dr. McLean glanced up from jotting some notes on a pad. "I know you're a responsible person, Rhiannon." He smiled kindly at her. "But in my long life, I've noted time and again how control can often be an illusion. We humans can set up our worlds as perfectly as can be, and yet still be faced with outcomes the opposite of what we intended. It's the grand irony of life."

This perspective was so counter to what she'd expected him to say that her mouth fell open at the simple truth of it.

She needed to digest this some more. She was certain he was referring to her agoraphobia, as well as her possible pregnancy.

Nothing was entirely controllable. Any person could be plucked up anywhere, surprised by a van of desperate and violent thugs intent on doing harm.

"Would you happen to have any recommendations for a

therapist who's trained to work with longtime agoraphobia clients?" she asked him.

He put down his pen. If he was surprised, he didn't show it. "I have someone in mind for you, yes. Would you mind if I speak with her first?"

Rhiannon fidgeted. She was longing to sit in her walled, secret garden and process all this. It suddenly seemed very scary again.

Through all the past work with her early therapists, she'd learned that the root of her agoraphobia was the fear that she wouldn't be able to escape if something bad happened to her again. That was why, as a child, she'd wanted to stay so close to the peace and safety of her home.

But really, if someone had wanted to hurt her again, wasn't that plan for control just an illusion, too?

Always, she'd longed for a love and family of her own, but she'd thought she couldn't have it because of her personal barrier—the agoraphobia. Now, with Colin's love and support, she had a gift. She needed to fight to keep it. She had to stop living in stasis and do battle with her agoraphobia, this time with fresh eyes and a fresh perspective.

"Yes," she said, standing, "please do contact the therapist. I'd like to begin working immediately, tomorrow, if possible. I'd like to work as hard as Colin does while he's away at his boot camp."

"Then I'll see what I can do. And I'll ring you personally with the results from the test."

"Thank you," she said quietly.

She felt a deep need to talk with Colin about everything. They'd spoken yesterday afternoon; he'd seemed tired and quiet then. He'd told her his plans to travel to Virginia to compete at his first tournament since he'd been working with his new coach. It would be the first real test of his training and commitment.

But she knew it wouldn't be wise to tell him just yet, because the best thing for him was to focus on his task at hand. If she called and told him her news over the telephone, it might overwhelm him. It might cause him to want to break off his plans and return to her, and she didn't want that.

She wanted what was best for them as a pair.

———

BEFORE RHIANNON MET with her new therapist, the results from her pregnancy test arrived.

Negative.

At first, Rhiannon was disappointed. But Dr. McLean reassured her she was a healthy young woman. He didn't see any medical reason preventing her from becoming pregnant when she stopped using birth control.

"Thank you," she said quietly, and hung up the phone.

The most important thing was that she keep her therapy appointment.

Cecily Lawson Wise arrived at the castle in a red, serviceable sedan that she parked carefully beside Rhiannon's drawbridge. Rhiannon watched her through the upstairs library curtains, but unlike usual, she decided to meet Ceci—as she preferred to be called—without going through the formal ceremony placing Paul as her barrier.

Rhiannon met Ceci at the front doors and then led her directly to her walled garden, at a table she'd set up beside the roses. What did she have to lose at this point?

Over tea, Rhiannon talked to Ceci extensively about her goals for therapy, and what she hoped to achieve.

"Because yours is such a long-term case, I'd like to start with medication," Ceci replied. "I know you prefer not to take drugs —I read it in your files that Dr. McLean sent over—but for the goals you've set out, I believe it's necessary. Later we can talk about decreasing the dosage."

Rhiannon swallowed. She'd been worried about addiction and losing control of her body. She'd been worried about a lot of things, she supposed, and surely that was a great part of her problem.

"All right," Rhiannon said softly. "But I'd like to work with other therapies as well, such as relaxation techniques—breathing, for example. A...continued shift in my thinking." She fell silent. Instead of painting, Rhiannon had begun writing in a journal, following prompts she'd read about online. So much was available over the internet these days. Much more than she'd realized.

"This is a lot for you all at once," Ceci warned.

"I know. But I'm extremely motivated to leave this estate for a trip to America. For personal reasons."

"Very well." Ceci smiled at her. Just the fact that she wasn't dismissing Rhiannon out of hand was remarkable to Rhiannon. She'd isolated herself so well that, until Colin, only people who enabled her seclusion were tolerated by her. She hadn't realized that fact until now.

"Have you worked at exposure therapy?" Ceci asked.

"What's that?"

"We'll leave the estate together in short, gradual walks with very modest goals. Down the lane, at first. To the village, eventually."

Ceci took a sip of tea, smiling gently at Rhiannon's shocked expression. "You can't expect to fly to America all at once, you know. Also..." She munched on a biscuit. "Do you have a support partner we can train? That will help immensely, especially if they can accompany you to America for your upcoming trip."

*Your upcoming trip.* Ceci did believe in her. "I have a cousin I could ask."

"Brilliant. See if she can come over and work with us one day next week." She gazed seriously at Rhiannon. "You'll be taking daily, increasingly longer walks. Eventually, you'll be doing it alone. But you'll need support throughout this change. It's quite a lot for a person to handle alone."

Rhiannon felt her muscles tensing with the fear of what Ceci described. But she *had* to let go and try the professional's techniques. "I do have support," Rhiannon said. She had Colin, especially.

"Very good." Ceci stood. "Shall we get started?"

---

OVER THE NEXT WEEK and a half, Rhiannon met daily with Ceci, pushing herself as she'd never pushed herself before. The first time she stood atop the hill over the property line, staring down at the castle beside Ceci, she had to pinch herself to believe it. The medication had helped, yes, but so had the gradual work she'd been doing on her therapies.

The last time Ceci accompanied her off the estate, they'd walked to the fairgrounds in the village where the Highland Games had taken place. On a Tuesday midmorning, the grounds were quiet. With each step, Rhiannon told herself to breathe. She thought of the peacefulness of her secret garden. She thought of Colin. Perhaps it was the medication as well as the gradual exposure, but she made it there and back again.

For the next test, Ceci accompanied her by mobile phone. Just for a walk past the guardhouse and over the lane.

Rhiannon was in the open, alone. Her palms were damp. Her breathing a little shaky. Cecily's voice in her ear walked through each step. Each breath.

Rhiannon took daily short walks and drives with Cecily.

Much like the way she supposed Colin hit golf balls, she performed her daily drills, as well.

Always, the payoff—*her* tournament—was to surprise Colin at *his* tournament.

And then before she knew it, her day was near. The plan that she and Colin had initially come up with had been a sound one: a private car, a private plane. Using the vision of "taking your secret garden into the world with you" that had so appealed to her.

During his lunch hour, she telephoned her brother on his private mobile phone.

"Rhiannon," Malcolm said, surprised. "I haven't heard from you in a while. Are you getting ready for Mum and Dad to return?"

"Actually, I'd like you to help me. Could you please arrange a flight for me and Isabel to travel to Virginia on Thursday, preferably an evening flight?"

"Sure," he said cheerfully. "I'll order that right up for you."

Rhiannon realized that he thought she was joking.

"I'm serious. I don't know if you were aware, but I've been working intensively with a private therapist. Isabel was here with us today, as well."

"That's...wow." Malcolm's voice seemed a bit hurt. "I didn't know."

"I asked Isabel not to tell you. I wanted to tell you myself as a surprise." Rhiannon paused. "You're still my big brother," she said softly. "You know I'll always love you best."

He laughed. "I understand. You and Isabel are friends now." His voice sounded relaxed. "I think that's great. Really great. But hey—you want to surprise Colin at his tournament, is that right?"

"Yes. It's his first tournament since the accident. The first round is on Thursday. I'd like to see him on Friday, for the second round."

"I know pro golf, Rhiannon. Getting admitted to watch Friday's play will be near to impossible. That's cut day—half the players are eliminated then. There's extensive crowd control, and it's unlikely you'll get near him. And why would you want to shock the hell out of him when he's trying to concentrate at work, anyway?"

She'd thought of that last bit, actually. "Because his first tee time isn't until noon on Friday—he told me so. In the morning he'll be at the practice range. It might be better for him to see me there."

"Still, there's heavy security at the official driving ranges on tournament day."

"Maybe if I had a Secret Service agent with me to smooth the way," she mused aloud.

There was a pause at the other end of the line. Malcolm seemed to be considering her idea, as well.

"That might work." Malcolm was silent for another moment. "Are you sure you really want to do this?"

She hadn't discussed with him about how she'd failed leaving the estate the first time, and she was glad he hadn't brought it up, even though he certainly knew. She wanted to stay positive and to *believe.*

"I want it all," she said softly. "Colin. A family with him. An estate of my own. Maybe even a gallery someday." She smiled to herself. "Look at you and Kristin. You both live and work together. And Isabel and Jacob have meshed their lives, too."

"Okay, I'm in. Will you let me talk with Jacob about the details?"

The fact that he'd asked her permission was an excellent sign. "Please do."

An hour later, Malcolm rang her back. "Isabel has cleared

her calendar, and Jacob said he can get a long weekend off, so he's coming. And, Rhiannon?" Malcolm coughed. "Kristy and I would like to go, too, if that's okay with you. I've, uh…come up with a reason to combine the trip with business so we can all take the company jet together."

Rhiannon's heart seemed to fill with happiness. "Thank you! I mean it. This trip means everything to me."

"I'm just glad you came to me and allowed me to help."

"You're welcome." Though that was Colin's influence.

Malcolm laughed. "All right. Then we're set to fly."

———

BY THURSDAY EVENING, Rhiannon had packed a small suitcase with clothing and filled a tote bag with her sketch pad and pencils. She'd dressed in jeans and a light cotton sweater, and had sat down with Paul to make sure everything was prepared and transitioned for her parents' return on Saturday.

Paul nodded, listening to her explain that she planned to stay with Colin for the next two weeks. *If he will have me,* she silently added.

"I watched you with your therapist, miss. You did very well, indeed."

"Thank you, Paul."

"May I help you pack?"

"Thanks, but I'm ready." She glanced at her watch. "Malcolm should be arriving shortly."

Paul nodded again. Then he did something out of character. He took her hands in his and quietly met her gaze. "I do believe that you'll make it to America this time, miss."

She blinked at the sudden moisture in her eyes. "I can't tell you what your support means to me."

"Your mother will be proud of you."

"It has been an eventful summer, hasn't it?"

Paul inclined his head. "May we tell Jessie about your trip?"

Rhiannon hadn't thought about that, but Jessie would always be family to her. "Yes, please do tell her and Jamie. They're welcome to see me off if they'd like."

"Very good, miss."

Rhiannon stood and went to the front of the castle to wait on the bench for her brother. Not long after, Jessie motored over, on her buggy, to join her.

"Paul told me everything." Jessie beamed at Rhiannon. "You're very brave. Well done for trying again."

"Your grandson is a handsome one. I couldn't completely stay away."

Jessie laughed. "If you make it this time, lass, then you'll have given me a challenge to overcome my own fear of flying."

That would be wonderful! "Colin would get a kick out of seeing you show up at a tournament of his, Jessie, I'm sure."

Jessie leaned in and hugged her. "You'll give him all our love, won't you?" she whispered.

"I will," Rhiannon said.

At the top of the drive, a long stretch limo with black-tinted windows pulled past the guard's gate.

"Well, that's me." Rhiannon stood, extending the handle on her suitcase.

"You'll be traveling in style," Jessie remarked. "Very posh."

"Yes, and it serves a practical purpose, too. See how people won't be able to look inside the car with those dark windows?"

"Oh, aye," Jessie agreed.

"That was Ceci's suggestion. Speaking of which..." Rhiannon craned her neck. Ceci's red sedan was just rounding the corner past the guard shack.

The limo came to a stop in the drive before them. Ceci pulled up right beside it.

Rhiannon dashed over and hugged her therapist. "Thanks for coming to see me off on my big day."

"I wouldn't miss it. And remember—you have my number. Ring me whenever you wish."

Rhiannon nodded. Breathing steadily, thinking of Colin, she focused like a laser beam on the limo door, and without any fanfare, opened it.

Inside, she saw Jacob Ross, wearing his dark suit and special agent's sunglasses.

"Rhiannon," he said, hopping out of the limo and making way for her.

"Thank you for coming to assist me." Taking a deep breath, she climbed inside.

Also inside were Malcolm, Kristin and Isabel. A driver was behind the front partition. The back of the limo was roomy and dark. Quiet and plush.

Rhiannon took a seat, her knees shaking a bit, but nothing she hadn't overcome before in Ceci's car during her therapy care.

She closed her eyes and thought of the cozy limo as a safe cocoon. Surrounding her, she imagined the serenity of her secret garden.

Isabel took her hand in reassurance. Rhiannon was vaguely aware of the engine running. Of the wheels slowly starting to move beneath her.

*I'm going to see Colin. I'm going to show him what he means to me. Everything I've ever wanted is unfolding now.*

Rhiannon said it over and over to herself, as lyrics to a song.

She kept her eyes closed and concentrated on breathing calmly and evenly. By the time they arrived at the airport in Edinburgh, she was tired. The anti-anxiety medication made her drowsier than usual.

Instead of worrying about being inside an airplane, she

mostly dozed through the flight. The interior of the cabin was silent. Rhiannon tucked a blanket about her and kept her window shade down.

When they landed in Virginia, it was still dark. Malcolm had a stretch limo reserved to whisk them to a hotel. Drowsy, Rhiannon again mostly slept.

She looked forward to more sleep, in the cool sheets of a luxury hotel beside the golf course.

They checked into a room with two beds, and her cousin Isabel shared this room with her.

"Thank you for being here," Rhiannon said to Isabel as she fluffed up her pillow.

"Thank you for inviting me." Before they turned out the lights, Isabel sleepily remarked to her, "You can be my in-person bridesmaid now, if you still want."

"Yes, I can do it, can't I?" Rhiannon murmured. Then, "Thank you for not telling anyone about the pregnancy test."

"You're very welcome." Isabel turned beneath her covers. "Are you feeling all right, honestly?"

Rhiannon's nerves were jangled and she'd occasionally broken out in a mild sweat, but as long as she kept focused on her breathing and visualization exercises, then she was doing far better than she'd anticipated.

"I'm just relieved we're here. I wasn't queasy during the flight, but I might be in the morning."

"I'll bet you're excited to see Colin."

"Yes," Rhiannon murmured.

But she wasn't there yet. The tournament would be the hardest test of all. A crowded event. Colin, focused on his golf play.

She hoped she'd done the right thing by coming. She'd hoped she hadn't flown all the way to America just to fail at the final test.

## CHAPTER SIXTEEN

COLIN HELD HIS PHONE to his ear and frowned. Rhiannon wasn't picking up—his call went directly to voice mail.

He checked for any messages from her this morning. Nothing.

This wasn't like her. For the millionth time, he wished they didn't have this gulf of physical and emotional distance between them. He felt powerless to do anything about it, other than to return home early, right after the tournament.

*Home?* He meant *Scotland.*

Strange how he had little desire to return to his digs in Texas, at least not without Rhiannon.

Maybe he should call Jamie to check on her.

"Are you ready?" Mack asked beside him. It was ten minutes till the start of his official practice time. They were at Day Two of the Mid-Atlantic Open. Friday, cut day.

By the end of the afternoon, Colin would know if he'd made the next round of play in pursuit of one of the tournament purses to be awarded on Sunday.

"Give me a minute." With a lump in his throat, Colin stowed

the powered-off phone at the bottom of his golf bag. Put on his glove and prepared to warm up on the driving range.

Mack hoisted Colin's bag over his shoulder and aimed for an open tee.

This was the new Colin-Mack partnership. A week before Colin had left boot camp in Arizona, he called for Mack to join him, wanting to get their golfer-caddie relationship off to a fresh start. A new professional seriousness.

Mack handed him his driver without asking. He knew Colin planned to start with his woods and work his way to a few hits with the smaller irons. Just an easy warm-up for the action to come later in the afternoon. Colin had a noontime tee-off, in the middle of the pack.

Colin made three easy long drives. Then he switched it up, moved on to his seven iron. From his peripheral vision, he saw Doc Masters approach him, waiting off to the side per golfing etiquette. But Colin didn't even acknowledge him, though the man was currently the top golfer in the world. Colin aimed to knock him off his pedestal. He was all business today.

Doc moved on. That was fine with Colin.

He finished his warm-up at the driving range and stretched his shoulders once more in the August heat. He felt good today. Confident of the work he'd put in.

"Ten minutes till twelve." Mack looked up from his watch. "You ready to head over?"

Now was Colin's time to cowboy up.

"Let's do it," he said to Mack.

———

RHIANNON SAT in her hotel room. One o'clock in the afternoon. She'd missed Colin's morning practice at the driving range. Then she'd missed his noontime start.

She'd woken up feeling shaken, as if she were outside her body looking in. She'd taken her medication and waited, working on her deep-breathing exercises. After an hour or two, she'd rung Ceci. "I think I need help," she'd confessed.

Ceci had instructed her to increase her medication dosage a bit. "It's natural, Rhiannon. You're doing beautifully, and now we'll take it step by step again. Please put your support partner on the phone."

Isabel had gladly taken Rhiannon's phone to talk with Ceci. Then, at Ceci's recommendation, they'd both taken a short walk around the parking area outside.

While Rhiannon focused on her breathing exercises, Isabel chattered about a tiny brown Chihuahua dog she and Jacob had adopted from a rescue center. "Barry" had been found wandering the streets in Edinburgh, hungry, sick and frightened. Isabel's mum was currently taking care of him while Isabel and Jacob were away for the weekend.

When Rhiannon and Isabel returned to the hotel room, Jacob poked his head in. He'd opened the adjoining door to his and Isabel's hotel room, and from inside, Isabel heard the low drone of the television announcer on the Golf Channel. The tournament was being broadcast live.

"How is Colin doing?" Rhiannon asked.

"Just finished putting on the third hole. A par five hole, and he hit an eagle. If he stays on course, he's headed for the leader board."

Rhiannon wasn't sure what all that jargon meant. She would have to learn. Once she had a better handle on her agoraphobia, familiarizing herself with golf terms was her next step.

"Is that good?" she asked Jacob.

"Damn good. The announcer said he's looking *in top form*. They don't usually show guys as far back in the ratings as Colin, but they kept the camera on him throughout his last hole."

Jacob paused. "I got hold of one of my guys. I was able to arrange special parking for us up front in the VIP area of the club. When you're ready to go, Rhiannon, we'll be close to the course. Nowhere near the general crowd."

"How'd you manage that?" Malcolm asked, standing in the doorway from the other adjoining room.

Jacob shrugged. "We're fairly close to Washington, DC, and Doc Masters is here. That's brought in some diplomatic VIPs from the capital who want to see him play up close. I still have friends on the protective details."

"Isn't he fabulous?" Isabel said to Rhiannon, grabbing a water bottle from their hotel refrigerator.

"Yes, he is. Thank you, Jacob." Rhiannon walked over to her unmade bed, kicked off her shoes and lay back on the pillows, closing her eyes.

The extra dosage hadn't affected her yet. She was too shaky. Too unsure. She wasn't ready to go to a crowded public event just yet.

*VIPs? General crowd? Protective details?* This was all rather more excitement than she'd expected. She just needed a bit more time to adjust.

She lay on the bed for another hour—or maybe it was two—breathing rhythmically and visualizing her peaceful nature scene. Her protective walled garden.

Maybe the medication was starting to kick in, because all of a sudden she felt better, happy, as if she was rolled back in time, playing on the estate with Colin. A lot of other friends, too. There was noise and laughter and...

Cheering sounded. Loud clapping. The musical trill of Isabel's laughter. Kristin's excited, feminine voice.

Rhiannon sat up. In the hotel room next to her, Malcolm, Kristin, Jacob and Isabel were engrossed in the televised golf event. Rhiannon stood in the doorway, smoothing her hair and blinking, waking up slowly, into reality. She felt utterly calm.

"What's happening?" she asked.

"Colin is on *fire,*" Malcolm said. "You should see him—"

"Yes, come see him," Kristin said. "Look! The crowd is totally on his side. All those people are following him, wearing red Colin's Crew T-shirts, but he's just powering through his game, and—"

"Look at Doc Masters." Jacob shook his head and laughed. "He is seriously ticked off."

"They just aired an interview with him," Malcolm explained to Rhiannon. "Doc was in an earlier threesome and he's finished now. He's the current leader, but Colin is close behind."

Rhiannon could only smile. Her family was finally seeing in Colin what she'd always known about him. Colin was special. One in a million.

She stood beside her brother and watched Colin on the television stalking down the fairway as if he owned it. His handsome face filled the screen and he looked utterly fierce. He concentrated on the course ahead as if it were a battlefield and he were the conquering general.

Without breaking stride, he dipped his head to hear a quick consultation from his caddie. Gave him a short nod.

Colin's eyes were squinted, his golf cap low, his lips pressed together. He showed no hint of a limp when he walked. He looked thinner overall, though a bit more muscular in the arms and shoulders. Her heart swelled.

Their hotel room fell to a hush as the cameras focused in on Colin. He teed a ball and lined up his stance. In a split screen, the announcers showed a comparison to Doc Masters—a taped version of Doc's swing, beside Colin's swing in real time. They looked amazingly close in technique.

"Rhiannon, you didn't tell me he'd been off working with Somer Grinks," Malcolm remarked to her.

"Well, he *was*." She shot a glance at Malcolm. "Where did you think he went?"

"I don't know." Malcolm shrugged. "Home to Texas?"

That bothered her enough to decide that she was ready to take action.

"Let's go to the tournament now," she said calmly to Jacob.

Jacob snapped to attention. Picked up his jacket and shrugged it on. She noticed that since breakfast, he'd changed into a dark gray business suit and blue tie, with an American flag pin on his lapel. The standard "uniform" of the US Secret Service, even if he was technically off duty.

"Let's go," Jacob said to them all. He seemed boyishly excited to be going to the golf game in person.

"What's the plan?" Malcolm asked.

"I suggest we head to the seventeenth hole. That should be better than the eighteenth."

"Why?" Rhiannon asked.

"Because the eighteenth is the last hole—the finish line, so to speak. There are stands set up and lots of press. Bigger crowds there."

Walking beside Isabel, Rhiannon made it to the vehicle Jacob had arranged—a huge black SUV. She sat in the front seat beside him, momentarily confused because the driver's seat was on the other side than it was in Scotland.

"That means we'll need to walk her down the rope line," Malcolm said to Jacob. In the backseat, he consulted a course map.

The drive to the iconic golf course at the beautiful, stately country club was a short one. As they turned into the access road and she saw the lots filled with cars, Rhiannon rolled up her tinted window and leaned her head back on her seat. She didn't stir again until the SUV had stopped and the engine cut out.

Malcolm helped her jump down from the tall step.

"You walk on her left side. I'll take her right," Jacob instructed Malcolm.

They were in a quieter area, and since Jacob constantly flashed his credentials, they were let in behind a series of rope lines. They followed the rope along a wide-open, rolling green golf course.

Rhiannon felt safe between the two familiar men. Isabel and Kristin walked beside them, too, and their presence gave her comfort.

"Here it is. The seventeenth tee."

There was a lull in the action on the course, but a small crowd was gathered a short distance from where Rhiannon and her friends stood.

In the crowd, a tall, familiar-looking blonde stood out, wearing cowboy boots and a Colin's Crew T-shirt.

"Wait," Rhiannon said. "That's Colin's mum. That's Daisie Lee."

Without waiting for Jacob and Malcolm, she headed toward the woman.

"Hi," she said to her. "I'm Rhiannon MacDowall. Do you remember me, Daisie Lee?"

Daisie Lee stared at her. "Little Rhiannon?" She pursed her lips and tilted back her head. "Are you here all the way from Scotland?"

"I am." Rhiannon beckoned to Malcolm. "My brother is here, as well. Do you remember Malcolm?"

Daisie Lee assessed Malcolm in a glance. "He's a CEO now, isn't he?"

"He's our company president, and let me tell you a secret. He was going to surprise Colin with the news, but I'll tell you first—

our management team voted to give Colin a sponsorship for our family brand."

Daisie Lee's smile widened. "They did? That's fantastic!"

A murmur grew in the crowd. Daisie Lee craned her neck. "Look! There he is."

A threesome of golfers, plus their caddies, approached the small hill where a few tournament officials waited beside the seventeenth tee.

Malcolm consulted a video feed on his mobile phone, and then whispered to Rhiannon, "He's currently in second place. He's one shot under Doc Masters. If he keeps that place, it'll be somewhat of an upset."

Daisie Lee jumped up and down. *"Go, Colin!"* she belted out, her hands cupped about her mouth like a megaphone.

Rhiannon cringed from the loudness, but had to smile at Daisie Lee's exuberance.

Colin appeared to have heard her, too. Though he was deep in concentration, seemingly blocking out the presence of the crowds, the faintest smile of recognition flashed across his face.

He glanced over toward them, just for a split second.

Rhiannon scooted behind Daisie Lee. *Please don't see me.* She didn't want to do anything to break his stride.

Colin glanced back to his business at hand. He seemed not to have seen her.

The crowd hushed as Colin made a beautiful yet ferocious swing. Like poetry. The ball arced high into the sky and disappeared from view.

"Come on," Daisie Lee whispered, tugging Rhiannon's sleeve. "He's moving to the eighteenth. Let's follow him."

Rhiannon resisted. "I...have anxiety in crowds," she explained to Daisie Lee.

"Anxiety? Oh, honey, been there, done that." Daisie Lee grimaced in commiseration with Rhiannon.

"Um...severe anxiety, actually," Rhiannon clarified.

"Do you need some meds?" Daisie Lee asked, searching through her purse. "You can borrow some of mine."

"No, thank you, I'm all set." Rhiannon felt a smile twitching on her lips. "I suppose I will walk with you, if you don't mind."

Daisie Lee was Colin's mum, after all. What would be more natural than to watch the rest of the tournament beside her?

Rhiannon gestured to Isabel. "I've decided to go to the eighteenth hole." Quickly, she made introductions all around.

Rhiannon reached for Isabel's hand. She was doing well—fabulously, actually—but she was eager to see Colin, so she could do even better.

He'd been so close to her she'd felt the urge to run over and touch him. They hadn't been together in weeks. Just the sound of his voice each evening on her mobile phone wasn't enough for her.

"So, how was the funeral?" Daisie Lee asked as they followed the path of the rope line in front of them.

Rhiannon stopped short. *What?* He hadn't told his mother? "What exactly did Colin say about it?"

Daisie Lee frowned. "Nothing, really. He only calls once a week now. He's been off training with his golf game."

Rhiannon nodded, relaxing a bit. She needed to trust Colin. He was setting his boundaries, as he'd said he would.

She only hoped that she was still included in his plans.

———

COLIN STOOD AT the edge of the eighteenth hole, waiting for his turn to sink his last putt. He stayed focused—avoiding thought or emotion over the holes that were behind him. Or the result that was in front of him. He'd been trained to take each moment as it came.

Finally, it was his turn. He went to the putting green, pulled up his marker and set down his ball. Then he studied the slope and distance in order to determine the best angle and force with which to sink the eight-foot putt.

From his squatting position, he glanced up to confer with Mack. In his peripheral vision, though, he saw a tall blonde woman jumping up and down. Daisie Lee. Colin smiled to himself. He was long used to his mom and her expressive cheering at his golf tournaments. That was okay with him—he wasn't embarrassed as an adult the way he'd been as a kid.

He was just about to snap his focus back to the business at hand when he realized who was standing beside his mom.

*Rhiannon!*

His mouth dropped open and he froze in place, dumbfounded. She seemed paler and thinner than when he'd seen her last, but honestly, he was just so happy to see her.

"Colin," Mack muttered, nudging him. He held out Colin's putter.

"Right. Thanks."

One more stroke. Sink the last putt.

He'd sunk thousands of putts over the last few weeks, and he was glad for that foundation of practice to fall back on.

Colin sighted the ball one last time, lined up his stance, drew his putter back and...

The ball circled the hole for a heart-stopping moment, but it went in at last. A loud cheer broke out from the crowd.

Mack ran at him in a bear hug. "Holy shit! Top of the leader board!"

"We made the cut? I figured we had, but—"

His words were drowned out by Mack's maniacal laughter.

Over Mack's shoulder, Colin scanned the crowd for Rhiannon. Her hands were clasped to her mouth, and she was beaming at him. Her entourage was with her—Jacob, Malcolm, Kristin, Isabel.

Colin broke away from Mack. "Give me a second, okay?"

He bounded toward Rhiannon. She took steps in his direction. They collided somewhere in the middle on the green. Colin caught her up in an embrace. Wrapped his arms around her and held her against his chest. She threw her arms around him and squeezed tight. He could have cried—it had been so long and it felt so good to touch her again.

"Colin!" Rhiannon choked out a sob. "You were brilliant, but I knew you would be!"

He kissed her hungrily, tasting her lips. It had been too damn long.

She pulled back and wiped her eyes. Tears had spilled over her lower lashes. "I think we're giving the crowd a show."

He was dimly aware of the Golf Channel guys hovering nearby, waiting for their interview. "Luckily, it's only Friday. The big crowds won't be here until tomorrow and Sunday."

"There's more to come?"

He laughed, brushing his lips against hers. "I haven't won the big purse yet," he teased. "All I did today was qualify for the final round."

He shook his head at her. "How did you get here, Rhiannon? When you didn't answer your phone this morning, were you on your way to see me?"

"Yes," she said, pausing briefly. "I'm sorry I couldn't go to Sedona with you like we'd planned. But I have news for you." She clung to him tightly.

He caressed her hair. Breathed deeply of her scent. Living alone in a hotel for the past weeks hadn't compared at all to living with Rhiannon. "I'm just glad you're here now." He drew back and faced her. "Are you sure you're okay? How were you able to leave the castle?"

"It wasn't easy, but I am okay now, finally." She smiled shakily at him. "Here's my news—Colin, you were right, I needed to work with a therapist. I planned it as a surprise for you. While you were at your golf boot camp, I was at my agoraphobia boot camp."

"That's fantastic!" He tried to laugh, but his throat was choked up. "Damn, I missed you."

"Me, too. Just thinking about you, constantly—missing you—and doing what you told me to, enabled me to finally leave the estate."

"What did I tell you?" he asked. "Remind me."

She leaned in and whispered in his ear, "I brought my secret garden with me."

He laughed in spite of himself.

"What's so funny?"

"Just that I have news for you, too. I'm playing the European Tour next spring. Kildrammond will be my home base."

"Oh, my gosh. But Daisie Lee will be—"

He put his finger to her lips. "You and I are a team, Rhiannon. Everybody else will just have to get used to it."

He kissed her again, for longer this time, not caring who saw them. He was pretty much sure that the whole world did, anyway.

Or at least, the people who were watching the Golf Channel on television that day—because they filmed the whole thing.

## CHAPTER SEVENTEEN

COLIN PLACED a surprising second in that tournament and earned a hefty prize purse.

He returned to the Highlands with Rhiannon and her group after the Mid-Atlantic Open. He met her parents again—they remembered him as a young boy. His reappearance as lover to their recluse daughter, coupled with the change in Rhiannon, created quite a stir.

But because of his upcoming tour commitments, he was only able to stay a few days, most of that time spent helping Rhiannon choose a small cottage she'd wanted to rent nearby in the village.

"It's close enough that I can return to my castle garden to recharge when I need to, but far enough away that I'll be able to develop my new, own life."

"That sounds like a good plan. Will you paint here, too?" he asked her.

"No, I'll go to my studio for that," Rhiannon said. "I'm just not sure what direction I'm taking yet. It's possible I'll go back to my landscapes, but they'll be of new places, I think."

Colin liked the sound of that. But still, she hadn't addressed his big question. His *elephant-in-the-room,* as she liked to say.

Namely, where did she think his place fit with hers?

She was quiet, not giving an answer to that question. "Colin, I want you to focus on finishing your season," was all she said. "That's your most important task right now."

"Will you ever travel with me, Rhiannon?" he asked wistfully.

"I wish I could say yes, but..." She sighed and traced her finger over his chest. They were in bed. In a hotel room, after celebrating his final day before leaving again.

"I need to work more with Ceci before I'm able to join you. I love you, Colin, I really do." She pressed her bare body to his, and it was all he could do not to groan.

"Can you wait for me?" she asked.

"Rhi," he murmured, kissing her deeply. "I missed you for twenty-two years. I can wait a couple more months."

"Besides," she said gently, "you have six more tournaments scheduled this autumn, all in America. I want you to continue to focus and do well. It's what you were made for."

"I'm more than just golf, Rhi."

"I know. I have every faith in you. It's me—let's see how I do these next two months, all right?"

He made the cut in each of those next six tournaments, and scored some more purses. On the golf front, everything had clicked into place for Colin. He was the man he wanted to be.

He'd managed to establish himself on the tour as someone to look out for—not for his good humor and jokes but for the talent and skill in the way he played the game.

He still had one major thing he wanted to do for Rhiannon, but it would take time. Her time.

———

*Two months later*

RHIANNON WORKED on three pieces of art while she and Colin were separated.

First, she completed two small portraits of Colin. One she sent to Daisie Lee, and the other she gave to Jessie.

Rhiannon had compassion for them—there would always be two women missing Colin almost as much as she did. Colin had told her that they would always be in his life—of course they would. But he'd carefully avoided saying the same of Rhiannon, though she knew that was because he didn't want to pressure her.

The third piece she painted was a landscape—a wedding gift for her cousin Isabel. It was a view of the firth from Isabel's back garden. Rhiannon had actually driven there, to Edinburgh, with her mother, part of proving to herself that she could stand as maid of honor to her cousin. And here she was...

Now...dressed in her bridesmaid dress, she paused just before entering the church in Edinburgh.

Colin had promised he would meet her later for the wedding reception. Fresh off the plane from his last travel commitment, she wondered how he would feel.

But when she saw him in his Black Watch kilt, surprising her just inside the foyer, he put his finger to his lips and drew her aside, a devilish smile on his face.

She pulled him to her and threw her arms around his neck, wanting to weep for seeing him. The familiar taste of his lips felt like home.

"I'm all done," he murmured, interlacing his hands in hers, "no more tour stops or travel commitments until next year." Then he drew back, marveling at her. "You drove yourself here? You're amazing. I can't believe the change in you."

"Neither can I." She sighed against his chest. She couldn't stop touching him, it seemed.

"Rhiannon," he murmured, rubbing her back. "There's something I need to tell you. I heard from my father. He's coming to visit Jessie for Christmas."

"That's wonderful! Right?"

"I hope so. I truly hope we can begin to patch things up. But whatever happens, I'll make it through, as long as you can be there with me."

"Of course I will," she promised. "I hope never to be separated from you again."

"Do you mean that?"

She nodded. She really had made so much progress. "I even hope to be able to join you in Texas sometimes."

A huge smile spread over his face.

"If you'll have me," she joked.

"If you'll..." He leaned back his head and laughed. "I love you, Rhiannon."

Then he led her outside the church, down the stone steps and across the busy street into a small garden surrounded by a low wall. It was late in the season and cold, and they were both shivering, but he protected her with his embrace.

"I was going to ask you in your secret garden," he said, "but I can't wait."

*Can't wait for what?* She felt breathless.

He presented her with a jewel case. She opened it with a huge grin, her heart pounding.

"Will you marry me, Rhiannon?"

She'd been hoping...oh, she'd been hoping. She felt a long way from that recluse who'd never thought she'd be able to share her life with someone. That it was Colin—her oldest friend—made it all the more special and amazing.

Her eyes felt misty with emotion.

He pressed his mouth close to hers, warming her with his breath. "I had the ring made especially for you. The diamond symbolizes enduring love. Those gems in the band—they're actually heathers and wildflowers from your castle grounds and your gardens, processed and hardened into gems. This way you really will be carrying your secret garden with you wherever you go."

"Colin, that's..." Her voice felt choked up, and she couldn't speak. The ring was so beautiful. But it was the part about the garden that above all touched her heart and made her see how blessed she was in loving him.

"I mean it to symbolize that in our marriage I'll respect your need to stay centered and protect yourself wherever you are and however you need to do it. You can count on me. We're a team, Rhiannon."

"We are a team, Colin. I'll always support you, too."

And then she flung her arms around him. With tears streaming down her cheeks, she considered herself the happiest woman in the world.

———

# ABOUT THE AUTHOR

Cathryn Parry writes from her home in central Massachusetts. She's an award-winning author of romance fiction with over a dozen novels published to date. Her books include small-town, sweet and clean, Scottish-set contemporary and sports romance series.

For more information about Cathryn's upcoming releases and to subscribe for new-book alerts, please visit her website at CathrynParry.com.